CLOSE QUARTERS

Barlow stepped into the shadows and watched Tiburon pass through a curtained doorway into the back.

Barlow reached the back door just in time. It burst open and Tiburon exploded into the alley, almost colliding with Barlow, then jumped back, astonished. Barlow didn't give him time to recover. He struck with the barrel of his pistol. Tiburon was quick—he jerked away and the barrel landed but a glancing blow. That was enough to daze him. Barlow lowered a shoulder and drove his body full-tilt into his adversary. Tiburon went sprawling in the rainwater that covered the alley's timeworn stones. He rolled over, drawing a pistol from under his peacoat. But Barlow was already on his feet and had his pistol aimed at Tiburon's heart.

"Drop it or I'll kill you," Barlow rasped.

WAR
LOVERS

Jason Manning

A SIGNET BOOK

SIGNET
Published by New American Library, a division of
Penguin Group (USA) Inc., 375 Hudson Street,
New York, New York 10014, U.S.A.
Penguin Books Ltd, 80 Strand,
London WC2R 0RL, England
Penguin Books Australia Ltd, 250 Camberwell Road,
Camberwell, Victoria 3124, Australia
Penguin Books Canada Ltd, 10 Alcorn Avenue,
Toronto, Ontario, Canada M4V 3B2
Penguin Books (N.Z.) Ltd, Cnr Rosedale and Airborne Roads,
Albany, Auckland 1310, New Zealand

Penguin Books Ltd, Registered Offices:
80 Strand, London WC2R 0RL, England

First published by Signet, an imprint of New American Library,
a division of Penguin Group (USA) Inc.

First Printing, April 2004
10 9 8 7 6 5 4 3 2 1

Chapter 1

Sam Houston arrived at the Hermitage on a horse that was nearly dead, and its rider wasn't much better off. He had come many miles in a great hurry, a journey that had taken many long days and nights. He had slept very little, beset as he was by anxiety, worried that he might arrive too late. And even before he reached the great white house, with its six grand Corinthian columns arrayed across the front portico, he knew that he was. Several of the house servants sat or stood on the broad front steps, weeping and trying to comfort one another. Houston's heart felt like a cold hard knot in his chest. He stepped down off the stumbling horse and stumbled himself as he passed, mute with a rising grief, past the servants and into the hall, with its scenic French wallpaper telling the tale of Telemachus in search of his father, Ulysses. Straight ahead was the staircase, with its elegant curve. To his left was a mahogany Empire sofa upholstered in black horsehair. A woman Houston vaguely remembered—he thought she was the sister of Andrew Jackson's daughter-in-law, Sarah—sat there comforting two small children. Houston assumed these children were related to Old Hickory, and he felt guilty that he did not know them, because his ignorance was a consequence of long and inexcusable absences on his part. At the foot of the stairs stood two men, one in a military uniform, the other, the older one, in a somber black suit, a medical bag in hand. Their heads were bent as they engaged in a hushed conversation. When the officer saw Houston, he abruptly terminated that conversation and came forward with hurried strides, hand outstretched, to greet him beneath the gold and crystal chandelier.

"General, I heard you were coming."

Houston nodded, forcing himself to ask the dread question. "Am I too late?"

It took Major William Lewis considerable effort to maintain his composure. "Yes," he whispered, his voice cracking. "He is gone. He breathed his last less than an hour ago."

Houston closed his eyes, sickened by despair. Less than an hour! He had been that close. That close to saying good-bye to a man whose fortunes had been so closely entwined with his, a man who had been a surrogate father to him. A man he had admired above all others. What a cruel twist of fate! It would have been better if he had missed his mark by a week or even a day. But now he would curse himself for being weak, for letting weariness slow his pace.

"Would you like a drink, General?" asked Major Lewis solicitously. He didn't have to add that Houston looked ill, or like he had come a long way in a great hurry.

"Later," said Houston, his voice hoarse. "I want to see him."

Lewis merely nodded. Shoulders slumped dejectedly, Houston headed down a narrow hallway branching off the main one. Andrew Jackson's bedroom was the first door on the right. Down at the end of the hallway was a door leading out to the garden,

where Jackson's beloved Rachel had been buried sixteen years ago. The garden had been a joy to her,
with its crape myrtle, roses, magnolias, honeysuckle,
Christmas ferns and goldenrain tree; it had been her
request that she be buried in it. Houston vividly recalled how grief-stricken Jackson had been by her
passing. He had been inconsolable for months. Later
he had employed an experienced stonecutter to build
a tomb along classic Greek lines—a copper-covered
dome supported by fluted columns. Jackson had long
planned to be buried alongside her.

Near the door at the end of the hall a young black
woman—another of the house servants—was sobbing
quietly all by herself. Houston noticed that the door
to the bedroom was ajar. He braced himself, took hold
of the doorknob, and pushed the portal open enough
to slip inside. The room was dark—the curtains on the
windows across the way had been closed. To Houston's left was a fireplace; it was early summer, and
there was no fire in the hearth. Above the mantel
hung Jackson's favorite portrait of Rachel, the one he
had taken with him to the White House. He had once
told Houston that he always hung the portrait directly
across from his bed, so that it would be the first object
to meet his gaze when his eyelids opened in the morning, and the last thing he saw when he closed his eyes
in sleep at night. Houston swallowed the lump in his
throat and looked to his right—at the bed, and at the
man who lay under the covers.

What first struck him was how frail and small and
inconsequential Andrew Jackson looked. It was as
though death had diminished him. He had always
seemed larger than life, but now that unconquerable
spirit was gone.

Now that he was alone, Houston let loose his emotions. Dropping to one knee beside the bed, he bowed

his head and wept silently. A few minutes later he regained his self-control. Wiping the tears from his cheeks, he looked idly around the room. A stray band of sunlight probed the curtains on the window and fell upon a pair of boots in the corner of the room. Houston was startled to note that there was a man standing in those boots. He stood up quickly, turning to face the man. As he did he brushed against the bed and Andrew Jackson's hand slid off the edge and dangled, palm up, as though making a gesture of silent introduction to the man in the shadows.

"Who is that?" asked Houston. "Show yourself."

The man stepped out of the corner, and Houston recognized him then.

"Timothy Barlow," breathed Houston. "By God, it's been . . . how many years?"

Barlow nodded. He was a man of medium height, in his late forties, his brown hair graying at the temples. He was slender except in the shoulders, which were broad. He wore the uniform of a major in the United States Army.

"Too many, Sam. Or should I call you Mr. President?"

Houston smiled ruefully. "I'm no longer president of the Texas Republic. And even if I were, you're too old and dear a friend for such formalities."

They clasped hands, and the memories came flooding back to Houston. He had been a young ensign when first he'd met Timothy Barlow. They had both been serving under Jackson's command on the campaign to end the uprising of the Red Stick Creeks. They had fought together—and both had been wounded—at the Battle of Horseshoe Bend. Later, when Barlow was promoted to captain, Houston had served with him in the campaign into Spanish Florida to deal with the Seminole threat. At the time, Barlow had been leading warriors from the Cherokee Nation who fought for Sharp Knife, as they called Jackson.

After the First Seminole War, Houston had gone on to become governor of Tennessee. For personal reasons his term was cut short, and he went away to live among the Cherokees who, by then, had begun their long and tragic relocation to lands west of the Mississippi. From there he had gone to Texas, to command the army of Anglo rebels who defeated General Santa Anna's veterans at San Jacinto and to secure independence for Texas. He became the republic's first president—a position he had only recently turned over to Anson Jones.

Despite the close friendship that had developed between him and Barlow, he had not seen Timothy since Florida, and he was shocked to realize just how many years had passed—over a quarter of a century! He had occasionally heard about Barlow, who had earned a reputation as one of Andrew Jackson's most stalwart lieutenants. It was Barlow whom Old Hickory had entrusted with a mission to Charleston during the nullification crisis, when South Carolina had teetered on the verge of open rebellion against the United States; with a handful of regulars, Barlow had defended the U.S. arsenal in Charleston against a mob of nullifiers. Later, Jackson had depended on Barlow to begin the difficult task of relocating the Cherokees; Houston's Indian friends spoke of the Army officer with respect, as one of the few white men who had treated them fairly and always been truthful with them. That had been ten years ago—and Houston wondered what his old friend had been up to since then.

Now, though, was hardly the time for catching up. Barlow was gazing at the gaunt face of Andrew Jackson, and Houston saw in his friend's eyes the depthless grief that he himself was experiencing. Barlow took

Jackson's hand and placed it, with a gentleness that bordered on reverence, back on the bed.

"I came as quickly as I could," said Houston. "If only I'd had an opportunity to speak to him, one last time."

"You had a long way to come. He left a letter for you. I believe Major Lewis has it."

Houston took a closer look at Barlow and recognized the exhaustion etched into the Army officer's features. "How long have you been here?"

"Six days." Barlow glanced at the curtained windows. "At least I think it's been only six."

"It's been . . . a long vigil."

Barlow nodded. "A difficult one. I thought we'd lost him several days ago. It was Sunday. He asked for the local reverend to come and give him Holy Communion. He said he felt certain death was close by, but he wasn't afraid of it."

"I don't think the general was afraid of anything," said Houston.

"But he rallied, to everyone's amazement, and looked much better on the following day. Then he began to swell. A doctor was called. An operation was performed. They tapped into his abdomen, released the pressure of fluids building up there. He suffered greatly that night. Of course he never complained." Barlow paused. His voice was flat, devoid of emotion. Houston supposed that his friend was emotionally drained. Barlow looked as though he hadn't slept the entire six days. His cheeks were gaunt and dark with stubble. His eyes had a glassy, faraway cast.

Barlow glanced at Houston, walked past him to the fireplace, and looked up at the portrait of Rachel.

"A couple of hours ago he regained consciousness. He spoke of his faith, called for his relatives and servants, and said his good-byes. Said he expected to meet us all in heaven. Then he was gone."

"At least he was free of the pain. And now . . . now he has rejoined his beloved wife."

Barlow turned and nodded. "I hope that's the case."

"You don't believe in the hereafter, then?"

Barlow was silent a moment, peering down at the worn carpet on the floor. "I'd like to," he said at last. He shrugged and forced a smile. "I'm sorry to have intruded, Sam. After a while, everyone left the room. It was my first chance to be alone with him. And, well, even though he had passed away, I didn't think he should be left by himself. I know. That doesn't make any sense. At any rate, I should have announced my presence when you walked in. I guess I . . . wasn't thinking clearly."

"You should get some rest," advised Houston.

"As should you, my friend, by the looks of you."

"We'll talk later?"

"Of course." Barlow took one last look at Jackson, tugged on the tunic of his uniform, and left the room, closing the door softly behind him.

Houston pulled an armchair closer to the bed and sank wearily into it. He gazed moodily at Andrew Jackson's face, reposed in an eternal peace. He knew that the old man had lived in pain for much of his life—more pain, probably, than most men could have endured. Old wounds and long, debilitating diseases had laid him low, but the man's imperious will had prevailed, had kept him on his feet and on the move when lesser men would have fallen.

Reflecting on all that Jackson had done for his country, and what the man had meant to his country-man, deepened Houston's sadness. On the field of bat-tle, Old Hickory had made the frontier safe, in the process earning for the United States the long-overdue respect of the European powers. And in the White House, he had dealt swiftly with South Carolina's dangerous challenge to the authority of the national government; had Jackson not done so, Houston was convinced that the republic would have disintegrated in a short span of time.

The republic still needed Jackson. Like Old Hickory, Houston was an intensely patriotic man, devoted to the United States above all else—in Houston's case, a devotion that exceeded even his love for Texas. And he was concerned for the future of the republic. War was coming—a war with Mexico. Sam Houston had no doubt that the United States would prevail when the conflict erupted. But he feared victory, in this case, more than defeat. Because in that victory lay the seeds for the nation's destruction.

Houston heaved a forlorn sigh. Yes, now more than ever, the country needed a man like Andrew Jackson to keep it on an even keel. But did such a man exist, now that Old Hickory was gone?

Chapter 2

The body of Andrew Jackson was laid out in the parlor of the Hermitage, and for the next two days people came from miles around to gaze their last upon the uncovered face of the Great Captain. In Nashville a public meeting was held at the courthouse, presided over by Mayor Maxey, at which Sam Houston, among others, spoke to the assembled crowd. The funeral was set for Tuesday. All business in Nashville would be suspended on that day. Minute guns would be fired from ten in the morning until two in the afternoon. The general's most trusted aides and closest friends would act as pallbearers—that included Barlow, Houston and Lewis.

Early on Tuesday morning the mourners began to arrive, and within hours hundreds of carriages and various other conveyances filled the front yard of the Hermitage. Barlow estimated that between twenty-five hundred and three thousand people were in attendance. At eleven the Reverend Edgar stood upon the front porch and gave his sermon. As he spoke of the character and accomplishments of the departed, many tears were shed. Afterwards, hymns were sung. Jackson's coffin was placed in another, made of lead, and the top was soldered. This was carried by the pallbear-

ers to the mausoleum in the garden, and lowered into
a tomb four feet deep and lined with brick and limestone. A slab of limestone was placed over the vault.
It was inscribed, simply: GENERAL ANDREW JACKSON.
Reverend Edgar read Psalm 90, and then the Nashville
Blues fired three volleys from their muskets. The wind
carried the faint sound of the minute guns and the
tolling of church bells from distant Nashville. The sun
was shining, but Barlow did not feel its warmth.

Late in the afternoon, Houston found Barlow, with
several other men, sitting on the ground near the
springhouse, in the shade of massive elm trees and
sharing a crock of corn liquor. Over in the nearby
slave quarters, someone was playing a mournful tune
on a mouth harp. The drinkers weren't talking, just
drinking, as Houston walked up. Barlow offered him
the jug, but Houston declined.

"I've been on the wagon for some time now," said
Houston ruefully.

Sensing that his old friend wished to speak to him
without the presence of others, Barlow stood up,
dusted off his trousers, and suggested that they take
a walk. He handed the jug to one of the other men
and fell in step alongside Houston.

"There was a time"— said Houston, with a sheepish
smile—"when I thought whiskey could dull bad memories. I believed I had it all; I was the governor of
Tennessee and I had a beautiful bride. Then it all just
fell apart. My wife left me on our wedding night. And
because of the rumors surrounding that event, I decided to leave the governor's mansion. I jumped
aboard the first riverboat—I didn't care where it was
bound. By the time I reached Arkansas I was so besot-
ted by that fatal enchantress, whiskey, that I couldn't
recall how long I'd been traveling. Then an odd thing
happened. I looked up to see an eagle soaring over the

river. It let out a cry, then winged its way westward. I took it as an omen. Only moments before I'd considered throwing myself into the river, drowning myself, ending the misery. Instead, after seeing the eagle, I threw the bottle of whiskey overboard."

"I'm glad it was the whiskey and not yourself," said Barlow.

"*Sic transit gloria mundi.* I think I was in the process of learning a very valuable lesson about life, and about myself. That even the most profound of tragedies can have an element of the sublime. All you have to do is learn to look beyond the hurt."

Barlow nodded. He had read several newspaper accounts of Houston's misfortunes in Tennessee, all liberally salted with rumors, most of them along the lines that Eliza Allen, the governor's bride, had been caught in the arms of another man. There was speculation that her marriage to Houston had been arranged against her will. Her brothers, heavily armed, had hunted Houston down, demanding that he make a written statement absolving their sister of any wrongdoing. But Houston had never said a word against her, and as far as Barlow knew, his friend had never strayed from his commitment to say nothing about the incident, even in his own defense. So Barlow wasn't about to delve further into the subject, regardless of his curiosity.

"I spent the next few years with our friends the Cherokees," continued Houston. "It got to the point where I avoided all contact with my own kind, because every time I met a white man I would be asked questions I would not answer, and it would resurrect the bad memories. The Cherokees called me Colanneh— the Raven. I dressed as a Cherokee. Lived as a Cherokee, at Neosho. I spoke only Cherokee. When I did have to communicate with a white man—like the good

Reverend Washburn at the missionary school near
Camp Gibson, I did so through an interpreter. Not
that Washburn had much to do with me. He considered me a menace to his proselytizing schemes."
Houston chuckled.

"But you returned to Nashville, I thought," said
Barlow. "I seem to remember something about a notice you posted in the newspapers . . . ."

"Oh yes." Houston nodded. "I really don't know
what got into me, but I did go back to Tennessee—
once. I had a portrait done. It represented me as the
Emperor Gaius Marius standing in the midst of the
ruins of Carthage." He glanced at Barlow, and
laughed at the perplexed expression on his friend's
face. "I don't know. A wild hare, I suppose. While in
Nashville I did publish a proclamation. 'I, Sam Houston, do hereby declare to all scoundrels whomsoever,
that they are authorized to accuse, defame, calumni-
ate, slander, vilify and' . . . something else . . . 'libel
(that's it) me to any extent.' Let's say it was a shout
of defiance. By that time the rumors had gotten very
much out of hand. People were indulging in the most
bizarre speculations! On the way back to Neosho I
overheard two men on the train speaking of Texas. I
decided on the spot to go there and make a new beginning." He put a hand on Barlow's shoulder. "But
that's enough about me. Tell me about yourself, Timothy. What have you been up to all these years? Last
I heard of you, you'd been involved in the removal of
the Cherokees from Georgia. I have not heard a single
Cherokee say a bad thing about you. The consensus
among them is that you are one of their few true
friends among the whites. They say you saved them
from a conflict with the locals."

"It had come to the point where leaving Georgia
was their only hope," said Barlow. "I only did what I

had to do. After that I stayed in Georgia. Got married."

"To a Southern Belle?"

Barlow nodded. "Rose Claybourne. We have a son. Joshua. He is nearly twelve years old."

"Good for you!" boomed Houston. "I always thought all you needed was a good woman to set you right."

"I love her with all my heart and soul. But the situation isn't without its . . . difficulties. I killed her brother, John Claybourne, for one thing."

"And she holds that against you."

"No. *She* doesn't. But just about everyone else who lives in Georgia does. To most of them, John Claybourne was a hero. A defender of the South. A true cavalier and a martyr to the cause of Southern rights."

"I see," murmured Houston. "Well, it's not in the Southern temperament to forget or forgive."

"It has occasionally made life difficult for Rose, and now for Joshua. The other children won't let him forget that he is the son of the damned Yankee that killed John Claybourne."

"And your career?"

"I am no longer on active duty. I didn't want to be apart from my family, and my wife was not inclined to leave Georgia for the wandering life of an Army officer's wife. I tend to various business concerns—a plantation, several merchant vessels out of Charleston, that sort of thing. My duty now is to make certain that my wife is happy and that my son, when he is grown, will want for nothing."

"Then you prosper," said Houston. "I'm glad of that." His keen gaze seemed to run Barlow through. "And yet . . . forgive me if I overstep my bounds . . . you haven't mentioned your *own* happiness."

"I am . . . reasonably content."

Houston laughed. "The warhorse out to pasture, reasonably content—but not doing what he was meant to do. You're one of those rare souls who understood early in life what you were made for. That's why you went to West Point in the first place. It's why you have made a reputation for yourself as a first-class soldier. You're not cut out to be a merchant, Timothy. You're a warrior, and you aren't happy unless you're at war."

Barlow looked at him, then looked away. They walked in silence for a moment. Houston could tell that he'd struck a nerve. He'd sensed Barlow's deep and abiding discontent when they'd met at Andrew Jackson's deathbed, but Houston had been too consumed by grief to do more than take note of it. Now he understood where that discontent was coming from; he had no doubt that he was on the money.

"But cheer up," said Houston. "As I suspect you already know, there will be war soon enough."

"You mean between the states? Between the North and South?"

"By God I hope *that* can be avoided," said Houston fervently. "No, I mean a war with the Republic of Mexico. In my opinion, it's inevitable."

"Because of Texas?"

Houston nodded. "Texas is part of the equation. A large part. But there's California, too. And all the land in between the two. Our people aren't going to be satisfied until they've arrived at the Pacific Ocean, my friend. That means stealing away a very large chunk of Mexico. And there are some who talk about taking the whole thing. The Mexicans aren't fools. They know what the future holds. The moment Texas is annexed by the United States, the blood will begin to spill."

"You speak as though annexation is a sure thing," said Barlow.

"It is."

"As I recollect, Texas formally requested annexation in 1837, and President Van Buren denied the
request. General Jackson himself agreed with Van
Buren's decision to abide by the Treaty of 1819, which
required us to recognize Mexico's claim to that territory." Barlow smiled. "In exchange for Spain surrendering Florida to us—after the general had wrestled
it from their grasp."

"With our help," added Houston, smiling warmly at
the memories of the campaign against the Seminoles.
Together he and Barlow had faced danger and hardship at every turn. Yet now, looking back, he considered those months fighting to stay alive in the Florida
swamps some of the best days of his life.

"I don't see that much has changed since 1837,"
observed Barlow.

"Ah, but it has. You see, the French and the British
have expressed a keen interest in Texas. The United
States will not take the chance that Texas might become the protectorate of some European power."

"Is there really any chance of that happening?"

Houston shrugged. "What matters is that the United
States believes there is a chance. When he heard that
about the British and the French, the general changed
his mind, the Treaty of 1819 be damned."

"Well," said Barlow ruefully, "the general never put
much stock in treaties once they ceased to be of any
practical use to him."

Houston abruptly stopped walking. "You know, I
have an idea. Why don't you come to Texas?"

Barlow was caught completely off guard. "Texas?"
He laughed, and shook his head. "And what would I
do in Texas?"

"You would be in the right place at the right time.
We're on the verge of annexation. And when that

happens, President Polk will contest the border with Mexico. As you may know, Texas has always claimed the Rio Grande, but Mexico insists that the boundary lies along the Nueces River. Polk will not settle for the Nueces."

"How can you be so sure?"

"Several reasons. Did you know that a naval squadron has arrived off Galveston Island?" Houston nodded, noticing the expression of surprise on Barlow's face. "Commodore Stockton is in command aboard the steam frigate *Princeton*. In addition there are three other warships."

"I've heard of Stockton—and the *Princeton*," said Barlow. Commodore Stockton had helped design the steam frigate to be the first warship driven with a screw propeller. He had also designed a pair of twelve-inch guns—larger than any then in use—and nicknamed them the *Oregon* and the *Peacemaker*. Secretary of State Abel Upshur had been killed when one of those guns exploded during a cruise on the Potomac River for then President Tyler and his cabinet.

"This isn't just about Texas, remember," said Houston. "President Tyler tried to purchase California from Mexico, and Mexico refused. What we can't buy we shall take by force of arms."

"You're saying that our government will provoke a war for the sake of expansion."

Houston nodded. "Exactly. A war we will carry into Mexico. And Texas will be the jumping-off point. It's the place for a warhorse to be in the months to come. Besides, you'll fall in love with Texas, Timothy. I guarantee it. Once you see it you'll never want to leave. She is a mistress whose seductions are too tempting for any mortal man to resist."

"I don't need a mistress," replied Barlow. "I have a wife. And a son. And a duty to them both."

"Yes, you and duty, always one and indivisible. One of your most admirable traits. But I hate to see you so discontented."

"I don't labor under the delusion that I am owed or even deserve happiness. And I am not discontented. I am content with my lot, Sam. Believe me."

Houston smirked. "If you say so, my friend. But I'll make you a small wager."

"And what might that be?"

"I'll bet that you'll be in Texas before the year's out."

Barlow shook his head adamantly. "That's a bet you'll lose."

"We'll see about that," said Houston.

Chapter 3

Timothy Barlow had spent the better part of twelve years on the Claybourne plantation, located near the thriving community of Athens in northern Georgia. In spite of that, the place still did not feel like home to him. He was glad to get back, nonetheless, because he had missed Rose and Jacob terribly. Still, as he turned off the road and up the tree-lined lane that led, between the cultivated fields, to the main house—a house, he noticed for the first time, not unlike the one Andrew Jackson had called home—he couldn't help wondering if he was one of those people doomed to live and die without knowing what it felt like to put down the roots. If he had put any down here they were very shallow; he had so quickly dismissed Sam Houston's suggestion that he come to Texas because he knew how easy it would be for him to leave this place. And he couldn't do that. It wouldn't be fair to Rose. Jacob, on the other hand, wouldn't mind at all. This was the only home the boy had ever known, yet Barlow sensed that his son would shed no tears were he called upon to leave the plantation. Especially if he were bound for a wild and exciting place like Texas.

Before marrying Rose and coming to live here, Barlow had called the Army his home—a rather euphemistic description for a succession of spartan quarters in faraway posts, with the occasional campaign thrown in for good measure. The 39th Infantry Regiment had been his family, and he'd thought himself quite content with that arrangement. But in those days he'd been young, thinking—as the young do—that he had all the time in the world. Now well past the halfway point in his life, Barlow had begun to brood about the things he'd missed. He envied Jackson—the old general had truly loved his Hermitage; it had become a part of him, and he a part of it, and now the two would never be separated. Gazing bleakly at the plantation house at the end of the tree-lined lane, Barlow indulged in a little self-pity. What a shame that he would never know that sort of communion with this place.

It was a nice enough home; in fact, a home far nicer than he had ever expected to have. And the fact that it was in Georgia and he was a Yankee, born and bred in Philadelphia, wasn't the problem. Nor was the fact that he had killed John Claybourne—his wife's brother, and a fugitive from the federal government, a traitor to his nation—on this very lane the problem, either: Barlow had long since come to terms with that act as one which had been unavoidable. It helped, too, that Rose had never given even the slightest indication that she held it against him. No, the problem was that this was and always would be a *Claybourne* home. Rose's father had built it, had toiled mightily to nurture it and make it grow, and had died in the process. Barlow had maintained it as a going concern, but Rose—or just about anyone else, for that matter—could have done that just as well as he. So when he looked at the house and at the fields, he did not see the mark of his own hand anywhere. Therefore it was not, and never would be, his home.

When the slaves in the fields saw the rider on the lane, they stopped and straightened from their back-breaking labors and, some shielding their eyes against the bright and broiling summer sun, watched his progress. He wasn't wearing his uniform—he seldom wore it these days—so it took a moment for someone to recognize him, and then the word spread like wildfire, and the slaves closest to the lane moved to the split-rail fence that ran beneath the trees and called out greetings to him, while those furthest away angled towards the main house, intending to catch him there. The affection they displayed was genuine, which Barlow found more than a little ironic. He was opposed to slavery, considering it a great moral evil, but he had become the beloved master of the forty-odd slaves who lived and worked on the Claybourne plantation. They liked him, he thought, because they knew without having to be told that he had no love for the peculiar institution that promised them a lifetime in bondage. In the past twelve years they had seen several overseers come and go, and one who had gone had done so because Barlow objected to the harsh, sometimes brutal, way he treated the hands.

Early on, Barlow had toyed with the idea of asking Rose to manumit the slaves; but he had procrastinated, sensing that if he insisted, she would do it, and the plantation would suffer as a consequence. Once freed, the hands would not stay. Oh, perhaps one or two might—the house servants like Jez, the elderly black woman who had rocked Rose in her arms when Rose had been just a baby, and who thought of Barlow's wife as her own daughter. And Jericho would probably remain, because he was devoted to both Rose and Barlow. But not the others. And now the opportunity was past. Barlow had waited too long. The Georgia legislature, two years past, had made a new law prohibiting slaveholders from freeing their human chattel. Were the Barlows to manumit now, these people would be snapped up by slave catchers; their manumission papers would not be legally binding, and they would be sold on the auction block, back into slavery. And then the authorities would come for Barlow and his wife. The situation was the same in many of the other slave states now. Barlow thought it was because the act of manumission implied that there was something wrong with slavery. These days one had to conform—or at least pretend to conform—to the prevailing opinion that slavery was a positive good, essential for the survival of the Southern economy, not to mention Southern society. The South didn't want to have to deal with three million freed slaves wandering about, some of whom might be inclined to seek revenge for the treatment they had received.

So Barlow had to come to terms with the fact that he was a slave owner. It was the last thing he had ever expected to become. His wife did not share his antipathy for the institution of slavery, but he didn't hold that against her. After all, Rose had been raised here, and she had learned to ignore the moral issues involved.

As he drew near the main house Rose emerged through the front door, and Barlow's melancholy musings were swept away by the sheer joy of seeing her again. The years had been kind to her—far kinder, he thought, than they had been to him. In his mind she had not changed one whit since he had first laid eyes on her. Her hair was still as black as a raven's wing, her eyes as green as emeralds, her lips as red as a ruby. She was of medium height, still as slender as she had been fifteen years ago, and she yet moved with a gracefully light step. But as beautiful as Rose Claybourne Barlow was, it was her character and personality that Barlow most admired and loved. For Rose was no shrinking Southern belle; she was bold and straightforward. She knew what she wanted, and when she wanted something she went after it with a passion. That was it, thought Barlow—her passion. For him, for her son, for her life. She possessed a magic about her that lent itself to every day spent in her presence. She had become as vital to Barlow's survival as breath itself. He refused to even contemplate how miserable life would be without her.

He quickened the pace of his weary horse. When he reached the main house he leaped from the saddle, dropping the reins, and she flew down the steps with a giggling laugh of pure delight and hurled herself into his arms. In her embrace Barlow felt a rare comfort. Sam Houston was wrong; he wasn't discontented, at least not always—not when he held Rose. He was able, then, to put everything else into perspective, and life became as perfect as he had any right to expect.

She kissed him, passionately, and he responded. Then she bit his bottom lip.

"Hey!" he yelped. "That hurt."

"It was meant to," she said archly. "You've been away for an entire month, and I'll have you know, sir, that every day was pure misery."

"I'm sorry. It couldn't be helped."

"I know," she said, suddenly full of compassion. "And *I* am sorry for being so selfish. You had to be there. I know how much he meant to you."

He nodded, wanting to change the subject, because the mere thought of Andrew Jackson brought the grief welling up in his soul, hot and strong and nearly overwhelming. Jacob showed up right on cue—running full tilt around the corner of the house with Jericho coming along as best he could, but limping badly and falling behind. Jacob Barlow had his mother's jet-black hair and Barlow's brown eyes; he was tall for his age, and slender as a reed, but there was plenty of strength in that lean body, as Barlow discovered when Jacob waded right into him, wrapping his arms around Barlow's midsection. Smiling, Rose stepped back and let her son and husband have their moment. Jacob was cut from the same mold as Barlow, and they were much alike. Best of all, in her view, they were completely dedicated to one another.

"Father!" exclaimed Jacob, excited to the point where the words that followed stumbled one over another. "You should've been here! Me and Jericho caught a bear cub!"

"Jericho and I," corrected Rose.

"Jericho and I caught a bear cub, Father!"

Barlow gave Jericho a querulous glance. "Sounds like that could be dangerous. What did its mother think?"

Jericho shook his head. He knew that, since the accident, his purpose in life had been to keep an eye on Jacob and keep the boy out of trouble. And the black bears who sometimes came down out of the foothills could be plenty of trouble. Barlow would have expected him to keep Jacob out of harm's way, not become the boy's accomplice in some hazardous enterprise.

"The mama bear was dead, Cap'n," said Jericho. He had no conception of Army ranks; all he knew or cared about was that Barlow had been an officer in the Army, and from that point on Barlow had become the *Cap'n,* especially as he would not brook being called *Master.* "Looked to me like a panther got the best of her. Dunno why that panther didn't kill the little one, too, but when we showed up it was alive and well and hungry."

"He was bawling up a storm," said Jacob. "So we

brought him home and gave him some warm milk. I wanted to keep him, but Mother won't let me."

Barlow looked to Rose, who was watching him with an amused smile on her lips, and an eyebrow slightly raised.

"Your mother is right," said Barlow. "You can't keep a bear as a pet, Jacob."

"But he's harmless, Father. And he needs me. If I don't feed him, who will?"

"He may be harmless now, but he won't be when he grows up."

"But we can't just let him go. He'll die, for sure, all by himself in the woods."

"Well," said Barlow, at a loss. "That *is* a problem."

"I can't keep him, and I can't just let him go," said Jacob, in emotional agony. "What's a person supposed to do?"

"I'm sure we'll think of something," said Rose, coming to her husband's rescue. "But don't bother your father with such things now, Jacob. He's ridden a long way, and he's tired."

She took Barlow by the hand and led him inside, with Jacob still clinging possessively to him. Jericho called out that he would take care of the Cap'n's horse. Inside the front parlor, Barlow sank onto a horsehair sofa and sighed with relief that he had something softer than a saddle under him for a change. He laughed ruefully.

"I'm getting old, Rose," he declared.

"No, you're not," she said, going to a sideboard to pour him a glass from the decanter of bourbon. "You were just as sore fifteen years ago, when you first showed up here, having come all the way from Washington."

"Was I?" he asked, gratefully taking the drink from her. "I don't remember."

"I remember every single thing about that day," said Rose, sitting beside him. "It's as clear in my mind as though it had happened last week. Just shows you what a big impression you made on me, I suppose." She put her hand on his knee. "I'm so glad you're home at last. You know, I think that's the longest you've been away from me since we moved back here."

Barlow nodded, appreciating the smooth fire of the whiskey as it trickled down his parched throat. "I think you're right."

"I know it must have been awfully difficult for you."

Once again Barlow found himself seeking a way to steer the conversation away from Andrew Jackson. "It wasn't all bad. Sam Houston was there. He rode all the way from Texas, so I shouldn't complain, should I? And he got there an hour too late, besides. But it was good to see him again. We go back a long way. When I first met Sam he was a wet-behind-the-ears ensign looking for his first fight. Which he got, at Horseshoe Bend."

"He's gone far since then," conceded Rose. "The hero of San Jacinto. President of the Texas Republic. What is he doing these days?"

"Trying to talk me into going to Texas, for one thing," said Barlow.

He knew immediately that he'd made a mistake in mentioning it. Rose stiffened, and she looked quickly away, so as not to let him see the expression—which he imagined was one of dismay—on her face.

"I told him there wasn't a chance of that happening," Barlow hastily added.

She looked at him then, having had a moment to compose herself, and her smile was convincingly serene; just the barest trace of discomfort lingered yet in her eyes. "And why is that?"

"Because I'd never go that far away for that long without you. And I wouldn't drag you all the way to Texas."

"I wouldn't want to be the cause of your not going, if that is what you wanted to do, Timothy," she said, very quietly and very earnestly.

"That's not what I want to do," he assured her, mentally kicking himself for being so loose-tongued.

"Are you absolutely sure?"

"Absolutely. Now why don't we just forget I mentioned it. It isn't important. Tell me, what happened while I was away?"

And she let him get away with it, let him change the subject, and proceeded to tell him about all that had transpired during his absence. But while she talked, he watched her closely and he could see the worry, there at the corners of her mouth. He knew he wasn't really off the hook after all.

Chapter 4

In the days to come, Barlow got back into the swing of things at the plantation, and before long thoughts of Sam Houston and his invitation to Texas—and the prospect of a war with Mexico—began to fade into the background of his mind. There was plenty to see to, and not because Rose had let the place go to ruin in his absence, for she hadn't; Barlow knew his wife was quite capable of running the day-to-day operations as well as he. And there was Carter, the new overseer, whom Barlow thought to be a very capable man, one who, thankfully, was stern but fair-minded when it came to treatment of the hands, who in turn liked him as well as a people in bondage *could* like someone who wielded absolute power over them.

The crops were doing well. The summer had been neither too hot or too wet, and the cotton was coming along nicely; Barlow judged that in a month's time it would be ready for picking. The tobacco was already being harvested. Once the fully ripe leaves were picked, they were bound together in pairs on curing sticks. The tobacco was then air-cured in large barns, protected from the wind and sun. One could mark the progress of the curing by the turning of the leaves from green to yellow as they and the stems slowly dried. Then would follow the many months of storage before the crop was ready for shipment. Keeping an eye on market prices in the newspapers, Barlow was confident they would realize a handsome profit from both the cotton and the tobacco. Southern cotton had been in high demand in England for some years; English textile mills consumed tens of thousands of bales. And Barlow had cultivated two firms that had been for several years reliable buyers for the tobacco: one in New Orleans, the other in Charleston.

In addition to the money crops there were the "provision crops" with which to be concerned—chief among them the vast fields of corn, used not just for human consumption but for the livestock as well. And there were some repairs needed on the main house and the stable before winter came. Fences and irrigation ditches needed to be mended in places. Despite all the work, Barlow made sure he set aside plenty of time to spend with Jacob. They went hunting and fishing on a regular basis. And every morning, unless inclement weather made it impractical, Barlow went riding with Rose. It was his favorite time of day, before it got too hot, with the new sun throwing its golden light on a ground that often glistened with dew.

It was while they were indulging in one of these morning excursions that they met a mounted soldier. Barlow assumed he was from Camp Gordon, located less than a day's ride to the west, on a site that had once been on the edge of Cherokee land. As he had been instrumental in its creation, Barlow was well aware of the history of the camp; a dozen years ago he and a handful of regulars had been given the task of preventing a war between white Georgians and the Cherokees from breaking out. The Cherokees were gone now, relocated west of the Mississippi just as Andrew Jackson—and a great many other whites—

had wanted. But the post remained, garrisoned by a company of troops under the command of Captain Martin Broward. Barlow considered Broward a friend—and he didn't have that many in this neck of the woods. Broward was a Southerner, born and bred in Virginia, and therefore tolerable to the civilians in the region. But he was a staunch Unionist, and, like Barlow, a graduate of the military academy at West Point. Occasionally Broward would come calling; he would stay overnight, and after dinner he and Barlow would repair to the veranda for brandy and cigars and talk well into the night on a variety of topics.

The rider this morning, though, wasn't Broward. He was a sergeant whom Barlow did not recognize, but apparently one who recognized him. He checked his horse and snapped a salute, even though Barlow was in civilian clothes and there was nothing about him to indicate that he was an officer.

"Good morning, Major, ma'am. Sergeant Rutledge, sir. Captain Broward has sent me with his compliments and to ask if you would visit the camp at your earliest possible convenience. He told me to tell you that it was a matter of some importance."

"What does this matter pertain to?"

Rutledge emphatically shook his head. "I don't have any idea, sir. The captain didn't confide anything else to me." He glanced at Rose. "I beg your pardon, ma'am, for interrupting your morning like this. But Captain Broward, he seemed to think it was real important that he see the major. Told me to get here quick as I could, and not to dally at Wiley's Crossing."

Barlow suppressed a smile. Wiley's Crossing, some ten miles from Camp Gordon, was notorious for its cheap whiskey and loose women. It was frequented by off-duty soldiers and men from Athens, as well as from the lumber camps that had recently sprung up in the hills. The sergeant would have had to pass right through that den of iniquity—Wiley's Crossing was also the location of one of the few reliable ferries on the upper Chattahoochee.

Barlow was a little perturbed. Broward requested his presence forthwith, but wouldn't give him a clue, through Rutledge, as to why. He knew it would have to be something important—the captain would not summon him so abruptly on some frivolous matter. Still, he was no longer on active duty, and if there were some military emergency he surely would have heard about it already. Perhaps Broward needed his advice regarding some vital business. Regardless of the truth, though, he could not refuse, if only because Broward was his friend.

"Fine," he said. "You can come back to our home, Sergeant, and wait while I collect a few things."

Back at the main house, Barlow handed Rutledge off to Jez so that she could provide him with a meal. Then he went upstairs to change into his uniform. Rose accompanied him. She had been unusually quiet all during the ride back. Now that they had some privacy, she asked him what he thought this business with Broward was all about.

"I have no idea," replied Barlow, who really didn't have a clue. "But whatever it is, I'll be back tomorrow."

"Are you sure?"

He looked at her. "Absolutely sure."

Rose nodded. She seemed about to say something, then caught herself. She smiled, a saucy smile, and came to him as he was buttoning his shirt. She unbuttoned it, ran her fingers through the dark curly hair on his chest. "Are you in a hurry to get away from me, Timothy?"

"Of course not."

"The sergeant needs time to eat his breakfast. And that gives me time to make sure you don't get it in your head to stop off at Wiley's Crossing."

"Rose, you know I wouldn't. . . ."

"I'm just going to make sure," she said, peeling the shirt off his back. "You don't mind, do you?"

Barlow smiled, desire stirring in his loins. "No. I don't mind at all. In fact, I think it's a damn fine idea. . . ."

He couldn't say anymore; Rose was covering his mouth with hers.

In the company of Sergeant Rutledge, Barlow arrived at Camp Gordon late that night. But for a few sentries, the outpost was sleeping. Rutledge escorted Barlow to a small cabin which proved to be the quarters of the commanding officer. Broward was asleep, but the sergeant's fist pounding on the door woke him up. Adjusting a suspender, he peered with half-open eyes into the darkness and recognized Barlow.

"Oh, it's you," he said gruffly. "I was dreaming about a young lady I met last time I was in Mobile. I thought for a moment I was back there, and it was her knocking on my door."

"If she knocks on doors like the sergeant does, I'd say you should have better taste in women," said Barlow, grinning in spite of his weariness.

Broward gave him a go-to-Hell look before turning his attention to Rutledge. "Thank you, Sergeant. Well done. He didn't give you any trouble, I see. You didn't have to hog-tie him."

"No, sir. Thank you, sir."

"That'll be all. Go get some rest. Major, if you'd step inside. . . ."

Barlow did so. Broward's quarters consisted of one room. There was a narrow bunk in a back corner, its covers rumpled, a big trunk, a table strewn with maps and correspondence, a couple of rocking chairs in front of a cold fireplace, a threadbare oval rug thrown over the puncheon floor. And that was it. The kind of spartan army life that Barlow was familiar with—and suddenly found himself glad that he no longer lived.

"Excuse the mess," said Broward dryly. "The maid hasn't been by lately." He took a bottle of bourbon from the log that sat atop a pile of firewood beside the hearth, fetched two glasses from the top of the trunk, and cleared a space for them at the table. He poured them each a drink. "I heard Andrew Jackson passed away," he said. "I assume you've been to Tennessee." He raised his glass in a toast. "To Old Hickory, a great soldier, a great patriot, a great man."

"I'll drink to that," said Barlow, raising his glass, then knocking back the whiskey. He put the empty glass down and peered at Broward. "So what's so important that you sent Rutledge to hog-tie me and bring me to this godforsaken place?"

"Yes, it is a godforsaken place—and since we're on the subject, thank you so much for creating it."

Barlow laughed. "Be warned. My wife thinks you're going to be the agent of a long separation from her husband."

"Not I." Broward searched the clutter on the table, found what he was looking for, and handed a letter across to Barlow. "You'll notice the seal."

Barlow noticed. The seal of the President of the United States was clearly imprinted in the red wax that secured the envelope. He turned the letter over and read the legend on the front. TIMOTHY BARLOW, MAJOR, U.S. ARMY, CAMP GORDON, GEORGIA.

"Why wasn't this sent to my home?" he wondered aloud.

Broward shrugged. "Maybe because anything that

goes to you there has to pass through Athens. Maybe the President didn't want everyone in northern Georgia to know he is in communication with you."

Barlow nodded. That was what he'd been thinking—and it worried him. A confidential letter from President James K. Polk? It brought back memories of all the times Andrew Jackson had summoned him for some special mission that, inevitably, wrought havoc with his personal life. Was it going to happen again? There was but one way to find out—he had to open the letter and read its contents. But he was reluctant to do so.

"You need another drink," decided Broward, reading the concern on his friend's features, and poured more bourbon into Barlow's glass.

Barlow broke the seal and opened the envelope. He read the contents of the letter. Broward waited impatiently. Finally, he could stand the suspense no longer.

"Well, for God's sake, what does it say?"

Barlow sighed, handed the letter to Broward. "All I can say is, Rose isn't going to like this."

Broward let out a low whistle. "Wonder what *this* means?"

Barlow drank his bourbon. "Whatever the meaning, I have to go to Washington to find it out."

"Surely your wife will jump at the chance to go with you."

"I can only hope so." Barlow reached for the bottle, poured himself another glass. Broward folded the letter, returned it to the envelope, and slid the envelope across the table.

"Now I remember why I never got married," he said wryly.

"It has some advantages."

"I'll take your word for it. At any rate, drink up. If

you pass out, I'll be sure to put a blanket over you before I turn in."

"Thanks," said Barlow. Getting drunk—and forgetting everything, at least for the night—didn't sound like such a bad idea. He knocked back another shot of bourbon. Yes, that *did* make him feel a little better. He wouldn't be feeling very good tomorrow morning, but then he was sick and tired of worrying about his tomorrows. It seemed like the more he worried about the future, the more likely it was that fate would step in and rearrange everything.

The envelope on the table before him was proof of that.

Chapter 5

Washington had not changed much in the years since Barlow had last visited. That had been during the second administration of Andrew Jackson. Old Hickory had given him a difficult assignment—to prevent a full-scale war from breaking out between the whites and Cherokees in Georgia. During that visit, Barlow had also helped foil an assassination plot, with the president as the target. And Barlow had rescued his first wife from the abolitionist leader Charles Marten, under whose spell she had fallen. He hadn't heard from Sarah Langford since, but he'd received two letters from her mother, telling him that Sarah was well. Barlow wondered if Mrs. Langford was still alive. She had been old and somewhat infirm when last they'd met. If she was gone, would Sarah be running the boardinghouse now? Barlow's curiosity almost got the better of him. It would have been a simple matter to ride by the house on his way to the executive mansion. But he exercised some self-discipline, and made his way at once to Gadsby's Hotel.

Getting a room, he exchanged his traveling clothes for his uniform. Then he took his horse to the nearest livery, and went down the street to a barbershop for a close shave. Looking about as good as he could ex-

pect after a journey from Georgia, he made his way
to the White House.

He was greeted by a man named Yarnell, who announced himself as the president's personal secretary,
and who informed Barlow that he was welcome, and
that the president had been expecting him. Would he
mind waiting a moment while Yarnell made certain
the president was ready to receive him? Barlow replied that he was at the president's disposal, and was
deposited in the oval room directly across a hall from
the foyer. It struck him that the president's house was
very nicely appointed; clearly it was benefiting from a
woman's touch, more so than had been the case during
the years when Andrew Jackson had been it's chief
occupant. Of course, Jackson had been a widower at
the time, and even though Emily Donelson, Jackson's
niece and the wife of one of his aides, had served as
the lady of the house, she had not been able to devote
her full attention to that task, with the result that at
times the Jackson White House had resembled a bar-
racks, filled, as it was, with the men—many of them
with a military background—whom the general had
most trusted. Barlow had heard that some were calling
Polk *Young Hickory,* and that this wasn't simply because both presidents hailed from Tennessee. They
said Polk had many of the same qualities as Jackson.
He knew his own mind, could be stern and uncompro-
mising, a man of principle and integrity, devoted to
duty, and wedded to the notion that the United States
should expand to the Pacific. For his part, Barlow disliked the fact that Polk bore that nickname. He'd
never met this president, but he was certain that no
man, no matter what his attributes, could come close
to comparing to Andrew Jackson.

He was not kept waiting long. Yarnell returned in
moments, and told him that the president would see

him now. Barlow was led upstairs, and down a broad
hallway to a tall paneled door upon which Yarnell
tapped. A staccato voice bade them enter. Yarnell
held the door open for Barlow, who stepped into the
upstairs oval room to see a short, spare man with long,
mahogany-brown hair, clad in a somber black suit,
bent over a pedestal table covered with maps. The
man did not look up. Yarnell glanced apologetically
at Barlow, then discreetly cleared his throat.

"Mr. President? Major Barlow is here to see you
now, sir."

Polk grunted something unintelligible, scowled at
the maps a moment more, then looked up at them.
The scowl remained on his face—Barlow would
quickly reach the conclusion that James K. Polk always scowled. He had the gaunt, stern features of an
ascetic. He gave Barlow a keen once-over with his
steely gray gaze, then stepped briskly forward and
stuck out a hand.

"Major, I've heard a good deal about you. Thank
you for responding to my summons."

"I'm at your service, Mr. President." What else
could he say? He hadn't wanted to come—hadn't
wanted to leave his family, or respond to a summons
that he suspected meant an extended period of time
away from home. But, even though he was retired, he
still felt it was his duty to respond. Especially when
the president, his commander-in-chief, called upon
him.

"Good, good," said Polk. "Mr. Yarnell, if you don't
mind, I would like to speak privately with the major."

Yarnell retreated discreetly, shutting the door softly
behind him. Polk motioned for Barlow to follow him
back to the map-laden table.

"I've been given to understand," said the president,
"that from time to time General Jackson saw fit to call

upon you to carry out a mission vital to the republic's welfare. Further, it is the consensus that you always got the job done—while conducting yourself at all times as befits an officer of the United States Army."

"Thank you, sir," said Barlow, uncomfortable in the face of such praise.

"As you may know, I was a great admirer of the general. His passing was a grievous blow to his countrymen. Not since George Washington has a man given more of himself for his native land. In my opinion he was our finest president. But he made one mistake during the years he occupied this great house."

"And what was that, Mr. President?"

Polk fixed his piercing gaze on Barlow. "He didn't hang Antonio López de Santa Anna when he had the chance."

"Pardon me, sir?" Barlow was taken aback.

"He had the Butcher of Goliad in his grasp—and let him slip through his fingers," said Polk fiercely. "Santa Anna, the man who had caused such grief and terror south of the Red River, and in his own country especially. When your friend Houston captured him at San Jacinto, many Texans wanted to see him executed for the murder of more than three hundred American prisoners of war at Goliad. And, I suspect, General Houston was similarly inclined. It was President Jackson, however, who prevailed on Houston to let Santa Anna live. Houston sent the man here, and President Jackson greeted him like a head of state rather than a prisoner of war. He was treated to dinners and receptions. The president offered Santa Anna six million dollars if Mexico would recognize the independence of Texas, and another four million dollars for all the land north of latitude 38 North, from the headwaters of the Rio Grande to the Pacific Ocean. I know this to be the case, as at the time I was Speaker of the House. I met Santa Anna—just before President Jackson put a corvette at his disposal so that the fellow could sail back home to Mexico. Santa Anna told the president he would give the offers I've just mentioned careful consideration. But I suspected then—and am certain of it, now—that he never intended to do anything of the sort. Instead he returned to Mexico, warned his people that the Americans intended to take all their land from them, and has spent the last few years raising and training a new army."

Polk turned his attention back to the maps. "I presume you are a Jackson man, Major, and I do not mean to offend you by being overly critical of the general. I bow to no man in my admiration for Andrew Jackson. His first priority was always the welfare of the republic. So is mine. He deemed it unwise to expand too quickly westward. The slavery controversy made him overcautious in that regard. He worried that the issue of slavery's expansion would be the one that might tear this nation apart. I do not happen to share that concern. In my opinion, the only way to prevent slavery from tearing us apart is to provide it with a safety valve." He jabbed a finger at the map. "And there it is, sir."

Barlow looked. Polk was pointing at the northernmost provinces of Mexico.

"But to get that," continued Polk, "we must have this." He slid his finger across the map to the Republic of Texas. "And that's where you come in, Major Barlow."

Barlow was perplexed. "What would you have me do, Mr. President?"

Polk paced restlessly to a tall curtained window and back to the table, hands clasped behind his back. Barlow sensed that this was a man of great ambition, but not for himself so much as for his country—a man determined to pave the way for the republic to realize its destiny. To that end he would work tirelessly, obsessively. He was a man who cared about one thing: results.

"As you may know, the annexation of Texas has been a political issue here in Washington for a good many years now. In 1844 we signed a treaty of annexation with Texas, but the Senate rejected it. Last year, Senator Benton of Missouri devised a plan which met with the approval of the Senate; it called for annexation once negotiations with Mexico regarding the disputed border were satisfactorily concluded."

"I'm familiar with the problem, sir. Texas claims the Rio Grande as its southernmost boundary, while Mexico insists that Texas ends at the Nueces River."

Polk nodded vigorously. "Exactly. Most recently, the House of Representatives has come up with a different plan, one that calls for annexation with certain conditions—that the boundaries of the new state would be determined by the United States; that all public lands in Texas would belong to the state rather than the federal government; that Texas would cede to the United States all property and means pertaining to defense, and several other plans. I have conferred at some length with my cabinet on the matter of which annexation plan to support, and have decided to support the House plan. The secretary of state, Mr. Buchanan, has prepared instructions for Andrew Jackson Donelson, our representative to Texas, to that effect. I would entrust that important document to your care, Major. In addition, there are certain instructions for Donelson that I dare not commit to paper, for if they fell into the wrong hands, well . . . when you are made aware of them you will understand. President Jackson relied on you, and I am sure I can do the same."

Barlow tried to conceal his dismay. If he traveled by sea it would take him the better part of two weeks to reach New Orleans, and sea travel did not suit him at all. But to go by land would take twice as long, and would be twice as dangerous. But an even greater source of dismay was the likelihood that, were he to accept this charge from President Polk, he would be gone from home for at least another month, and probably longer.

And yet, how could he refuse the president? Most men, in his place, would look upon the mission as a tremendous honor. It sounded to him as though this would be a crucial event in the history of the republic's "manifest destiny" to stretch from sea to shining sea. Polk was right: Texas was the key. Without annexation the goal of reaching the Pacific would be thwarted.

But Barlow was well enough acquainted with the facts of the matter to understand what the president's acceptance of the House annexation plan meant. It meant war. If the United States brought Texas into the fold with a disputed boundary, Santa Anna would have no choice but to march at the head of his army to defend Mexico's honor. He would not be the kind of man who would settle for making a toothless protest over the confiscation of thousands of square miles of Mexican soil. And then there was that other condition—that Texas would cede to the United States all property and means pertaining to its defense. That meant all forts and arsenals, which would, in turn, obligate the United States to fight for the disputed territory to which Texas was so adamantly laying claim. To do otherwise would be seen as betrayal by the Texans.

In short, Barlow was perfectly clear on the fact that,

if he accepted the mission, he would be instrumental in starting a war. And if war broke out, would he be satisfied sitting safe at home in Georgia?

Polk seemed to sense Barlow's uncertainty. He stopped pacing, and fixed that gaze upon his visitor once more.

"I know I'm asking a lot of you, Major. I understand that you have retired from active duty in order to be with your family, and that what I am asking you to do will take you away from your loved ones, not to mention your business affairs, for a period of time. But it was Sam Houston's opinion that there was no better man for a task of this importance, and I am inclined to agree with him."

"Houston?" Barlow was startled. What did Sam Houston have to do with this? Before he could ask, Polk gave him the answer.

"Some time back I received a letter from Houston. He wrote of the crisis we now face where Texas is concerned, and he mentioned that were I to require the services of a man whose courage, discretion and patriotism were beyond reproach, I should call upon you."

Barlow smiled ruefully.

"Did I say something amusing?" asked Polk.

"No, sir. It's just that Sam . . . General Houston . . . made a wager with me not too many months ago. He bet that I would end up in Texas. It looks like he hedged that bet. I'll deliver your messages to Major Donelson, Mr. President."

"Excellent. Now come and sit down, Major, for I want you to be comfortable, and able to concentrate on what I am about to tell you. The British and the French are trying to snatch Texas away from us, and they've made promises that many Texans find appealing. You must thwart the efforts of the British and the French, Major, and to do that I will authorize you to make certain promises yourself, in the name of the United States government. But this information must not reach the wrong ears, or else my political enemies— and those opposed to the annexation of Texas and our acquisition of California—would be howling at my heels like a pack of starving wolves. Do you understand?"

Barlow was beginning to. There could be more to this than just delivering some confidential messages. There would be enemies all around him. The British. The French. The Mexicans. And even those Americans who were dead set on expansion. The stakes were extremely high, and high stakes made for desperate men. He realized then that he was already at war.

Chapter 6

Barlow reached New Orleans in twelve days—a quick voyage aboard, first, a mail schooner bound for Savannah, and then a merchant brig that made good time under favorable winds as it rounded the Florida peninsula into the Gulf of Mexico. As swift as the journey was, however, it wasn't fast enough for Barlow. He had sailed only once before, on an American frigate from Chesapeake Bay to Charleston, and had been deathly ill from start to finish. This time was no different. So he was grateful to arrive in New Orleans, even though the weather was dismal. Torrential rains fell from a surly gray sky when he disembarked from the brig and set foot on solid ground. At least he hoped it was solid. He had never been to New Orleans before—he had missed the famous battle fought nearby in 1815, when Andrew Jackson whipped the British to put the finishing touches on the War of 1812; Barlow had been stuck in Washington on a mission for Jackson when that heroic struggle had taken place. But it appeared to him that the city was built mostly on swampland, and the heavy rain had quickly flooded the streets.

He found himself in the Vieux Carré, the old French Quarter, and eventually located the house where he'd been told Andrew Jackson Donelson was residing. It was Emily Donelson who answered his knock on the door. She was a slender, dark-haired beauty, uncommonly tall, and with a gentle, refined nature that endeared her to everyone who met her. Barlow knew her—Donelson had been one of Andrew Jackson's most trusted lieutenants for many years, and in that coterie of young men who had hitched their wagons to Old Hickory's star many lifelong friendships had been forged.

"Timothy!" she exclaimed. "We were expecting you, but not this soon! Come in, before you drown!"

Barlow stepped into the foyer and stopped, leaving a puddle of water on the floor. Andrew Jackson Donelson emerged from a room off the downstairs hall, and advanced with an outstretched hand and a smile of delight on his angular handsome features.

"Major! Good to see you again! My God, you look positively wretched."

Barlow laughed, and Donelson joined him. For his part, Barlow liked Donelson, and knew him as a man who was as honest as the day is long. He was a straight talker, and a man who got things done. His devotion to Jackson had not made him a sycophant; he had been quick to speak his mind if he'd disagreed with Old Hickory. That attribute was one Jackson had admired. So had Barlow. When Donelson told you something you could rely on its verity.

"I *am* wretched," replied Barlow. "I've just spent nearly a fortnight draped over a ship's rail. How do you think I feel?"

"The things we do for God and country," said Donelson, still laughing. "Here. Tiburon will show you to your room. Get some dry clothes on. We'll have some food and a good stiff drink waiting for you when you get back downstairs."

"I'm not sure about the food," admitted Barlow. "But the drink sounds attractive. I have a trunk outside in the carriage."

"Tiburon will see to it."

Tiburon was a tall, lean black man with a shaved head, gaunt cheeks and a ring in his ear. He had the sort of fierce buccaneer gaze that scarcely seemed appropriate for a house servant. Barlow allowed himself to be escorted upstairs to a well-appointed room. Tiburon drew back the curtains on the pair of French doors providing access to a covered wrought-iron balcony that overlooked the cobblestoned street. Then he left, having uttered not a sound the entire time. Barlow shed his wet clothes and donned his uniform, which had been packed away in the valise he carried. He was just buttoning up the tunic when someone knocked on the door. It was Tiburon, with Barlow's trunk slung on one shoulder. Barlow told him to put it down by the bed. Tiburon handled his heavy burden with surprising ease for one with so spare a frame. Barlow thanked him, and Tiburon merely gave a curt nod and left the room again.

Barlow had left home for Washington without any expectation of having to embark on another journey, so he'd bought the trunk and stocked it with some new shirts, two pairs of trousers, several maps of Texas he had purchased from a bookdealer and a few books besides. The trunk also contained his saber, shako and a wooden case containing a set of English-made pistols—a present to him from Rose on his last birthday. Also inside the trunk was a leather pouch wrapped in oilskin. Secretary Buchanan's letter to Donelson was inside the pouch; there were other letters inside as well, all of them pertaining to official government business and produced by various members of Polk's cabinet, as well as by the president himself.

Barlow had been instructed to hand them all over to Donelson, who, presumably, would see to it that they were delivered to the intended recipients. But for now Barlow removed only the letter penned by Secretary Buchanan—the one meant for Donelson's eyes only— which conferred the information that the administration had decided to support the annexation plan of the House of Representatives. Barlow tucked it away under his tunic. Then he stepped out onto the balcony, giving himself a moment to collect his thoughts before going downstairs. The rain was falling in sheets. Before him stretched the rooftops of the French Quarter, and beyond them he could see the masts of ships at anchor in the Mississippi River. The rainwater flowed like a river in the street below. The carriage that had brought him from the docks was gone, and the street was virtually deserted.

Emily Donelson had prepared him a plate of food, and Barlow was surprised to discover that he had an appetite after all. Donelson sat at the table while Barlow ate, and read the letter from James Buchanan, his face set in a scowl of concentration. Finally he sighed and folded the letter, returning it to the envelope, and looked across at Barlow.

"Do you have any idea what this contains?"

"The president told me he was prepared to support the House annexation plan. I assumed it had something to do with that."

Donelson nodded. It may be too little, too late."

"Too late for what?"

"Annexation."

"I thought that's what the Texans have wanted all along."

"They did. Many still do. But I'm not sure it's enough. Their pride was hurt when we declined the offer to annex them some years ago. And now that

Anson Jones is the new president, well, it becomes even more complicated."

"This Jones is opposed to annexation?"

"Fundamentally opposed. That's why the French and the British see an opening. Jones seems quite willing to listen to their offers."

"Are these serious offers?"

"Oh yes," said Donelson. "Make no mistake about that. The offers range from a special trade arrangement to military support in the event that Texas is attacked to the British suggestion that Texas become a protectorate. Part of the British Empire."

Barlow shook his head. "I can't imagine that Texans would opt for becoming subjects of Queen Victoria."

Donelson shrugged. "Texas is worried about fighting another war with Mexico alone. What makes the British so attractive is that they may be able to mediate an end to the border crisis. And if they can do that, Texas won't need the United States anymore. Of course, this kind of rhetoric doesn't help, either." He tossed a recent edition of the *New Orleans Commercial Bulletin* in front of Barlow. The front page editorial was prominently displayed below a bold headline: WE MUST HAVE TEXAS! Barlow glanced over the editorial. The gist of it was that if Texas refused the United States offer of annexation then it should be occupied, just as President Madison had occupied West Florida. It went on to surmise that the Texas people were all for annexation, but that they might be prevented from the expression of their will by the machinations of Anson Jones and the Europeans.

"The president has given me a message to deliver to you verbally," said Barlow. "There are certain things you are authorized to promise Texas if she accepts annexation. But he cannot put them in writing at the present time."

Donelson leaned forward. "I'm listening."

"The president is willing to guarantee large appropriations to be spent on Texas, should annexation occur," said Barlow. "There will be money for roads, harbors and to buy up Indian land."

"That's good. One thing Texas has always been short of is money."

"There's more," said Barlow gravely. "The president wants you to know that the Navy Secretary, Mr. Mason, has sent verbal instructions to Commodore Stockton authorizing him to begin the formation of a military force in Texas, which the United States will pay to provision and arm. This force will exist in order to block any aggression launched by Mexico."

Donelson was astonished. "The United States is going to foot the bill for a private army in a foreign country? No wonder the president doesn't want that in writing! Can you imagine the commotion that will make once word leaks out? The British and the French both will be outraged. But that explains the last part of this letter from Secretary Buchanan." He held up the envelope. "It authorizes me to request that you undertake a journey along the coast of Texas, to identify strategic points between Galveston Island and Matamoros."

"What!" Barlow stared at Donelson, then at the envelope. "You're playing a game with me."

Donelson shook his head. "Read it for yourself if you wish."

Barlow took the envelope, opened the letter, and did just that. Watching him, Donelson noticed the anger darkening Barlow's cheeks.

"I take it," said Donelson, "that the president didn't see fit to inform you of anything like this."

"No, he didn't," said Barlow curtly.

"Don't do it," said Donelson. "It would be a difficult journey through dangerous country. You would be in the disputed area much of the time. And, of course, your true identity would have to remain a secret, for your own safety. Texas is filled with spies and assassins, Timothy. This is a game of high stakes—and high stakes make for desperate men."

Barlow shook his head, returned the letter to Donelson. "No. This is where I draw the line. I won't accept this job. I wrote my wife from Washington, told her that I was coming here to deliver important documents to you, and that afterwards I would be coming home. And that's exactly what I intend to do."

"That's fine. You're welcome here, of course, for as long as you wish to stay. As for me, I must be off to Texas in the morning. The information you have provided me must be delivered to President Jones at once. If you're finished, why don't we step into the parlor for a drink?"

Barlow rose from the table. "I have other letters in my trunk, which I was told to give to you, with the understanding that you would put them into the proper hands. I'll go up and get them."

Barlow went upstairs to his room. He was preoccupied, still fuming over what he considered to be subterfuge on President Polk's part. There was no doubt in his mind that the president had known about the request included in the letter to Donelson. Yet he had given Barlow no inkling of it during their meeting in the White House. Perhaps, mused Barlow, the president had sensed that just getting him to agree to journey to New Orleans would be the best he could hope for, and was content to leave any further persuasion up to Donelson. What had Polk been thinking? That once Barlow had gone as far as New Orleans he would readily accede to venture into Texas, forgetting the obligation he had to his family? If so, thought Barlow grimly, the president had misjudged him.

Because he was preoccupied, Barlow stepped into his room and stared at the open trunk at the foot of his bed, taking precious seconds to realize that something was wrong. He was sure he had closed the lid of the trunk. But had he locked it? He was pretty certain that he hadn't. Someone had . . . .

In the silence Barlow thought he felt a whisper of air against his neck, and he was turning, every nerve ending in his body on fire, instincts warning him of danger, when the blow fell. He crumpled to the floor, dazed, fighting to remain conscious. His vision blurred, he could vaguely make out the shape of a man looming over him, and he was pretty sure the man had a pistol in his hand. If it was a pistol, the man didn't fire it—instead he bolted out of the room. Barlow could hear him pounding down the staircase. Rolling over, Barlow pushed himself to his knees, then to his feet. The room tilted and whirled madly, and he fell against the door, rubbing the back of his skull. His fingers came away sticky with warm blood. His assailant had been concealed behind the door. Only then did Barlow put two and two together. He stumbled to the trunk, fell to his knees, rifled through it, trying to clear his vision. The letters were gone. The letters that his government had entrusted to him. Stolen, right out from under his nose!

Barlow got to his feet again and headed out into the upstairs hallway, catching himself on the staircase railing before he fell. There was a shout from downstairs—he thought it was Donelson—then a crash, and the slamming of a door. Donelson appeared at the foot of the stairs, looked up, saw Barlow, and turned ashen.

"Who was it?" asked Barlow.

"Tiburon. I . . . . What's going on?"

"He stole the letters."

"My God," muttered Donelson—and vanished.

By the time Barlow had negotiated the stairs, Donelson was emerging from a downstairs room—a pistol in either hand, a grim expression on his face. Emily appeared, asking what the commotion was about. Donelson brusquely told her that he would explain later. He handed Barlow one of the pistols.

"Are you badly hurt?" Donelson asked him.

"My pride, worse than anything. Let's go. We have to catch him and get those letters back."

They left the house.

Chapter 7

It was still raining, though not as heavily as before. Barlow thought that would be to their advantage, as the streets were still largely empty. But with one glance along the street as he emerged from the Donelson house, Barlow realized that they would have to be very, very lucky to find Tiburon. The French Quarter was a labyrinth of narrow streets and alleys and courtyards. Tiburon probably knew it quite well—better than Donelson and certainly better than Barlow. But Barlow beat down the rising despair he was experiencing, and turned to Donelson, his voice and expression resolute.

"You go that way," he said. "I'll go the other."

Donelson nodded, started off to the right as Barlow went left. The first intersection was but thirty yards away, and when he reached it Barlow looked both ways. There was a carriage coming his way from the left, the horse plodding along with its head lowered in the torrent. To the right a man was hurrying away from him, covering his beaver hat with a newspaper. Barlow knew immediately that it wasn't Tiburon. He turned left, making straight for the carriage, and grabbing the horse's harness. The driver protested, but Barlow cut him short.

"Did you see a large black man, in a hurry?"

The driver shook his head, water dripping from the brim of his hat. Perturbed, a male passenger inside the carriage called out, demanding to know why they were being delayed. Barlow let go of the horse, stepped back as the driver whipped the leathers against the animal's haunches to get him moving again. Shod hooves clattered on cobblestones. Barlow took one more look down the street, then turned and ran the other way.

This was taking him towards the river, only a few blocks away. Barlow paused at the next intersection, took a long, careful look in all four directions. Nothing. He ran to the next street, paused, and did the same. He caught the barest glimpse of a man ducking into a doorway—he thought it was a black man, bareheaded. Barlow turned in that direction, striding quickly along the narrow sidewalk on the opposite side of the street from the doorway. He'd gone a hundred feet when he realized that the doorway led into a tavern. He could see into the establishment, thanks to a large window of plate glass that bore the legend *Café Chartres*. He stepped into the shadows of a recessed doorway, behind a sheet of falling rain, and watched Tiburon, his back to the window, speaking urgently to the portly mustachioed man wearing an apron who stood behind the bar. The man listened a moment, then gave a curt nod to one side. Tiburon went to the end of the bar and passed through a curtained doorway into the back.

Barlow was crossing the street when he saw Donelson coming round a corner to his right. Motioning for his friend to hurry, Barlow went to the café's entrance and waited.

"He just went inside," said Barlow, when Donelson arrived. "The bartender let him into the back."

Donelson nodded. "I know this place. I'll go around back. You go inside, make a commotion, and that will flush him out to me."

"You speak French, don't you? You go in the front. I'll take the back."

Donelson grabbed his arm as Barlow started to turn. "Take care, my friend. The word is that Tiburon was with the last of the pirate gangs to operate off this coast. Don't underestimate him."

"Believe me, I won't."

Two doors down, Barlow found an extremely narrow passageway that took him to the alley running behind the café. He reached the back door just in time. It burst open and Tiburon exploded into the alley. He almost collided with Barlow, then jumped back, astonished. Barlow didn't give him time to recover. He struck with the barrel of his pistol. Tiburon was quick; he jerked away, and the barrel landed but a glancing blow. That was enough to daze him. Barlow lowered a shoulder and drove his body full tilt into his adversary, driving Tiburon into a wall, knocking the wind out of him. Tiburon brought an arm down across Barlow's back. As far as Barlow was concerned, an anvil being dropped from a great height on his spine could not have hurt worse. The blow drove him to one knee, gasping. Tiburon tried to run. Barlow made a desperate grab for the man's legs, tripping him. Tiburon went sprawling in the rainwater that covered the alley's timeworn stones. He rolled over, drawing a pistol from under his short peacoat. But Barlow was already on his feet, and had his pistol aimed at Tiburon's head.

"Drop it or I'll kill you," he rasped.

Tiburon hesitated, but only for an instant. He could tell by the expression on Barlow's face that the threat wasn't an idle one. He tossed the pistol away and lay there, a trickle of blood from the gash on his skull mixing with rain to curl down his cheek.

"Give me the letters," said Barlow.

"I don't have them." Tiburon's face showed no emotion. His tone of voice was flat, revealing no anger, no fear, nothing.

"Where are they?"

Tiburon's eyes, bright like obsidian, fixed on Barlow. "A Frenchman." He pointed with his chin at the café. "In there. Don't know his name. Didn't want to know it. He paid me, that's all I care about."

"Paid you to steal the letters? How did he . . . ? Never mind. Stand up."

Tiburon got to his feet. Barlow motioned toward the café with the pistol. Tiburon turned, and when he did Barlow pistol-whipped him, knocking him out cold. He crumpled facedown at Barlow's feet.

"Now we're even," muttered Barlow.

As an afterthought he wedged a foot under the unconscious man's shoulder and rolled him over on his back, so that he wouldn't drown in a puddle of water.

Entering the Café Chartres through the back door, Barlow found himself in a short, narrow, dimly lit corridor, at the other end of which was the curtained doorway to the front room. To his left were two doors. Donelson was coming through the curtains. He took three strides, then whirled and leveled his pistol at the beefy, apron-clad man Barlow had seen through the plate glass window. The bartender froze in his tracks. Donelson spoke brusquely to him in French. Barlow didn't have to understand the language to comprehend that a warning had been issued. And clearly the bartender received it—he backed up slowly, passing back through the curtain.

"Tiburon doesn't have the letters," said Barlow, and

kicked in the nearest door. The small storeroom was filled with casks and crates. Donelson kicked in the second door. This room was lamplit, and occupied. A small, balding man with a grandiose mustache was standing behind a desk, busily stuffing something into a brown leather dispatch case. When he saw Donelson and Barlow, and the pistols they were aiming at him, he made an incoherent noise and backed up until he was pressed against a wall and could go no further. He raised his hands and stammered in French. Barlow assumed he was pleading to them not to shoot. Donelson spoke to the man in his native tongue, and he replied readily.

"He says his name is René Bonnière," Donelson told Barlow. "He is the owner of this café."

"He's also a spy." Barlow had moved to the desk, and dumped the letters that had been stolen from his trunk out of the dispatch case. "For France, I assume. Tiburon said this man paid him to steal these."

"How did they know you were carrying them?" wondered Donelson. Again he spoke in French to the café owner, and again Bonnière replied without hesitation. He was too frightened not to cooperate.

"He says they knew you were coming," Donelson said, translating for Barlow. "And that you were carrying important documents. So that's why he bribed Tiburon."

"Maybe you should pay your servants more," said Barlow wryly. "Then they might not be so susceptible to temptation."

"I have a feeling," replied Donelson grimly, "that Tiburon holds no allegiance to anything *but* money. Where is he?"

"Out back—and out cold." Barlow was checking the letters. He was relieved to find that none had been opened. His government's secret correspondence had not fallen into enemy hands. They'd been lucky to retrieve the letters before that happened.

Donelson was conversing with Bonnière once more. "He says his orders were to deliver anything of value that he acquired to the French chargé d'affaires here."

"Nice of him to be so cooperative."

"He thinks we're going to execute him on the spot."

"Why bother?" asked Barlow. "We know who he is now. His secret is out. And we've got what we came for."

"And what about Tiburon? He might have killed you."

"He had a chance when I walked in on him back at your place. He didn't take it."

"I doubt that was motivated by a humane impulse," said Donelson. "He knew a shot would alert me, and reduce the likelihood of his getting away."

Barlow shrugged. "Do what you will with both of them. I don't care." He shoved the pistol under his belt, gathered up the letters, put them back in the dispatch case, and placed the case under his arm. From the café proper came voices raised in alarm. "Sounds like they're planning to rescue Mr. Bonnière," he told Donelson. "Whatever you want to do, I suggest you do it soon."

"To hell with him," said Donelson. "I'll make sure everyone I know in New Orleans is acquainted with his true line of work. Come on. Let's get out of here."

Barlow led the way into the corridor, then out the back door. Tiburon still lay unconscious in the alley.

"And this one?" asked Barlow.

"Leave him," rasped Donelson angrily. "He's where he belongs."

They hurried down the alley. A few minutes later they were back at the Donelson residence. They retired to their respective rooms, changed into dry clothes, and met in the parlor downstairs so that Emily could pour them each a good stiff drink while trying not to show how worried she had been. Donelson related to his wife what had happened, leaving out mention of the pistol-waving. "As for Tiburon," concluded Donelson, "he won't be coming back to work for us."

"I hope not," said Emily, "for if I see him again I shall kill him, if you don't do it first."

Donelson saw the look of surprise registering on Barlow's face, and chuckled. "People tend to forget that she's the daughter of a Tennessee frontiersman."

Emily left them. Donelson finished off his drink, and rose to pour himself another. "I'm relieved we got the letters back. No one else need know about this."

Barlow shook his head. "No. I'm going to include everything in my report. Tiburon isn't your fault, Andrew. But I made a mistake by leaving the trunk unlocked. It was unforgiveable carelessness on my part."

"You're too hard on yourself. No harm's been done. Tomorrow I'll be off to Texas, as planned. And you can go home."

"I've decided to go with you," said Barlow. "I'm going to do what the president asks."

Donelson stared at him, surprised. "What changed your mind? This business with the letters?"

"That's part of it. If I don't take on this mission someone else will have to. And, like you said, it's going to be dangerous."

"But why should you be the one?"

"Because that's the kind of work I do best," said Barlow. *I'm far better at it,* he mused, *than I am at being a plantation owner and slaveholder.*

Donelson smiled. "What happened today has got your blood churning. You've forgotten what it's like to be in action. For men like you, it's an essential ingredient to life. But don't get me wrong. I'm not going to try to dissuade you. I'll be happy for the company to Washington-on-the-Brazos, and I'll give you every assistance I can in your undertaking. I can't help but wonder, though, what your wife will think when she finds out you won't be coming home any time soon."

"She'll be upset," replied Barlow frankly, "and angry at me. But she'll get over it. I hope."

Donelson carried the decanter over and refilled Barlow's glass. "A toast, then." He raised his own glass. "To Mrs. Barlow's forgiving nature."

Barlow drank to that.

Chapter 8

It would have been possible for Barlow and Donelson to travel by ship from New Orleans to Galveston, the principal port of the Texas Republic, but the weather continued foul, and many of the vessels in the harbor were delayed in their embarkation in hopes of improved sailing conditions in the near future. A few skippers were willing to risk rough seas, but Donelson decided they should go overland. This would add a few days to their journey, but, as he pointed out to his companion, if they ended up at the bottom of the Gulf of Mexico the delay would be considerably greater. Barlow was quite willing to go by land, as he had no desire to ever set foot on the deck of a ship again.

The rain persisted for the first week, and they found crossing swollen rivers an adventure, even when a ferry was available. The roads, such as they were, had been reduced to stretches of bog. On the third day out of New Orleans the wind turned, coming out of the north, and the nights became not only wet, but cold—and doubly miserable as a result. A few nights were spent in inns along the way; the rest of the time they made camp under the open sky.

There was plenty of time for conversation, and by

the time they reached their destination Barlow thought he was well-versed in the diplomacy and intrigue that attended the fate of Texas. He learned the extent to which Britain was committed to stopping American expansion westward. Several of her most prominent statesmen had publicly declared that the domination of the Gulf Coast by the United States had to be stopped at the Sabine, the river that formed the border between Louisiana and Texas. British animus toward the idea of American expansion hinged on slavery. The British Empire had indulged in an antislavery crusade for the past decade. She had freed the slaves who lived and worked in her West Indies possessions, placing those possessions at an economic disadvantage when competing with the goods produced by the American States. But many Britons were more concerned with the moral crusade to end slavery, and they feared that if the United States acquired Texas the "peculiar institution" would be guaranteed a future safe from the growing abolitionist movement in the North. Finally Britain had hopes of sponsoring a second North American nation that would rival the United States. The price of their support, though, was steep—Texas would be required to emancipate her slaves. Otherwise, London could never justify to the British population measures to promote and protect Texas.

"Most of the people who settled Texas were from the South," Donelson told Barlow, "so it's not likely they will readily dispense with slavery. It depends on whether they feel there is an alternative other than being subjugated once more by Santa Anna."

"Which is where you come in," said Barlow.

"Right. I've got to convince the Texas government that the United States will annex the republic with the

Rio Grande as her southernmost border, and that we're willing to go to war with Mexico to protect her."

"What about the French? What are they after?"

"France, too, wants to curb our expansion westward. Louis Philippe wants a new nation that is obligated to the crowned heads of Europe for its survival. Both England and France have capable men in place in Texas. Captain Charles Elliot represents the former, while the Comte de Saligny represents the latter. Captain Elliot, I'm told, is a worthy adversary, but an honorable man. I don't know that the same can be said of Saligny. They say he bears a striking resemblance to Napoleon Bonaparte, and that he is just as great a conniver. You'll want to be careful around them both, but especially with Saligny, I'd think."

As luck would have it, they met Elliot and Saligny on the road to Washington-on-the-Brazos, only miles away from the Texas capital. The British and French envoys were traveling together. Captain Elliot was an angular gentleman, whose polished urbanity did not distract Barlow from what a close look made evident— the captain was smart, observant and cool as ice. The Comte de Saligny had the look and manner of the pampered French upper class. He was as short as Elliot was tall, as plump as the Britisher was lean, and had affected the hairstyle of the late emperor—the dark hair was slick with pomade and curled forward to cover a receding hairline. Barlow noticed that while Saligny had a manservant on a horse that trailed along behind, who was in charge of a pack horse laden with luggage, Elliot traveled with a single small valise strapped to his saddle.

"Ah, Mr. Donelson," said Elliot, "what a pleasure to meet you again. We were introduced two months ago, in New Orleans at the home of Jacques Delacroix."

"I remember," said Donelson. "May I introduce my friend and companion, Timothy Barlow. Timothy, this is Captain Charles Elliot, representative of Her Majesty the Queen, and the Comte de Saligny, from the court of Louis Philippe."

Barlow figured Donelson had a reason for leaving his rank out of the introductions. But one glance in Elliot's direction told him that the captain wasn't fooled. They were both military men, and as such could usually spot one of their own kind; Elliot, he thought, knew that he was a soldier.

"We are on our way to Galveston, and from there back to New Orleans," announced Elliot.

"Back to civilization, thank God," muttered Saligny effusively.

"Is President Jones in the capital?" asked Donelson.

Elliot smiled. "Indeed, he was this very morning. We bade him farewell."

"And the Congress—is it in session, by any chance?"

"No," said Saligny. "Is there some reason why it should be?"

"None that I know of," said Donelson vaguely.

Bemused, Barlow watched all three men. They were engaged in some sort of verbal fencing match, trying to get the other to divulge information without resorting to direct questions. If the stakes weren't so high, Barlow would have found this diplomatic game-playing rather amusing.

"Well, we won't detain you," said Elliot. "And we must be on our way. Poor Jean here doesn't want to spend one more hour in Texas than is absolutely necessary."

"*Mon Dieu,* at least the weather is improving," sighed Saligny, gesturing in what Barlow imagined was a very Gallic way at the clearing sky. "It is the first time I have seen the sun in a fortnight, gentlemen!"

They rode on. Donelson sat his horse and watched them go, an expression of disgust on his features.

"Damn them," he muttered. "They've done some mischief."

"How can you be sure?"

"Elliot is entirely too smug."

"Then we'd better go on and find out what kind of damage has been done," suggested Barlow.

Washington-on-the-Brazos was not what Barlow had expected of the capital of the Texas Republic. It was a small collection of log and clapboard cabins, nestled in rolling prairie, interspersed with bosquets of pecan and oak trees. There wasn't much coming and going—it struck Barlow as a sleepy town unaccustomed to big doings. Hardly the sort of place one would expect to hold the key to the future of the United States.

Anson Jones wasn't what Barlow had expected, either. As he and Donelson approached a small whitewashed clapboard cabin near the center of town, a small, white-haired man with the beginnings of a paunch and wearing a rumpled suit of broadcloth emerged and peered at them. Donelson had told Barlow that the Massachusetts-born Jones had struggled through medical school before launching an unsuccessful practice in Philadelphia. He next appeared in New Orleans, where he gained a reputation for hard drinking and high-stakes gambling. Not long after that, he arrived in Brazoria with a few dollars in his pocket and, since that community lacked a doctor, set up a practice there—one which met with more success than his first attempt in the North. Jones had volunteered as an infantry private in the army during the Texas Revolution, and had been made regimental surgeon because of his medical background. After independence was won, he was dispatched to Washington as the new republic's envoy. Once back in Texas he became a senator. Donelson had warned that while Jones looked like a benevolent uncle he was in fact a cunning political infighter. He disliked Sam Houston, whom he believed did not deserve to be elevated to hero status by the vast majority of Texans; as far as Jones was concerned, it wasn't Houston's greatness, but rather the weaknesses of his enemies that had resulted in the great victory at San Jacinto and the winning of independence from Mexico. In spite of this opinion, Jones had become secretary of state during Houston's presidency.

But while Houston was committed to the annexation of Texas by the United States, Jones—according to Donelson, at least—was just as committed to Texas remaining an independent nation. Not just any independent nation, however—Jones envisioned Texas as the greatest power in the western hemisphere, and he would be its chief architect. To this end he had been trying to wean Texans from their affection for the United States; it was Jones who had first solicited British interest in the republic's future.

"Be careful what you say about yourself and your purpose here," Donelson muttered to Barlow as they rode nearer the white clapboard cabin. "Rest assured it will reach the ears of the British, and probably the French as well."

Barlow merely nodded. As they arrived at the cabin, Dr. Jones smiled with what appeared to be genuine pleasure and warmth and stepped out of the shade of the porch to extend a hand of greeting to Donelson as the man dismounted.

"Ah, Colonel Donelson, what a delight it is to see you again!" said Jones effusively.

"It is not only a delight but also an honor to see

you again, Mr. President. May I introduce my friend and companion, Captain Timothy Barlow?"

Jones shook Barlow's hand vigorously. "Captain, my pleasure. What brings an officer of the United States Army so far from home?"

Barlow smiled. "I'm not on active status, sir. I'd heard so much about Texas I wanted to come see her for myself. Mr. Donelson was kind enough to invite me along on this trip." He glanced at Donelson. "And I jumped at the chance."

Donelson suppressed a smile.

"I trust you've not been disappointed by what you've seen of Texas thus far," said Jones.

Barlow was wary. This was no casual question posed by the republic's leader. "It seems to be a bountiful land," he replied. "Also, of late, very wet."

Jones laughed. "You've crossed a number of rivers to get here—all of them treacherous when running high. But indeed, you are correct. This is a rich land, and one that is generous to those who are worthy of her. Please, come in." He gestured towards the cabin.

Donelson and Barlow preceded him inside. The cabin was furnished in a spartan manner, with a hand-hewn table and desk, ladder-back chairs, a rolltop desk in a front corner, a narrow bed behind a make-shift curtain in a back corner. Barlow was surprised; these were not very prepossessing quarters for a president of the Republic of Texas. Jones offered them some wine and apologized for not having stronger spirits, reminding Donelson that he himself did not indulge, and so was prone to being remiss in keeping a supply of whiskey. Barlow declined the offer, as did Donelson.

"You'll forgive me for getting right to the point, Mr. President, but I have important news from Washington," said the latter. "News which, in my opinion, will warrant calling the Congress to session."

"Is that so?" asked Jones, guarded.

"I recently received a letter from President Polk. He wanted me to inform you that he has decided to support the annexation plan of the House of Representatives. In addition, there are certain commitments he is willing to make to Texas. He is willing to guarantee that large appropriations will be made for building roads, bridges and harbors."

"All things we are sorely in need of," murmured Jones.

Barlow glanced at Donelson, wondering if his friend was going to mention the other commitment made verbally by Polk and passed on by Barlow—that the United States was preparing to finance a private army to protect the southern border of Texas from Mexico. Instead, Donelson abruptly changed tack.

"We met Captain Elliot and the Comte de Saligny on the road east of here," he told Jones.

He went no further. He didn't need to. Jones understood what he was after.

"Yes, we had a pleasant visit," said the Texas president.

"So it was just a social call."

"Not exactly. We did conduct a little business." Jones sighed. "I signed an agreement, authorizing England and France to negotiate with Mexico for Mexican acknowledgement of our independence. In return, while those negotiations remain viable, Texas will not annex itself to any country."

Donelson could not disguise his shock and dismay. "You did this without the consent of the Congress, sir?"

"It is within my power to conduct foreign policy as I see fit," said Jones, stiffly.

"But on such a matter—one that is of vital interest to all Texans. . . ."

"I assure you, sir, I have the interests of Texans at heart."

Donelson looked at Barlow, who could tell that his friend was having a difficult time keeping his anger in check.

"How long do you suppose these negotiations will take?" Barlow asked Jones pleasantly.

Jones shrugged. "Captain Elliot assured me he would leave for Mexico at once. I have in turn agreed to dispatch Ashbel Smith to Europe to see to the arrangements there."

"I still say you should have called the Congress to session, Mr. President," said Donelson curtly.

"In fact, I cannot do so. As part of the agreement, I agreed not to call the Congress for ninety days."

"Because you knew it would never approve of such an agreement. The Congress, if given a choice, would vote overwhelmingly for annexation."

"I do not know that to be the case," said Jones. "The people elected me to do what I think is best for the republic, and that is precisely what I am doing."

"Even if it runs counter to their will?"

"If they really think that, they can remove me from office."

"But not before the damage is done."

"Really, Colonel. What damage can arise from peace negotiations with Mexico? A war is not in our best interests."

"Mexico will not agree to anything as long as Texas claims the Rio Grande for its border."

"That remains to be seen. It is not my wish to create animosity between Texas and the United States. But your country's opportunity to annex this republic has passed. Texas offered herself, and was spurned. Now

you can hardly blame her for turning to another
suitor—one who promises to keep her out of a war."

Donelson rose abruptly from the table and turned
to Barlow. "It's time to go," he said briskly. To Jones
he gave a perfunctory bow. "My thanks to you, Mr.
President, for taking time out of your schedule to
see us."

Jones smiled benevolently. "It is always a great
pleasure to see you, Colonel. And I am pleased to
make your acquaintance, Major Barlow. Do you intend to stay long in Texas?"

"No, not long," said Barlow pleasantly. "I have a
family waiting for me back in Georgia, and I'm eager
to get home."

Jones escorted them out. They mounted up and
rode away. Barlow was a little surprised that Donelson
seemed uninterested in stopping off at a general store
that they passed; they were in dire need of provisions
if they were embarking on the return trip to Louisiana.
But he waited until they were out of town to speak.

"If you really believe what you said about the Congress," he remarked, "why don't we find some of the
members and let them know what Jones is up to."

Donelson shook his head. "That would be inappro-
priate. No, we'll ride at once to Huntsville. General
Houston lives there. Hopefully we will find him at
home. We will tell *him* what Jones has done. The general knows every member of the Congress—and he
won't stand by and do nothing while Jones sabotages
the will of the people."

"Let's say Jones has his way, and annexation fails.
Do you honestly think the United States will attempt
to take Texas by force?"

Donelson looked at him bleakly. "I can only hope
it doesn't get to the point where such a decision must
be made. As for you, my friend, Huntsville would be

a good place for you to begin your survey of the coast." He smiled. "You did well back there, by the way. That wily old fox was trying to get information from you about your reason for being in Texas. He suspects that you're here for more than just a little sightseeing. But you gave him nothing. I especially liked the bit about your family and going home to Georgia."

"It wasn't a lie. They *are* waiting for me—and I *am* eager to get back."

"But you are intending to carry out the president's request. . . ."

"Yes," said Barlow. "And the sooner I get started, the sooner I'll be finished."

"I take it you have no intention of staying around for the war with Mexico that's bound to come."

Barlow peered suspiciously at his friend. "None whatsoever. I presume you don't have further secret instructions regarding me from the president?"

Donelson laughed. "No, I swear. No more surprises."

Chapter 9

A fortnight later, Barlow was on the Texas coast, having accompanied Donelson to Huntsville where they'd found Sam Houston, as hoped, at home. Houston was disgusted, but not surprised, when Donelson told him of the agreement Anson Jones had signed with the British and French envoys. He promised to inform as many members of Congress as possible of the president's secret negotiations. And he was pleased with what Donelson told him of American commitments to Texas. Knowing he could depend on Houston's complete discretion, Barlow informed his old friend of his mission. Houston provided him with excellent maps and the names of several people he could rely on, who lived in various communities along or near the coast. He also warned Barlow to be careful.

"There used to be cannibals along the coast," said Houston, "back in the days of the Spanish conquistadores. Pirates, too—and they lingered until fairly recently. The remote islands and palmetto swamps are still hideouts for cutthroats and renegades, and the towns where there is any law to speak of are few and far between. Trust no one, except for the gentlemen whose names I have just provided to you. Avoid all others, keep your eyes open, and watch your back. I'd hate to have to write your wife to tell her you never returned from this little excursion. But I can't think of a better man for the job."

"Well, you had a lot to do with my being here, I understand," said Barlow dryly.

Houston laughed—booming, infectious laughter that made Barlow smile even though he was trying to appear disgruntled. "And I've won that bet we made at the Hermitage."

"You cheated," said Barlow.

From Huntsville, Barlow struck out due south, reaching the coast at the mouth of the Colorado River. He found the maps Houston had supplied to be invaluable. They showed where every crossing and ferry was located—and there were plenty of rivers and streams to cross. He made his way around Tres Palacios Bay, staying as close to the coastline as he possibly could, but finding that he often had to detour inland to avoid an impenetrable swamp or find a way across a river. It was along this stretch that Matagorda Island stretched parallel to the coast for more than twenty miles. Barlow found a man who lived in a cabin at the tip of the peninsula between Tres Palacios and San Antonio bays who informed him that, at low tide, he could cross to the island at a certain point. At the southern end, he would be able to cross to San Jose Island at low tide, but he would have to be wary of the undertow, which could carry horse and rider out to sea. Barlow thanked him, and crossed to the island without difficulty.

The island was quite narrow—in most places no more than a few hundred yards wide—and consisted entirely of sand dunes, some as high as ten feet, and in most places covered with grass. The mainland was visible from anywhere on the island, but inaccessible

due to the intervening body of water, which was infested with sharks. Barlow saw no one while he tra-
versed the length of the island; he spotted, on the far
horizon of the gulf, a sail that appeared for only a
few moments before disappearing beyond the curve
of the earth.

He was impressed by the wild and magnificent soli-
tude of the place, the endless panorama of sea and
sky, and thought that in fact Texas *ought* to be part
of the United States, that perhaps it was destined to
be so, because the United States was a great country,
and Texas would make it greater still. To some that
would have seemed a frivolous reason for annexation,
especially when the debate raged over more serious
matters, such as slavery and the security of the republic and keeping the European powers from reestablish-
ing themselves in the New World. But he had been
brought up to believe that the most important matter
of all was the perpetuation of the nation to which he
owed an unshakable allegiance. He was here out of a
sense of duty, but the duty was to more than a flag
or a man who happened to reside in the White House.
It was a duty to a far grander concept that moved
Barlow to make great sacrifices and undertake such
risky ventures: the concept of the United States being
the greatest nation on Earth. The acquisition of this
land, rich in resources and strategically located, would
contribute greatly to that end. In Barlow's mind, issues
like slavery, or the ambitions of men like Anson
Jones, or the envy of European courts which wanted
to stymie the growth of the United States, should not
be allowed to interfere.

Barlow took detailed notes of everything he saw in
a small leather-bound book. He knew what to look
for, what President Polk was looking for. The private

army, if it ever came to exist, would require an easily defensible position, and also one that was readily accessible to the sea, because it was by sea—or more precisely, by Commodore Stockton's fleet—that supplies would most likely come. Thirdly, the location had to be large enough to contain several thousand men; that was the number, according to Donelson, that was being bandied about as a goal. And those thousands of men would have to be able to march, without too much difficulty, from the location to the Rio Grande, which meant Barlow had to take into account any possible obstacles between that river and the location he picked.

He concluded that Matagorda Island would not be suitable. It was accessible to the sea all along its length, and easily defensible, as there were only two places to reach it from the mainland without boats. That fact also made it a trap—an enemy force could be positioned on the mainland at either end of the island and prevent anyone from leaving it except by boat.

Night fell when he was still on the island, so he made camp on the beach, taking the chance of building a fire out of driftwood, and sitting for a long while gazing at the stars and listening to the waves lapping at the stretch of white sand. He felt as though he had the island completely to himself; he hadn't seen any sign of another human. But, just to be on the safe side, he took the precaution of sleeping among the sand dunes, rolled up in a blanket, well away from the dying fire.

He left the island the following morning. The crossing at its southern end was just as had been described to him. At ebb-tide there was a strong current pulling through the straits and out to sea. He and his horse had to swim a hundred yards against it, but made it to the next island south, San Jose, without too much difficulty.

Thoroughly drenched, he shed his wet clothing and laid it out on the grass that covered the dunes, then stretched out on the sand to dry himself. The warmth of the sun on his chilled body lulled him to sleep. It was the horse that woke him—a whicker of alarm. Barlow sat up quickly, looked around, and thought he caught the barest glimpse of movement up among the dunes. Grabbing his pistol, he investigated. He didn't see anyone, but he knew that someone had been there: they'd left their footprints in the sand. He knelt, examined the tracks, and concluded that they had been left by a woman of slight stature, or an older child. He put on his clothes and rode away, unwilling to waste time searching for the person who'd been spying on him, assuming it had been a local, curious about a stranger.

From the northernmost end of the second island, another crossing was successfully negotiated, and Barlow found himself on the mainland once again. A few miles further down the coast, he reached a small settlement consisting of a half-dozen cabins, one of which contained a general store. It appeared to Barlow to be a place that was enough out-of-the-way that he wouldn't have to worry about British, French or Mexican spies. By the looks of the boats pulled up on a nearby beach, he assumed the settlement was inhabited by fishermen. It was possible that he might learn something valuable from them regarding what lay in store further down the coast.

With this in mind, he rode into the settlement and dismounted in front of the general store. An old, white-bearded man sat on the rickety porch smoking a corncob pipe, watching Barlow through sun-faded blue eyes sunk deep below bushy white brows.

"Afternoon," said Barlow.

"Howdy," rasped the old codger. "Where you from?"

"Georgia."

"Where you headed?"

"South."

The old man nodded, puffing vigorously on his pipe. "Got any tobakker you can spare?"

"Sorry, I don't have any."

"Damn. Well, reckon I'll have to break down and buy some." The old man tilted his head in the direction of the store's entrance. "Plug of tobakker costs too damn much inside, you ask me. That Daniel, he's a thief. Watch he don't rob you blind with his high prices and all. I say that even if he is my son-in-law?"

"Your son-in-law."

"Yep. Everybody here is related to each other in some way or tuther."

"I see. And what's this place called?"

"Ain't got a name. We're all Fullers. Maybe we should go to callin' it Fullertown."

"Maybe so," said Barlow.

"If you're headed south, you got two choices. You can go all the way around Copano Bay or make a crossing at low tide to a peninsula on the other side of Aransas Bay. We got water on three sides of us, y'see."

Barlow took out his map, consulted it. "Do you mind showing me where we are on this?"

The old man looked at the map for a moment, pipe clenched between yellowed teeth, brows knit. He scratched his head, then shook it.

"This map ain't all it could be, on account of it

don't show Copano Bay atall. We're here." He pointed. "And Copano Bay is here, north of us."

Barlow nodded, then turned and looked out beyond the beached boats and the sand dunes to the sea. Matagorda Island was barely visible up the coast, and San Jose Island was directly across what he assumed was Aransas Bay from the settlement.

"So, if the tide is low, you can get to San Jose Island, and from there to Matagorda," posited Barlow, "or you can cross over the narrows that divide Aransas and Copano bays and you're still on the mainland."

"That's about right. Or, you can ride northeast for about ten miles and then circle around Copano Bay."

"Thanks for your help."

"Don't mention it."

Barlow went inside the general store. There were two counters, and on the walls behind these were shelves sparsely laden with goods. In front were a bench and a couple of chairs arranged around a potbellied stove. A man was stretched out on the bench, a hat over his face. He didn't stir when Barlow entered. A second man was behind one of the counters, working on a ledger. Barlow went up to him.

"What can I do for you?" asked the man, closing the ledger.

"I'll take some coffee and flour. Oh, and I'll need a plug of tobacco, too."

The man behind the counter—Barlow assumed his name was Daniel Fuller—nodded and gathered up the order. As he painstakingly scratched out the bill on a piece of paper, he kept glancing curiously at his customer.

"Haven't seen you around here before, have I?"

"No."

"Didn't think so. Not too many folks come through here. What brings you to these parts?"

"Just passing through. How much do I owe you?"

"Five dollars if you're paying with Texas banknotes. Eight bits if you've got American money."

Barlow nodded, took a small sack of hard money from the pocket of his coat, and paid the man in American coin.

Eyeing the sack, Daniel Fuller said, "Sure I can't interest you in anything else, mister? Got a whole crate of good Kentucky bourbon in the back. And some mighty fine ladies' dresses, if you want to take something special home to the missus."

"No thanks." Barlow gathered up his purchases and turned to leave. The man on the bench hadn't moved. Neither had the old man on the porch. Barlow handed him the plug of tobacco. "In exchange for your help," he explained.

The old man looked up at him with surprise registering on his deeply lined face. Then his gaze flickered to something, or someone, behind Barlow. A heartbeat later Barlow heard the creak of a loose porch plank and started to turn. It was the storekeeper, who was in the process of swinging an ax with intentions of separating Barlow's head from his shoulders. Barlow dropped the goods he had just purchased and ducked. The ax missed him by inches. He tugged at the pistol in his belt and had it aimed at Daniel Fuller before the latter could swing that ax again.

"Drop it," rasped Barlow, "or I'll put a bullet in your head."

"Wouldn't do that if I was you," drawled the old man. He had gotten to his feet, using a cane to support his weight. He had a pistol in his free hand, and now he planted the barrel against Barlow's skull, directly behind his right ear. "He's a scoundrel and a thief, but he's still kin, so I'd have to kill you."

Barlow entertained no doubts as to the old man's

sincerity, and lowered his pistol. The old man pressed harder with the barrel of his own gun.

"Throw it down and kick it out into the street," he said.

Barlow did as he was told.

"Stand back, Zeke," growled Daniel. "I'm goin' to lop his head off right here."

"You'll do no such thing," replied Zeke calmly. "There's children and womenfolk around, and that ain't the kind of thing they should see."

"They've seen us kill strangers before," protested Daniel.

"Not when I had anything to do with it. Now put that ax down or by God I'll let him put another hole in your head."

Keenly disappointed, Daniel lowered the ax. Behind him, the man who had been sprawled on the bench emerged from the general store. He looked with complete ambivalence at the three men, then walked to Barlow's horse and looked it over.

"Good, solid piece of horseflesh," he drawled. "Who gets the cayuse?"

"We do it like we always have," said Zeke. "Sell the horse and saddle and anything else of value to Moke Lewis up at Refugio. Split the proceeds and any money he's got on him equally."

"He's got American money," said Daniel. "A sack of it in his coat pocket."

"And what about me?" asked Barlow.

"You? We're going to have to kill you, young man," said Zeke. "Sorry, but we can't have you coming back here with the law—assuming you could *find* any law within five hundred miles of here."

"I take it you boys make a living doing this," said Barlow. He had to keep them talking, delay his execution, while he sought an opening, an advantage, a chance to survive.

"Ain't much of any other way to *make* a living out here," said Zeke. "Tried my hand at mustanging, but Churacho and his gang put me out of business."

"Churacho?"

"He's stalling," growled Daniel. "Let's take him out to the dunes and kill him. The crabs'll pick his bones clean in two days."

"He was kind enough to buy me a plug of tobacco," said Zeke, "so I reckon the least I can do is return the favor and answer his questions."

"You old fool," muttered Daniel.

"Shut up, Daniel," said the third man, who was in the process of untying Barlow's valise from the saddle. "That's my father you're insulting."

"I don't care who he is," said Daniel truculently. "He talks too much. And we're wasting time. Let's kill him and get it over with."

Zeke sighed. "Fine, then. You've got an ache to do some killin' today, Daniel, you do it."

"Don't bother me none," said Daniel.

"Yeah, but it bothers me," said Zeke. "Take him out into the dunes to do it; I won't have it done here."

"I didn't know you'd been made the boss around here," said Daniel.

"Just do like he says," said the third man, thoroughly exasperated. He reached under his coat, brandished a pistol, and handed it to Daniel. "Here, use this."

Daniel put down the ax and took the pistol, aiming it at Barlow's midsection. Zeke instructed the third man, whom he called by the name of Joshua, to relieve Barlow of his sack of hard money. With the barrel of Zeke's gun still pressed against his skull, Barlow didn't move while Joshua searched his pockets and discovered the sack.

"I want it counted out now," said Daniel.

"What, you don't trust us?" asked Joshua.

Daniel looked him straight in the eye. "Hell no, I don't trust you. I don't trust nobody. Not when it comes to money."

"No honor among thieves," murmured Barlow.

"Shut up, son," advised Zeke. "You're in enough trouble as is. Go ahead, Joshua. Count it out."

Joshua shook his head. He poured the coins into the palm of his hand, counted them. "I make it out to be two bits over eighteen dollars. Slim pickings, if you ask me."

"Hardly worth killing somebody for," remarked Barlow.

"He's a cool customer, this one," said Zeke, chuckling. "Give Daniel six dollars and the two bits, Joshua. Then he'll stop bellyaching."

"How much you reckon Moke Lewis will give us for the horse and saddle?" Joshua asked the old man.

"Not half what they're worth," replied Zeke dryly. "But it ain't like we've got anyone else to go to, and Moke knows it. He knows he's got us over a barrel."

Daniel looked sourly at the coins that Joshua placed in his hand. "He's right. It ain't hardly worth the trouble."

"Well," said Barlow, "we can just forget the whole thing. Give me back my money and I'll be on my way."

Zeke laughed out loud. "No, not you. You'd come back and give us hell. Make us sorry we'd ever met you. Go ahead, Daniel, get it over with."

Daniel motioned with the pistol. "Start walking," he told Barlow. "You try anything, and I won't mind putting a bullet in your back."

"I'm sure you wouldn't," said Barlow. He started walking toward the dunes and Daniel fell in behind him, keeping a safe distance between them. Barlow realized that if he was going to do anything to prevent his own murder he would have to act soon. At least now all he had to worry about was one man, not three. The odds were as good as they were going to get. But he had to wait until they were out of sight of the others, so he trudged obediently away from the collection of shacks. In moments they were in the dunes. On the far slope of the second dune he lost his footing and fell. Daniel paused at the crest of the dune, looking down at him, and laughed harshly.

"You think I'm dumb enough to fall for that? Now get up, and don't try anything."

Barlow got up and kept walking, fairly certain that Daniel had failed to notice that his belt buckle was now undone.

They negotiated a few more dunes, and were about fifty yards from the beach when Daniel called to Barlow to stop.

"That's far enough. You got one minute to make peace with your Maker."

"That's not necessary," said Barlow.

"Suit yourself. Get down on your knees."

Barlow did as he was told, half-turning his head so that he could see Daniel out of the corner of his eye as his would-be executioner stepped closer. He had one chance, and he wanted to make sure it counted. When Daniel was only two steps away, Barlow made his move. Lashing out with the belt, he whirled, rising at the same time. The broad strap of leather caught Daniel full across the face. He spun away with an incoherent shout of alarm, and pulled the trigger reflexively. Barlow felt the burn of the bullet in the upper part of his left leg. The impact knocked him off balance, but he didn't fall. He didn't dare. He moved in on Daniel, grabbing the other end of the belt with his left hand and letting go of the buckle with his right. Swinging the belt again, he laid the buckle across Daniel's skull just as the latter was recovering from the stinging surprise of the first blow. This time Daniel fell, partially blinded by the blood that flowed from a deep gash just above his right eyebrow. Barlow lunged at him, dropping on top of him, planting a knee into his chest and driving all the wind out of Daniel's lungs. Then he took a flailing blow to the shoulder, warded off another, and wrapped the belt around Daniel's neck. He got up and, both hands around the belt, dragged Daniel down to the bottom of the dune. There he put one foot on the man's shoulder and coldly, methodically strangled the cutthroat. Daniel made strange noises as he clawed ineffectually at the leather strap biting deeply into the flesh of his throat, and when his windpipe collapsed, he kicked and flailed about for a moment. Then he died.

"Damn you to Hell," muttered Barlow angrily, releasing his grip on the belt. He staggered away, two steps, three, then sat down, shaking uncontrollably. He'd been shot before, and recognized the symptoms—he was going into shock. But he couldn't let that happen. There had been one shot, and presumably, if they'd heard it, Zeke and Joshua would assume that Daniel had done his dirty work and would reappear shortly. How long would they wait before walking into the dunes to find out why he hadn't returned? Barlow examined the wound in his leg. The bullet had not passed through, but neither had it crushed bone or severed the major artery. It did, however, hurt like Hell, and the wound was bleeding profusely. Barlow used his belt as a makeshift tourniquet to quell the flow of blood.

He wanted to go back to the general store and retrieve his horse and saddle and deal with Zeke and Joshua. But that was just pride talking, and pride could get him killed: he was in no condition to do battle with those two. Zeke was a crippled old man, it was true, but Barlow wasn't about to sell him short; old or not, he was an extremely dangerous individual. On the other hand, there was still plenty of daylight left, and it was unlikely that he could elude those two if they came looking for him, especially in his condition. His only option seemed to be to head back to the collection of shacks—to return to the snake pit— if not to wreak vengeance then to at least get his hands on a weapon, or better yet to find a horse, either his or someone else's, that would give him the means to effect an escape.

He reached the back of the nearest shack unseen, and lay with his back to the wall, resting for a moment. The bleeding had slackened thanks to the tourniquet, but every movement was an ordeal. Dragging himself to the corner of the building, he took a careful look at the other buildings; from this vantage point he could clearly see the general store, about fifty yards away. His horse was gone, and he saw no sign of Joshua or Zeke. But a moment later they both emerged from the store, to stand on the porch and gaze out at the sand dunes, wondering, no doubt, what was keeping Daniel. They talked for a moment, then Joshua went back inside, coming out a minute later with a double-barreled shotgun under his arm. Accompanied by Zeke hobbling rapidly along on his cane, he headed for the dunes. Their course took them no more than a stone's throw from where Barlow was hiding, but they didn't see him, for their attention was riveted to the dunes ahead of them.

Barlow steeled himself for more pain and got to his feet as soon as Zeke and Joshua had vanished from view. He had no idea how many other people resided in the small settlement, but he couldn't worry about that. Instead, he focused on reaching the general store. He didn't stop or waste time looking around until he was inside the store; only then did he dare to look back at the other shacks. He saw no one—and apparently no one had seen him. Amazed by his good fortune, he quickly searched the store, but could not find a firearm. He found a back room, though, with a door to the outside, which he opened to peer out at an expanse of rolling grassland. Nearer at hand was his horse, tethered to an iron ring attached to the back wall. Barlow dared to think he might actually get away with his life.

He went back into the store, picked up an ax— probably the same one, he thought, that Daniel had been intent on using to chop his head off—and cracked open several small casks of gunpowder he'd found in the back room. Then he cracked the top of another cask and poured a trail of gunpowder to the back door. The back room was windowless, and there was an oil lamp sitting on a small table in the center, the wick turned down low. Barlow removed the glass chimney, turned up the wick, and watched the flame strengthen. He carried it carefully to the back door, untied his horse and climbed—with some difficulty and no little pain—into the saddle. The lamp's flame flickered in the sea wind. Barlow tossed the lamp through the door, spun the horse around as soon as he saw the flash of burning powder, and kicked the cayuse—with his good leg—into a canter, and then a gallop.

He was expecting the explosion; nonetheless, when it came, he ducked instinctively, shoulders hunched. Throwing a look over his shoulder, he saw with tremendous satisfaction that Daniel Fuller's general store was engulfed in flames, a plume of black smoke billowing into the sky. He noticed that the roof of the adjoining structure was already on fire. With any luck the whole place would go up in smoke. And he made himself a promise—that one day he would return, just to make sure that nest of vipers no longer existed.

Chapter 10

By the next morning Barlow knew that the gunshot wound in his leg had become infected, and he came to terms with the realization that, in all likelihood, he was going to die as a result.

The pain was steadily becoming more excruciating—a throbbing, relentless agony that became almost unbearable when he loosened the tourniquet, as he had to do on a regular basis—but he managed to ride throughout the day, keeping to the coast, hoping against hope that he might find someone willing to help him. By midafternoon he'd decided that he couldn't wait any longer. If he was going to survive he would have to get the bullet out himself and cauterize the wound. He rode down to the dunes along the beach, where he was certain to find plenty of driftwood for a fire. He managed to build a fire, and to fetch a clasp knife from his belongings—the Fullers hadn't even bothered removing the valise from his saddle in the brief time they'd been in possession of his things. He cut open his trouser leg and stared with dismay at his wound. Ugly red streaks radiated away from the bloody hole. Heating the blade, and wishing he had a shot of whiskey to steady his nerves, he tried to steel himself for the task ahead. Even though he knew the alternative was death, he could hardly bring himself to attempt the task—but after twenty-four hours of incessant pain he wasn't sure he could stand any more. But he did it—sliding the knife into the wound, screaming himself hoarse, and actually touching the bullet with the tip of the blade—before passing out.

He woke up screaming, a guttural noise engendered by the excruciating pain from his leg. Someone was looming over him—someone was digging a blade deep into his wound. Barlow instinctively tried to squirm away. A fist plowed into his chin; he saw a flash of bright light, then blacked out again.

When he came to, the first thing that greeted him was a dawn sky, streaked with purple and old rose. The pain now was a constant, throbbing agony, but not as intense as the last thing he remembered. He was very weak; his body ached from head to toe, and he wasn't even sure if he could lift his head. He was lying flat on the ground, a rolled blanket beneath his head. He heard the sound of horses, the crackle of a fire and the muted voices of several men. He could smell the aroma of strong coffee. Wondering if he'd been followed and found by Zeke and Joshua and perhaps more of the treacherous Fuller clan, he tried to sit up. Hands on his shoulders gently but firmly pushed him back down. And then her face came into view—a strong, stubborn chin, high cheekbones, a wide, full-lipped mouth, slightly parted, and large, honey-colored eyes. Tangled black tresses cascaded over her shoulders.

"You must rest," she said, in English, but with an accent. Barlow figured her roots were in Mexico.

"Who are you?" he asked—or tried to ask it; his voice was a hoarse whisper. His throat was parched and sore.

"My name is Therese. Do not talk now. You need rest."

"I need something . . . I could use some coffee. . . ."

"No. No coffee." This came from a man who suddenly appeared to loom sternly over Barlow. He was tall, broad shouldered, wearing a short *chaquetilla* or short jacket, and chino pants. He wore a pistol on one hip and a coiled whip on the other, the latter tied to a broad leather belt by a thong. A sombrero hung by its neck-strap between his shoulder blades. He had long, unruly black hair—nearly as long and unruly as the young woman's, the same stubborn chin and cheekbones and odd-colored eyes. He had a mustache, too—partially obscuring a knifc-slit of a mouth—and a shadow of a beard.

"He can have a little water, but not much," the man told the young woman.

Barlow lifted his head enough to see that his wound had been dressed. "What happened?"

"I finished the job you started," said the man curtly. "I took the bullet out of your leg. Cauterized it with gunpowder. We will have to wait and see, though, if the infection goes away. If it grows worse, you will have to lose the leg."

A chill ran up Barlow's spine. The man spoke so matter-of-factly about amputating his leg that he felt a surge of anger.

"You won't take my leg," he said.

The man might have smiled—Barlow wasn't sure if his lips curled beneath that ferocious mustache or not. Then he shrugged. "It does not matter to me. You can die if you want to."

"It matters to me," said Therese, with a flash of defiance in her eyes as she looked up at the man. "You will not let him die, *hermano*."

Hermano. Brother. Barlow didn't know much Spanish, but he knew enough to translate that word. As much as the two looked alike, he wasn't surprised that they were kin.

"If he does not want to lose his leg, who am I to take it from him? He is a man—let him decide if he wants to live or die. That is none of our concern."

"He will not die," said Therese fiercely, as though by willpower alone she would keep Barlow alive.

The man shrugged again. "We must go now. The *mesteñas* are close by. We drew straws, and Julio lost. He will stay here with you. But when I return, this one must be well enough to travel, or he will be left behind. *Comprende?*"

"He will be well enough," said Therese.

The man looked at Barlow, and his expression was inscrutable. "In a day or two you will know. If he dies before I return, bury him, and wait for me."

With that, he turned away. A few moments later Barlow heard the thunder of hooves, and turned his head in time to see five riders disappearing over the dunes. A man with a rifle cradled in his arms came over to look down at Barlow. Then he spat to one side and trudged to the top of the dune and stood there, silhouetted against the rising sun, scanning the horizon.

"Don't mind Julio," said Therese. "He is just angry because he drew the short straw and cannot ride for the *mesteñas.*"

"*Mesteñas?*"

"The wild horses."

"I should have thanked the other man—your brother—for what he did."

"You can thank him when he comes back."

"I hope," said Barlow, wishing he could be as confident about his recovery as Therese seemed to be.

He spent the next several days resting under her

scrupulous care. And after three days he began to feel better about the chances of keeping his leg. The cauterization of the wound seemed to have worked to quell the infection. By the time Therese's brother and the other mustangers returned, he was sitting up on a regular basis, and could even stand, as long as he didn't put any weight on the bad leg. By this time he had also learned that Therese's brother was known as Churacho. He'd heard that name before—Zeke Fuller had told him that it was Churacho who had forced him out of the mustanging trade. Therese had been unable to supply him with any information about the relationship between her brother and Fuller, except to say that Churacho had for years warned the men who rode with him to stay away from Zeke and his kin. Barlow told her that, in his opinion, this was very good advice, and went on to relate all the details of his run-in with the Fullers.

Therese informed her brother that Barlow's wound had been the result of a clash with the Fullers, and this interested Churacho greatly. That day he asked Barlow to relate the story to him, which Barlow was glad to do, leaving out only the purpose for his being on the Texas coast. Churacho nodded with satisfaction when Barlow got to the part about killing Daniel Fuller.

"They are a bad bunch, all of them," said the mustanger. "But the man you killed was probably the worst of them. I knew Zeke Fuller many years ago, when he first came to this country with two brothers. I should tell you that my father, and his father before him, chased the *mesteñas*. So did the Fullers. This was in the days when Mexico had given grants of land to Anglo settlers, and the Fullers hunted horses for the Anglo settlements that had started to spring up to the east of here. In those days, thousands of wild horses roamed the prairie. There was more than enough to keep many *mesteñeros* busy. But of course the Fullers, being Anglos, did not see it that way."

Churacho paused to light a cheroot. He did not offer one to Barlow. The latter wasn't sure if this was an intended slight or not—Churacho's mind seemed to be somewhere else. His eyes held a faraway gaze, as though he could see back through the passage of years to the time of which he spoke.

"One day, Zeke Fuller and his men ambushed my father and some of his *mesteñeros.* There was a big fight. Fuller's two brothers were killed. My father was mortally wounded. He died in my arms. I was only sixteen years old at the time, but I had been a *mesteñero* for several seasons. I cried out for vengeance on Zeke Fuller. But my father spent his last breath talking me out of it."

"Fuller told me you put him out of the mustanging business."

Churacho nodded. "This is true," he said, with deep satisfaction. "I promised my father I would not kill him. But I did catch him one day, and crippled him forever. He was a very good rider before. After I was done with him, he could hardly stay in the saddle."

Barlow was curious to know what Churacho had done to Fuller to cripple the man, but decided not to ask.

"By that time," continued Churacho, "Fuller had married and had children. He brought some of his other relatives to Texas. They began to rob and murder travelers. They have done this for many years now. But they do not bother me or mine, and I no longer bother them. What they do is none of my business. I catch the *mesteñas.* That is all." He gave Barlow a long look, and Barlow knew what was coming next. "What do *you* do?"

Barlow had had several days to prepare for this moment. Churacho was in Texas, but he was a Mexican, and Barlow had no idea where his loyalties lay. If he told the mustanger the truth it could be the last thing he ever did.

"I used to be in the American army," he replied, without a moment's hesitation. "Now I'm a planter. I live in Georgia. I came to Texas with a friend of mine. He asked me to ride along the coast as far south as I could. To make notes of what I saw."

Churacho nodded—and produced Barlow's leather-bound book from beneath his *chaquetilla*. "These notes," he said flatly.

Barlow nodded. It rubbed him wrong that Churacho had seen fit to rifle through his belongings. But he tried not to let it show.

"Why does your friend want these notes?" asked the mustanger.

"He and some other men are thinking of building a new town on the coast," said Barlow, the lie rolling effortlessly off his tongue. "Someplace where there is a good harbor. They envision a town that will someday rival Galveston."

"There is only one such place. I know every inch of the coast from Matagorda to the mouth of the Rio Grande. The place I speak of is a couple of days to the south, where the Nueces River empties into the sea."

"Thanks. I'll have a look at it."

"We are going south along the coast. You will ride with us. It is not safe for a man to go alone. Especially an Anglo." Churacho put the notebook back under his jacket. Barlow wondered if he would ever get it back.

"I appreciate the offer," said Barlow. But he wasn't sure if it really was an offer so much as an order. It sounded very much like Churacho was telling him what to do. Barlow had a hunch that the mustanger had not yet decided whether he was telling the truth about his reason for being here. And until he was sure, he intended to keep Barlow close at hand. But, for the time being, Barlow was willing to go along. He was in no condition yet to travel alone. And he couldn't be sure that the Fullers weren't still looking for him. He'd killed one of their own, and families like that tended to live by the Old Testament rule of an eye for an eye.

Churacho and his *mesteñeros,* he learned, had found the *querencia,* or stomping grounds, of a band of mustangs. They had managed to capture the stallion, a magnificent blood-red beast with black points. The eighteen mares who constituted the rest of the *manada,* or band, did not have to be captured—they would follow the stallion wherever Churacho took him. They would not leave him even if he wanted them to, even if it meant they were going to their deaths. Therese told him that she knew of one band of mares that had followed their stallion over a cliff. The stallion, she believed, had chosen to kill itself when it realized there was no escape from the ropes of the *mesteñeros.* It chose to die free rather to live in captivity, and the mares had followed its lead.

In the days to come, Barlow learned a great deal about the mustanging trade. No one knew for sure how many wild horses existed in Texas. There were tens of thousands, that much was certain. They were the offspring of the fine Arabian chargers brought over by the Spanish conquistadores centuries before. The horse—which the native peoples had never seen before—was the reason a handful of Spanish adventurers managed to conquer the great empire of Montezuma. A few had escaped their masters; running free, they reproduced, and spread across the prairie. The mustang was a creature of the wide-open spaces, avoiding canyons and mountains and wooded bottoms unless it was being pursued. It had few enemies; it was too quick and strong and wary to fall prey very often to the predators of the plains—the wolf and the cougar. Conditions were ideal for the rapid increase of the mustang population. The only limitation they recognized was the one placed on them by their need for water. They rarely strayed more than five miles from a water source. In Texas, with its numerous rivers and lakes, water and good graze were as abundant, so that a *manada* was usually able to remain within a *querencia* no larger than twenty miles square.

That didn't mean they were easy to catch. Quite the contrary. The mustang had sharp eyesight and a sharper sense of smell. *Mesteñeros* had to approach a band from downwind and under cover. No creature was more watchful, more incessantly vigilant, than the mustang stallion. Sometimes a band would consist of one stallion with all the rest being mares; occasionally a stallion would tolerate a wild mule or gelding horse in the band, for both the mule and the gelding were excellent sentinels. When challenged by a band of wolves, the *manada* would form a circle—the colts, if any, protected in the center, and the adults displaying a formidable front of flashing hooves and snapping teeth. But when man approached, the band would take flight. They could run all day without stopping; they would outrun any mounted mustanger, no matter the caliber of the horse beneath him. So a band of *mesteñeros* had to use subterfuge. Churacho's method was, upon locating a *manada,* to divide his men into four groups. Each group would position itself several miles from the band of wild horses, at the four points of the compass. Then the group located downwind would approach. Once they were spotted, the mustangs would begin to run. But no matter which direc-

tion they ran, there was at least one group of
mesteñeros in place to turn them. If done properly,
the mustangs would soon be running in a giant circle,
perhaps ten miles in diameter. The groups of mustangers would take turns pursuing them. Eventually, the
mustangs would tire. Then it would be time for all
four groups to close in and, with skill and luck, capture
the stallion. This was how Churacho and his men had
taken the band of wild horses they were now moving
south to the border country. At night the mustangs
were either hobbled, sidelined or necked together in
pairs to discourage flight.

Barlow was allowed to travel for the first few days
in the wagon which carried the *mesteñero* gang's provisions. Then he felt strong enough to ride part of the
day. When a week had passed he was riding the entire
day. The wound healed rapidly. Every evening, Therese would put a foul-smelling poultice on it, and in
the morning most of the pain would be gone. Barlow
asked her what the poultice consisted of; she assured
him that he did not want to know, and he believed
her.

He thought that the attention Therese paid him
went above and beyond the call of duty. She was never
far from him, and when he happened to glance her
way, she was usually watching him, and sometimes
would look away shyly. In night camp, she would
make sure he was fed first, which annoyed some of the
mesteñeros. Barlow really didn't blame them; they'd
worked hard from sunup to sundown, and he'd done
nothing all day. But there was more to it than that.
He got the distinct impression that many of the men
in Churacho's band had eyes for Therese. And why
not? She was a pretty young woman, and they were
young men who spent many weeks on the prairie without recourse to feminine company. Of course none of

them made advances towards her—not with the ever-vigilant Churacho around. Barlow assumed that any man who tried to get too familiar with Churacho's sister would live just long enough to regret it.

For her part, Therese hardly seemed to notice that anyone but Barlow existed. That worried him, for a couple of reasons. He felt an obligation to her; after all, she had interceded with Churacho on his behalf—without her advocacy the *mesteñero* leader would have left him to die. She had nursed him back to health. So he certainly did not want to cause her any distress, and if he let her obvious attraction to him get out of hand she would end up getting hurt. She didn't know that he was happily married, and madly in love with his wife; the topic had simply never come up. But now it needed to. Barlow wondered, though, how to do the least amount of damage when he *did* bring it up.

And then there was Churacho to worry about. If he hurt Therese in any way he would have to answer to her brother.

Chapter 11

The place that Churacho had mentioned to Barlow, where the Nueces River emptied into the Gulf of Mexico, had much to recommend it. The bay made for a fine natural harbor. The river provided excellent protection of an army's flank, in the direction from which any threat from Mexico was most likely to come. And the entrance to the bay was sheltered by an island, but there was a passage, just to the north, deep enough for deep-draught sailing ships. Best of all, there was no sign of habitation. Barlow elicited from Churacho that the bay was located approximately halfway between Galveston and the mouth of the Rio Grande. And it did not escape Barlow that the Nueces river was the northern limit of the disputed territory. If an army was landed here, Mexico could not complain that it was landing on their soil. And if Mexico launched an invasion of Texas, an army landed here would be in a perfect position to cut off its lines of supply. After spending half an hour scouting the location, Barlow was pretty well convinced he'd found the spot that President Polk had asked him to find.

According to Churacho, a Spanish expedition had landed here long ago, with the idea of building a mission on the headlands. But the Karankawa Indians had attacked, slaughtering many of the Spaniards, and forcing them to retreat to their ships. They had called the bay Corpus Christi, body of Christ. Churacho thought there was some irony in that, as the Karankawa were notorious cannibals, and had, he suspected, eaten the flesh of some of their Spanish victims.

Barlow continued southward with the mustangers for the remainder of the week. But, just as Churacho had said, he saw nothing along the coast that came close to matching the attributes of Corpus Christi Bay. He decided it was time he took his leave. He was well along in his recovery, and considered it very good fortune that they had not run into trouble now that they were beyond the Nueces and in the disputed territory. One night he informed Churacho that he was ready to go home.

He chose a moment when Therese was not within earshot. They had just made camp, and while some of the mustangers tended to the horses, Theresa and the old man who drove the wagon began preparations for the evening meal. The stallion, staked out and guarded, was pacing restlessly round and round, whinnying to his mares, calling them in; even with ropes around his neck, he was concerned first and foremost with the safety of his harem, and while he distrusted the *mesteñeros,* he knew that this was the time of day when the mares were most at risk from the predators that prowled the prairie.

Churacho was silent a moment. His expression was fathomless as he looked at Barlow, then across the camp to the wagon where his sister worked.

"I think you should stay longer," said the mustanger, at last. "Join us. Who knows? Maybe I can make a *mesteñero* out of you." And for the first time Barlow saw him smile.

"I'm tempted," said Barlow. "There's much to be said for the life that you lead."

"There is much freedom in it," said Churacho, nodding.

"But I have to go back. I have a home, back in Georgia. A family that I have not seen for many months."

"You have a wife, and children."

"A wife and one child. A son. Do you have children?"

There was a trace of pain, a hint of sadness, in Churacho's voice. "I had a family, too, once. But they were all killed, thirteen years ago, by Santa Anna's dragoons."

"My God. I'm sorry."

"It was a long time ago," said Churacho, lifting his chin defiantly. He gazed again at his sister. "Therese . . . will be sorry to see you go. But perhaps it is better if you leave."

"I think so, too." Barlow thought he understood what Churacho meant. To remain even one day longer would make things even more difficult for Therese.

Deep in thought, Churacho was again silent for a while. Then he said, "Santa Anna—he is the reason I helped you."

"I . . . don't think I understand."

Churacho took the leather-bound notebook from beneath his jacket, handed it to Barlow. "You did not tell me everything, I think, as to why you are here. You said you were once in the American army. Maybe you still are. Maybe that is why you write such things in this book."

"You're right," said Barlow. "I'm here because the president of the United States asked me to come, to explore the coast—to find a place where an army could be positioned, in case Santa Anna decides to war once again with Texas."

This time there was no doubt in Barlow's mind—it was a genuine smile on Churacho's face.

"Bueno," he said, nodding. "You look surprised. You think, because I am Mexican, I am for Santa Anna? No. There are many Mexicans, on both sides of the border, who support the independence of Texas. Most do so because they see Santa Anna for what he is—a tyrant. If any part of the country that can free itself from that tyranny it is a good thing."

"Why did his soldiers kill your family?"

Churacho's smile vanished, and Barlow thought for a moment that he had erred in asking for details.

"Santa Anna's soldiers had fought rebels in the southern provinces before coming to Texas. He had always let them prey on innocent people—to loot, rape and murder. This is how Santa Anna makes war. I had not done anything. My family had not, either. They were . . . just in the way."

"In the wrong place at the wrong time."

"Yes. I should have been there, but I was gone, chasing the *mesteños*."

"I doubt you could have done anything to change the outcome."

Churacho looked at him, his face like stone. "I could have killed my wife and daughter so that they did not fall into the hands of the dragoons."

Barlow felt a chill run down his spine. He didn't doubt that the mustanger would have done just that, if he'd been there, once he'd seen that it was hopeless. The courage, the strength of will, that such an act would require was almost beyond Barlow's comprehension.

"So you will go," said Churacho, changing the sub-

ject. "Maybe you should leave tonight, when Therese
is asleep. In the morning I will tell her."

"Tell her what?"

"That you went home."

Barlow shook his head. He didn't cotton to the idea
of sneaking away under cover of darkness, like some
coward. "I should tell her myself. It would be easier
on her."

"It would be easier on *you*," corrected Churacho.
"But I am thinking maybe she would learn to hate
you for going away without saying good-bye. And that
would be a good thing, no? Not for you, but for her."

Barlow grimaced. He could sense that Churacho
was going to be adamant on this point. The mustanger was asking him—or rather, telling him—to
sacrifice his peace of mind for Therese's sake. To
play the role of the ingrate and coward, so that Churacho, perhaps, could try to convince his sister that
her feelings for such a man were misplaced. Barlow
had learned long ago—when he had fallen in love
with Rose Claybourne, even though he'd been married to Sarah Langford—that taking the easy way
usually turned out to be the most difficult of actions
to live with. He could see Churacho's point. The man
was only trying to look out for his sister's welfare.
And maybe he was right. Maybe Therese would learn
to hate him, and that would be a crucial first step in
getting over him.

So, reluctantly, Barlow agreed.

In the early morning hours, having slept not at all,
Barlow quietly rose from his blankets. Churacho was
the only person in camp who was awake. The mustanger sat by the dying embers of the cook fire, smoking his pipe. He said nothing to Barlow, only nodded
as the latter went to the horses picketed nearby and

saddled his own. In moments he was gone, vanishing into the night.

He assumed it would be the last he saw of Churacho. But he was wrong.

On the morning of the second day following his departure, he checked his backtrail—as he had often done, being aware through recent experience of the dangers that lurked along the Texas coast—and was startled to see a distant rider. At first he couldn't make the man out, but it was evident that the rider was pushing his horse hard, judging by the spray of dust and shorn grass raised by the animal's hooves. Barlow threw a quick look around. He was in open prairie, and there was very little cover. It occurred to him that he might be able to outrun the man—he had been traveling at a cautious pace, and his horse was fresh, while it seemed a safe bet that the other's mount was not. But Barlow thought he'd done enough running away for a while—the whole business with Churacho and Therese and slipping away in the middle of the night had been rubbing against the grain for the last forty miles, and he was not in a good frame of mind because of it. So he drew the pistol from his belt and grimly waited for the rider to arrive.

A moment later, the horseman was near enough for Barlow to recognize Churacho.

He couldn't imagine what it was about, why Churacho had come after him. He'd done what the mustanger had wanted, despite the damage it had done to his self-image. Barlow experienced a surge of anger as he put away the pistol. Maybe Churacho's plan where his sister was concerned hadn't worked out the way he'd expected it to; maybe now he was looking for Barlow to help him with Therese. . . .

Before Barlow could indulge in further idle speculation, the mustanger was upon him. Churacho slowed his horse to a canter at the last instant, then launched himself from the saddle at Barlow, knocking him off his horse. Caught completely off-guard, Barlow landed poorly. The wind was knocked out of him, and shooting pain radiated from his barely healed leg wound. Thus his attempt to defend himself was feeble, and in a heartbeat the mustanger had him pinned to the ground with a knee in his chest. Brandishing a knife, Churacho pressed the blade against Barlow's throat.

"Where is she?" rasped the mustanger.

"Damn it . . . get off me . . . you bastard . . . ."

"*Where is she!?* What have you done to her?"

More angry than scared, Barlow mustered all the air he had left in his lungs and shouted, "I don't know what you're talking about!"

Churacho glowered at him, the blade of his knife pricking Barlow's skin and drawing blood.

"Now use that knife or get it the Hell away from me," gasped Barlow.

Churacho, reluctantly, removed the knife from Barlow's throat. He stood up, backed away. But he didn't put the knife up. Barlow felt his throat, looked at the blood on his fingers, and tried very hard to control his temper as he got to his feet. He noted that his pistol was gone, he quickly scanned the ground for it, assuming he had become separated from it in the fall, but couldn't find it in the tall grass.

"Therese is gone," rasped Churacho, his tone accusatory. "When I told her you had gone, she became convinced that I had driven you away—that I had *forced* you to leave against your will." He shook his head, disgusted. "I do not understand how women think. When I went out to check the *manada,* she ran away. She took a horse and came after you. I sent the others on and found her trail." With bleak eyes he swept the rolling prairie.

"I haven't seen Therese," said Barlow.

"She must have found your trail—or crossed it without knowing. I am a fool. I thought that I was following her all this time, but somewhere along the way I started following you and not her."

Barlow's anger began to ebb, replaced by a growing concern for Therese.

"Is she armed?"

Churacho shook his head.

"Damn," muttered Barlow. "We'd better find her."

Churacho looked at him with surprise.

"Just because you're an idiot," said Barlow dryly, "doesn't mean I won't help you find her. What were you thinking? That I'd done away with her because she followed me?"

"I was not thinking straight," snapped Churacho. "I am sick with worry. She is all the family I have left."

"Fine," said Barlow. "Then help me find my gun so we can start looking for her."

Chapter 12

Barlow figured that they had to work under the assumption that Therese had found his trail and followed it. She had grown up with *mesteñeros,* living on the wide-open plains, and knew how to track someone. Knew better, it seemed, than her own brother, as Barlow was quick to point out. So their best course of action was to backtrack.

It wasn't that easy tracking someone across the coastal prairie. The grass grew thick and tall, and it was more a matter of looking for the damage done to the grass by a horse's hooves than relying on the imprint of hooves on the ground. Though they proceeded carefully, Barlow thought they made good time for the remainder of that day. But as the sun began to sink lower in the western sky, he despaired of finding a clue before night fell. He didn't relish sharing a night camp with a Churacho who was almost crazy with worry about his sister. And if something *had* happened to Therese, they could scarcely afford to while away the hours until dawn.

Then they had some luck—they found where a single rider had cut across Barlow's trail. Another rider, presumably Churacho, had come along some hours later; it is at this point that the mustanger had been thrown off his sister's trail and onto Barlow's. Somehow, Therese had missed Barlow's sign altogether. It would have been easy to do. His trail was hours older, and he had been traveling at an easy pace, with less disturbance to the grass as a consequence. Therese's trail angled off to the northeast. They turned to follow it, and just before dawn found more signs. Three, maybe four horses. They were shod, which meant, at least, that it wasn't a Comanche hunting party. The riders had cut Therese's trail and then set out after her. Try as he might, Barlow couldn't come up with any reason why any group of riders would do that— at least not one that gave him any comfort. He kept hearing the words of warning Houston and Donelson had spoken regarding this country. How it was infested with cutthroats and renegades. The kind of men who would think of a lone rider as a potential victim.

Churacho said nothing; his features were a stoic mask—and yet Barlow was pretty sure the mustanger was thinking along the same lines. He pushed his sturdy horse mercilessly, and it was all Barlow could do to keep up. He was about to speak out on the subject of just how foolhardy it would be if they killed their mounts when night fell and they were unable to proceed further, lest they lose the trail altogether.

They didn't risk building a fire. Barlow rolled up in his blankets and tried to sleep, with miserable results. Churacho sat up all night, sometimes smoking a cheroot, waiting impatiently for the night to run its course, and speaking not a word until the eastern sky began to gray. Then he was on his feet, telling Barlow that it was time to go.

They had traveled but a couple of hours when they found the dead horse. Churacho identified it immediately as the one Therese had taken.

It had been shot several times. Barlow figured the

men who had been pursuing Therese had gotten close enough to kill her horse out from under her. With a knot of fear in his belly, he helped Churacho search the grass all around. Barlow half-expected to find Therese's battered, abused corpse. But there was nothing. The men had carried her off.

They picked up the trail quite easily. Therese's captives were headed straight for the coast. After two more hours had passed, Barlow shared with Churacho his observation that the men had evidently ridden through the night; he based the assumption on an educated guess—that they had caught up with her right before nightfall. Considering the time that had elapsed and the distance covered, it couldn't have been much earlier, or much later, than that. But it was clear that the men hadn't made a night camp, which meant, encouragingly, that they were too busy traveling to bother with Therese too much.

All of this he told Churacho. The mustanger's only reply was that he hoped Barlow was right.

By midafternoon they reached the edge of a broad expanse of water. Barlow realized that he had passed this way before, and when Churacho told him it was Copano Bay, he had a premonition that set the hair at the nape of his neck on end.

"I think they're headed for the Fuller settlement," he said.

Churacho stared at him. "Zeke Fuller would not dare to take my sister."

"Zeke Fuller's probably not one of the men we're chasing. You said yourself he can't ride much now. And maybe whoever did take her didn't know who she was." Barlow thought about it some more, then added, bleakly, "Or maybe they do know. Maybe they took her because they knew I was riding with you."

"To trade for you," said Churacho slowly.

Barlow nodded. "Yes. It's a possibility."

They rode on, and a short while later were belly down at the top of a low, grassy swell, gazing at the collection of shacks just their side of the dunes. A pile of charred timber marked the place where the late Daniel Fuller's store had once stood. Barlow studied his handiwork and would have felt a sense of tremendous satisfaction but for the fact he thought it likely that Therese was in danger because of him. There were four horses in a pen behind one of the shacks, and even at a hundred yards it was easy enough to see they had been ridden hard. One man sat in a rocking chair on a porch of another cabin, a rifle across his knees. Barlow almost didn't see him because he was in deep shade, sheltered from the high, hot sun by the porch roof. But Churacho didn't miss him—Barlow doubted that the mustanger ever missed much of anything.

"She must be in there," muttered Churacho, meaning the cabin in front of which the guard was stationed. "The question is, how many of them are there?"

"At least five men," said Barlow. "The four riders we've followed here, and Zeke Fuller. I didn't see any while I was here, but I wouldn't be surprised if there were a few women, too. And they may be as dangerous as their menfolk."

"They are all vermin," said Churacho.

"I'll grant you that."

"I am going to get her."

Churacho started to stand up. Barlow grabbed his arm and pulled him back down. "Don't be a fool. You can't do her much good shot full of holes."

"I will not leave her in their hands any longer than I have to."

"Well, you'll have to a little longer," said Barlow

curtly. He checked the sun. "At least a couple more hours. Until dark."

"No," said Churacho. "I go now."

Barlow sighed. "There's one other way to do this," he said.

A quarter of an hour later he found himself leading his horse into the Fuller settlement, a length of driftwood with a piece of white cloth tied to the end in one hand, reins in the other. The guard in front of the cabin saw him and got up slowly, staring, as though he couldn't quite believe what he was seeing. Then he called inside, and a moment later several men emerged, including Zeke Fuller and his son, Joshua. The old man was using a cane to get around. Barlow halted about thirty paces away and waited. He could only hope that Zeke wouldn't shoot first and ask questions later.

It was Zeke who broke away from the others and stepped out into the slanting, late afternoon light— Barlow had made sure to come in from such a direction that the sun was directly behind him.

"You got a lot of brass, mister," said Zeke admiringly, aiming the cane at Barlow. "Just waltzin' in here like this, after what you did to Daniel."

"I didn't have much choice about that," said Barlow. "He was about to kill me. You would've done the same."

Zeke nodded. "Probably. But I'm still going to have to kill you, son."

"I know. But not yet. I want the woman freed first."

"And what if we don't want to let her go?" asked Joshua. "What's to keep us from just killing you right now, you son of a bitch, and keeping her?"

Zeke turned and looked at his son. "Shut your trap, Josh," he said.

"I'll give you one good reason for not doing it that

way," said Barlow. "I don't think you know this, but that's Churacho's sister."

Zeke's head snapped around. "Churacho!" he breathed.

Barlow nodded. "That's right. And if any harm comes to her, you know what will happen. You of all people should know what Churacho is capable of, Zeke. There won't be a Fuller left alive in the state of Texas."

Zeke looked at Joshua again, who turned defensive. "Hell, Pa. I didn't know who she was. All I knew was she come out of that mustanger bunch."

"That's what I told Churacho," said Barlow. "That's why you have this chance to let her go and put things right. I told him I figured you tracked me down, found out I was with the *mesteñeros*. Came back here for reinforcements, and when you rode out again you cut her trail. You thought it might be me, but when you saw her you knew who it was—you'd seen her before."

Zeke squinted at him. "Who are you anyway?"

"The name's Barlow. I'm a major in the United States Army."

"That figures. Explains why you was asking so many questions when we first met. And the American money you were carrying. You're some kind of scout."

"Something like that."

"But what's an Army officer doing riding with the likes of Churacho?"

"That's your doing. Or rather your kinsman's. The one named Daniel. He shot me in the leg. Right before I strangled him."

Zeke was looking very grim. "Bring the woman out," he told his son.

Joshua knew better than to argue. He went inside the cabin, emerging a moment later with Therese, her hands bound behind her back. When she saw Barlow her face lit up . . . and then she looked scared—realizing, figured Barlow, exactly what he was doing. He was relieved to see that she didn't look much the worse for wear; he didn't think the Fullers had molested her in any way.

"Cut her loose," Barlow said, "and let her ride away."

"I say we keep her," opined one of the men Barlow didn't know. "We could have some fun. . . ."

"No," snapped Zeke. "Like the man said, he's the one we want. Cut her loose."

Joshua produced a hunting knife, cut Therese's bonds. She walked to Barlow, rubbing her wrists, which were raw from struggling against the hemp rope they had used.

"You shouldn't have come," she said, looking into his eyes.

"Get on the horse and get out of here."

"I want to stay with you."

"Then you're a fool," he said bluntly.

She was hurt by his words, but then, that was what he had intended. He took her by the arm and turned her towards the saddle and would have lifted her bodily onto the horse if he'd had to, but she jerked her arm free, her temper flaring, and mounted up without his assistance.

"Whatever you hear, whatever happens, don't look back—just keep riding," said Barlow.

Tears welling in her eyes, she turned the horse sharply, kicked it into a gallop, and rode away. Barlow kept an eye on the Fullers, thinking they might try something—like shoot his horse out from under her—but they didn't. They kept their weapons trained on him. He didn't mind—that was the whole idea.

"You want to try for that pistol?" asked Zeke, "Or

you can throw it down, and maybe live a few minutes longer."

Barlow thought it over. He could finish it quickly by reaching for the pistol in his belt. But he wasn't quite ready to concede that he was going to die. Maybe he was just fooling himself; he realized that this was a distinct possibility, but he clung to the notion that he might, somehow, be able to survive. If he touched the pistol, they would kill him on the spot. That, and nothing else, at this point, was a certainty. Moving very slowly, he brought his left hand up and removed the pistol, tossing it to one side. Joshua walked over to retrieve it.

"I wouldn't be going around calling anybody a fool, if I were you," said Joshua, with an unpleasant grin.

The bullet hit him in the forehead—Barlow saw the hole suddenly materialize before the sound of the long rifle reached his ears. Joshua Fuller lived long enough to look surprised, then the pistols—his and Barlow's—slipped from his numb fingers, and he crumpled like a rag doll.

Barlow was as surprised as Joshua had been—he'd told Churacho to take his sister and leave. Obviously the mustanger hadn't listened; Barlow had no doubt it was he who had fired the shot. He dove for his pistol, heard a shotgun roar, and rolled as the buckshot kicked up dust around him. Miraculously, he was unscathed. He came up to one knee and fired at the man with the shotgun, hitting him high in the shoulder and spinning him around. Then he moved again, because Zeke and the other Fuller were recovering from the shock of seeing Joshua killed. They had instinctively crouched and looked around for the sharpshooter, thinking they would be next on his list of targets. Now, though, they were aware that Barlow was an equal threat. Zeke fired his pistol as Barlow scooped up Joshua's and ran for the cover of the nearest shack. Zeke's bullet splintered wood, missing Barlow by inches. Barlow chanced a look around the corner of the shack, hoping to find a target, but hesitated to shoot, because Zeke and the other man were on the move, seeking cover themselves. The man he had wounded was crawling under the weathered planks of the cabin porch; Barlow figured he was out of the fight for the duration.

Then he heard the thunder of horses' hooves, and looked back the direction Therese had just taken—to see why.

Churacho was riding Hell-for-leather into the Fuller settlement, and Therese was right behind him. While the mustanger rode right past Barlow's position, heading for the cabin into which Zeke and the other man had dodged, and fired through the solitary window, Therese angled her mount over to Barlow. Sliding a foot out of the stirrup nearest him, she held out her hand.

"Come on!" she said. *"Andale!"*

Stepping into the stirrup and taking her hand, Barlow vaulted into the saddle behind her. She had been standing up in the other stirrup—now she sat, virtually on his lap. As she turned her head, he thought he glimpsed a faint smile tugging at the corner of her mouth.

"Reach around me and take the reins," she advised.

He did, kicking the horse into motion and riding away from the settlement, trusting that Churacho would have the good sense to follow. If not, that was his problem—at least until Barlow could get Therese out of harm's way. But a quick look over the shoulder confirmed that the mustanger was coming after them.

Barlow didn't stop until they'd reached the top of a low rise south of the settlement, well out of long-gun range. Looking back at the settlement, he could see Zeke Fuller standing over the body of his son; the old man was pointing his cane in their direction, and shouting something that Barlow couldn't make out.

"I wonder what he is saying," murmured Therese.

"I killed his son," said Churacho bleakly. "That means he won't rest until he has killed me."

Barlow nodded. "And he's still got a score to settle with me."

"We will both be hunted men, my friend," said the mustanger. "Not just the old man, but all of his kin, will swear a blood oath. It is their way."

Chapter 13

"My God!" exclaimed Andrew Jackson Donelson when he opened the door of his Vieux Carré residence and saw Barlow standing there. "Timothy! You're alive!"

"More or less," said Barlow with a grin. He knew he looked like warmed-over Hell, having trekked by horse to Galveston and then, subduing his innate fear of sea travel, boarding a merchant brig bound for New Orleans. He'd done the latter for one reason and one reason only: he was in a hurry to get back home to Rose and Jacob—in such a hurry that he was willing to suffer the misery that afflicted him as soon as the ship set sail, and continued without abatement until it had docked and he, pale and wretched, had stumbled down the gangplank.

"To be honest, I thought you were dead," admitted Donelson. He turned his head and shouted for Emily, who appeared seconds later at the top of the staircase in the main hallway. She looked delighted when she saw Barlow, hurried down the steps, and gave him a warm embrace, even though he warned her in advance that he was a little "ripe" after several days at sea and weeks—he wasn't really sure how many weeks had passed—since he'd crossed the Sabine into Texas.

"I'll have a hot bath drawn for you, and we have plenty of ham left over from dinner," she told him, and hurried off to turn her words into action. Donelson escorted Barlow into the front parlor, and poured him a glass of good Kentucky whiskey.

"You met with no trouble along the coast, then?" asked Donelson.

Barlow's smile was rueful. "Well, I wouldn't say that. But I believe I did find what you and Commodore Stockton and President Polk are looking for." He took a drink, put aside his glass, and removed the notebook from under his jacket, handing it to Donelson. Then he drank the rest of the whiskey, savoring the smooth flame that exploded in his belly, while Donelson pored through the voluminous notes Barlow had made.

"This is excellent work," said Donelson. "The president knew what he was doing when he chose you for this task."

"Don't even start," said Barlow, holding up a hand. "I've done what was asked for me—on two occasions. Now I'm going home. So if you or the president have something else in mind for me to do, you can forget it."

Donelson laughed. "No, there is nothing else. I didn't mean to alarm you, my friend."

Barlow looked disconsolately at his empty glass, then motioned in the direction of the sideboard. "Do you mind if I help myself?"

"Make yourself at home." Donelson watched Barlow cross the room. "Is it my imagination, or are you limping?"

"It's nothing." Barlow wasn't at all interested in revisiting his experiences with the Fullers. "I drew several maps in that notebook. The best location is at

Corpus Christi Bay. It's located where the Nueces river flows into the gulf."

"Commodore Stockton will be excited to hear the news. He is in New Orleans at present. I'm certain he would like to discuss your findings with you. That is, if you're up to attending a soiree this evening."

"That's fine. But I'm leaving for Georgia in the morning. If you're going to have a war in Texas, Andrew, you'll have to fight it without me."

He spent a long while luxuriating in the hot bath that one of the Donelsons' servants had prepared for him in a big cast-iron tub located in a small room off the kitchen and, for the first time in many days began to feel civilized. The tension started to drain out of him, and he indulged in reflecting on his Texas experiences. Much of the reflection had to do with Therese, and what had transpired between him and Churacho's sister following their escape from the Fullers. . . .

They had ridden south for an hour, and then Churacho called a stop, and they spent the rest of the waning day keeping an eye on their back-trail, watching for pursuit. There was none. Barlow wasn't surprised. They had hurt the enemy, killing one—Joshua Fuller—and wounding another. Zeke Fuller would want to give his son a proper burial before setting out for vengeance. And he would probably wait for reinforcements as well, because he had to know he'd be taking on not just Churacho but Churacho's entire mustanging crew. Barlow wondered how many kin Zeke Fuller had in Texas—and how many of those he could count on to ride for revenge.

They had continued on until well after dark, finally stopping to make camp in a grassy hollow, surrounded by prairie. There would be no fire—its light could be seen for miles, and would serve as a beacon for unwanted company. But the moon was three-quarters full, and there were countless stars in the sky, so they had plenty of light to see by. Churacho told Barlow they needed to keep watch through the night; Barlow agreed, and volunteered to take the first watch. He had pulled the mustanger aside.

"I haven't thanked you for saving my life back there," he said. "But you took a big chance. You'd have been smarter just taking your sister and riding out."

"She would not go." Churacho's smile was rueful. "*Sí,* I could have forced her to leave with me. But she would have hated me for a very long time." He looked past Barlow at Therese, who was watering the horses with water she had fetched from a creek a stone's throw away from the campsite—looked at her and sighed. "Our father and mother died when she was very young. She has led a hard life, riding with *mesteñeros.* But she never complains. So I . . . if she wishes me to do something, I try to do it."

Barlow smiled. "You have a heart after all, Churacho."

"And you," said Churacho, his eyes glinting in the darkness. "You were willing to give up your life for hers."

"She was in that mess because of me."

"I owe you a debt I may never be able to repay."

"I'd say we're even," said Barlow, and headed for the highest point in the rolling sea of grass, to take up his four-hour vigil.

The night turned cold, with the grass bending and rippling at the mercy of a steady breeze out of the west. Churacho and his sister took to their blankets and were soon, assumed Barlow, asleep. All he saw in the first two hours were a half-dozen dark shapes moving furtively, silently through the grass, circling the camp. It was a pack of wolves, attracted, he supposed, by the smell of the horses. But they also smelled man, and eventually moved away.

Not long after that he heard a whisper of sound behind him and whirled, rifle at the ready—to find Therese standing just a few yards away. He put the rifle down and apologized. She smiled, and draped the blanket she was carrying around his shoulders.

"You saved me from those men," she said, barely above a whisper. "You shouldn't have traded yourself for me."

"And you shouldn't have come after me in the first place, Therese." He made it a simple statement of fact, and not a scolding.

She looked away, embarrassed. "I thought my brother had lied to me about why you left."

"He told you the truth."

She found the courage to look squarely at him then. Her tone was plaintive. "But why didn't you say good-bye?"

Barlow grimaced. "It didn't even occur to me," he said gruffly.

She smiled. "You are lying. My brother told you to go without saying good-bye. He hoped I would hate you for it. Admit it. This is the truth."

"No."

She gasped, and then laughed softly. "You're *still* lying! My brother made a mistake. I could never hate you, no matter what you did." She glanced over her shoulder, down into the hollow, and saw that her brother was still rolled up in his blankets. Then she sat next to Barlow—uncomfortably close, in his opinion. But he didn't move away.

"Why do you have to go?" she asked.

Barlow sighed. "I have a wife and son back home. I haven't seen them for a very long time."

"Oh," she said, in a small voice. She looked across the moonlit prairie. The wind blew her long black hair away from her face, and Barlow stole a glance at her profile to see if she was crying. But she wasn't, and he thought that maybe he wasn't giving her the credit she was due. Therese had to be made of stern stuff, to have led the life of a mustanger. It was a life of great freedom but also, he imagined, a lonely life, especially for a young woman.

"One day," she said finally, "you will come back."

Before he could argue that point, she had turned to him and—her eyes bright with passion, even in the darkness—she kissed him, pressing her lithe, eager body against his, and nearly pushing Barlow off balance. He took her by the shoulders and pushed her firmly away. Her dark, windswept hair was like a veil across her face, across her blazing eyes and breathlessly parted lips.

"Don't do this, Therese," he warned.

"Lay with me tonight. Just this one night."

"I can't." He made the mistake of gently brushing the hair out of her face. Then he made another mistake, this time with words. "If things were different . . . If I could, I'd stay with you. But I can't."

He knew immediately that it had been the wrong thing to say. It gave her hope where there was none. His only defense was that he was searching for something that would give her solace. He didn't want to tell her that he didn't love her, that he loved Rose, and Rose alone. He desired Therese—what man wouldn't? But he was old enough to know the difference between lust and love. He wasn't angry with her for trying to tempt him. She was merely listening to an instinct she shared with all women—to use her femininity to lure the man she wanted into her arms. He didn't want to hurt her. And so he was a coward after all.

She sat there beside him for a while, saying nothing. Perhaps, he thought, treasuring what would be—even if she didn't realize it now, thanks to his foolish words—their last few moments together. Barlow felt sorry for her, and when she started trembling from the cold, he shrugged the blanket off his shoulders and put it around hers. She smiled and lay her head on his shoulder and he let her—what was he supposed to do?—and for a while she slept, so that Barlow started to worry about Churacho waking up and finding them like this. There was no telling what the mustanger would do if that happened. But soon Therese sighed and rose, handing him his blanket back, gazing at him a moment, her hair again veiling her face, before returning to the camp.

Wide awake now, Barlow decided to let Churacho sleep, and stood watch the remainder of the night. Just before sunrise he shook the mustanger awake. "I'm going home," he said. Churacho nodded, glanced at Therese, who seemed to be sound asleep in her blanket. He waited until Barlow had mounted up, then stepped forward and extended a hand. Barlow shook it. No words passed between them. Barlow felt as though he was parting company with an old and dear friend. He knew he would never see Churacho—or Therese—again. But in spite of all the peril and pain he had survived during their time together—or perhaps because of it—Barlow had a hunch he would look back on his days with the *mesteneros* as one of the most exciting times of his life. It had been many years since he had felt so . . . alive.

He reluctantly let go of Churacho's hand. With a

brief nod he turned his horse and rode north across the awakening prairie.

The water in the tub had turned cold. Barlow sighed and got up, dried himself, and put on his uniform, which had been cleaned by one of the Donelson house servants. Then he went to the window and spent a long time gazing out across the rooftops at the forest of masts that marked the nearby waterfront. He was a little surprised to find that he regretted having to leave New Orleans—and Texas—behind. Or maybe, he mused, it was just that he didn't relish returning to the mundane life of a plantation owner, whose only concern was whether it would rain or shine, or what the price per cotton bale might be at the end of the season. He missed Rose and Jacob—missed them so much that it hurt. But he also knew he would miss living on the edge, which he'd been doing ever since his arrival in this city, carrying secret messages for the president, engaged in what just about everyone knew was a prologue to war.

Chapter 14

The "soiree"—as Donelson had called it—was held in a grand old house but a few blocks away, a house built around a large courtyard with a handsome fountain that featured lions rampant as its centerpiece. The host was an American businessman named Bennett Anderson, who had grown immensely rich off a fleet of merchant schooners that plied the coastal region, carrying goods to remote communities and bringing pelts and hogs and corn liquor and a dozen other products back to the city. Barlow figured there were at least a hundred guests, the cream of New Orleans society, in attendance. But the guest of honor was Commodore Robert F. Stockton.

Barlow knew a good deal about Stockton, thanks to Donelson and his own assiduous reading of newspapers. The commodore was the grandson of a signer of the Declaration of Independence. He had joined the United States Navy in 1811 as a midshipman and had seen action during the war with Great Britain that followed shortly thereafter. Later he served in the Mediterranean, and fought with distinction against the Barbary Pirates, during which time he also managed to fight a couple of duels with British naval officers. Committed to the recolonization of slaves to Africa, it was Stockton who had scouted the western coast of the "dark continent" and obtained the territory that had come to be known as Liberia.

Inheriting the family fortune, Stockton had dabbled in politics, but met with greater success in business, investing heavily in the construction of the Delaware and Raritan Canal and serving as the first president of that highly profitable venture. With John Ericsson he had designed the *Princeton*—named for Stockton's hometown in New Jersey—the first warship to be driven with a screw propeller. He had also designed two 12-inch guns, the largest naval ordnance of the times. President John Tyler had offered Stockton the post of secretary of the navy, but Stockton had declined, preferring to go back to sea. According to Donelson, he was an avid expansionist, a man of action, a close friend of Andrew Jackson's, and a great patriot. According to others, he was a flamboyant and unconventional braggart. Barlow was eager to meet him, and to draw his own conclusions.

He soon had the chance. He and the Donelsons had only just arrived when a young naval lieutenant approached them, bowed stiffly, and informed Barlow and Donelson that their presence was respectfully requested in the drawing room. Donelson looked at Barlow and shrugged, indicating he had no idea what it was all about. Emily went off to join a group of women. The lieutenant escorted them into the house. There were six men gathered around a pedestal table in the center of the lavishly appointed room. Three were in uniform, and three were in civilian dress. When the lieutenant presented Donelson and Barlow to this company, and performed the introductions, Barlow learned that the three civilians were prominent businessmen—their host, Anderson, among them. Of the three naval officers, two were captains and the third, a big, barrel-chested man with thick sideburns covering his fleshy jowls and piercing blue eyes under bushy brows, was the commodore himself.

That gaze was fixed on Barlow as soon as the lieutenant mentioned the latter's name.

"Barlow?" The commodore's voice was gruff—perhaps, imagined Barlow, from years of shouting commands at a ship's crew over the roar of cannon or heavy seas. "Seems I've heard that name before. By God, yes, now I remember. General Jackson spoke of you on several occasions. He seemed to have high regard for your abilities, Captain."

"I held the general in high esteem."

"As did we all, sir, as did we all."

"Captain Barlow just returned from a mission to Texas, Commodore," said Donelson. "He was chosen by the president himself to survey the Texas coast, in search of a likely place for a base of operations." He produced Barlow's notebook, opened it to a particular page. "The captain informed me that, in his opinion, this was the location he preferred."

Stockton scowled at the scribbled notes. "Yes, yes. Corpus Christi Bay." He consulted a large map opened on the table. "Right here, gentlemen," he told the others, pointing. "At the mouth of the Nueces."

"That would be ideal," said one of the civilians.

Stockton gave him a scathing look.

"I could be wrong, of course," said the civilian hastily. "I have no military experience from which to draw."

"No, you're right, it would be ideal," said Stockton. He turned his attention back to Barlow. "As you have been on the trail for, I imagine, many weeks, you may not be privy to the most recent developments. Things are moving quickly, Captain, as they tend to do when the fates of entire nations hang in the balance. An army of eight thousand Mexican troops has arrived at the Rio Grande."

Barlow glanced at Donelson, who shook his head. "This is the first I've heard of it. Where did you come by this information, Commodore?"

"A reliable source," insisted Stockton. "A captain in the Texas Rangers. And this just came into my possession today." He handed Donelson a letter. Barlow read it over his friend's shoulder—and noticed that there was no signature. It ended merely, *Yr. obdt. svt., W.*

"I'll be damned," murmured Donelson. "The Texas Congress has rejected the peace treaty with Mexico that President Jones proposed. Furthermore, it has accepted the United States plan for annexation, and sanctioned calling an annexation convention. This is excellent news."

"I trust this fellow, *W.*, is also a reliable source," said Barlow, with a trace of sarcasm in his voice, which, apparently, Stockton missed.

"So as you can see, gentlemen, circumstances require us to change our plans," said the commodore. "We no longer have need of a private army, supplied by the United States. I suspect that in a matter of weeks President Polk will dispatch our own troops to Texas, especially since the Mexicans are poised to invade. The president has, after all, promised Texas that if she joined the Union she would be protected." He looked again at Barlow. "But your efforts will not be in vain, Captain. The area around Corpus Christi Bay will be a perfect landing point for such an army, and I will make that very recommendation."

"I propose that we have a toast, my friends," said Anderson. He gestured for an old black man in a white jacket, who had been standing inconspicuously in the shadows that had gathered in a corner of the room. "Eben, bring us a bottle of my best cognac at once."

Eben bowed and hurried away. Stockton and the others engaged in spirited conversation while they awaited his return, but Barlow scarcely heard what they were saying. Donelson drew him aside.

"I suspect that this *W.* is Charles Wickliffe," Donelson told him. "A lawyer from Kentucky. He served in the House of Representatives, and went on to become the governor of Kentucky. And he was President Tyler's postmaster general. He is a man with many important friends, some of them now residing in Texas. The president sent him down six months ago. I met him briefly, before he crossed the Sabine."

"So I wasn't the president's only spy in Texas," remarked Barlow.

"You don't seem all that pleased by these developments," observed Donelson.

Barlow glanced beyond Donelson at the men at the table—and shrugged. "I think I'm the only one who isn't."

"I don't understand you," admitted Donelson, without rancor. "Do you want Texas to fall to Santa Anna? Or to be allied with England?"

"Of course not. Texas should be annexed. She belongs in the Union. But are you convinced that there is no peaceful way to secure that result, Andrew? War should be the last resort, not the first choice."

"That strikes me as an odd thing for a military man to say."

"Not at all. Military men are well acquainted with the hardships and horror that war brings. No, it's men like our host, Anderson, who are the war-lovers. They look at war as a means to an end, and that end is profit. Once Texas is secured, so are their markets. She will grow, and their profits will grow right along with her. And then . . . then there are the slaveholders, who see the acquisition of Texas as the salvation of the South."

"I think you sell them short," said Donelson. "Once war is declared, many civilians will rush to volunteer, to do their duty for their country."

"Because they think there's glory on the battlefield. I've been on the field of battle, and I've seen very little glory there."

Donelson sighed and shook his head, like a parent who has given up trying to reason with a recalcitrant child.

The slave named Eben returned with a bottle of cognac and six glasses on a tray. Once he'd placed the tray on a table, Anderson waved him aside and took over, pouring generous portions of the liquor into each glass, and handing them to each of the men present, taking the last one for himself.

"Commodore, would you do the honors?" he asked.

"Gladly," said Stockton. He raised his glass, and all the others followed suit. "To Texas. May the Lone Star become another glorious addition to the Stars and Stripes."

"Hear! hear!" said Anderson.

They drank. Barlow took a sip so as not to draw attention to himself.

A short while later, Commodore Stockton took Barlow aside and questioned him regarding what he had seen in Texas. The latter kept his answers as concise as possible. All he wanted to do was complete the interview, return to the Donelson residence, get a good night's sleep, and embark on his journey home in the morning.

"Of all the men I know," concluded Stockton, "you are probably the one best acquainted with the Texas coast. Your knowledge will be invaluable, and I trust you will be available when the time comes for us to land an army there and deal with the Mexicans."

"Everything I know and saw is in that notebook, sir," replied Barlow. "You don't need me anymore, now that you have it. I've done what the president asked of me. Now I'm going home."

"I sec." Stockton pursed his lips and looked him up and down with what Barlow suspected was disapproval.

As soon as he could do so without being discourteous, Barlow took his leave from the Anderson place and returned to the Donelson home, leaving the Donelsons themselves behind. He went immediately to bed, and fell asleep moments after his head touched the pillow. Early the next morning he said his farewells to Donelson and his wife. Eschewing another sea journey, he had decided to travel overland, and Donelson provided him with money sufficient for the purchase of a good horse.

"Don't worry about paying me back," said Donelson. "I'll mark it down as part of my expenses. There's something to be said for being in the employ of the United States government. Not that I take advantage of the situation. But it seems to me that, considering all you've done for the republic, this is the least it can do in return."

Barlow accepted the gift with good grace. At the most convenient livery he found a sturdy, two-year-old bay mare and purchased her, along with a serviceable saddle. The day was still very young when he put New Orleans behind him.

Chapter 15

Barlow was glad to be going home at last, and he had
no second thoughts about leaving the war-lovers and
their plots behind. He'd done his duty—and barely
survived. He'd had his adventure, and now he could
return to the Claybourne plantation and—of this he
was convinced—be content with his mundane existence as planter, husband and father. Upon his return
Carter, the overseer, showed him the ledgers, and Barlow was pleased by the price that year's cotton had
brought. There was money in the bank, and it was
Carter's opinion that they should attend the upcoming
slave auction in Athens and purchase several new
hands. With more slaves they could cultivate more
acres next year, and make an even greater profit. The
English textile mills seemed to have an insatiable appetite for Southern cotton, and Carter surmised that
the prices would continue to rise for some time to
come. Barlow agreed with him on that score, but he
balked at the idea of buying more slaves. In all his
years at the Claybourne plantation he hadn't been in
a position where he had to, which was some small
consolation, at least, for a man who found the "peculiar institution" of slavery distasteful. He put Carter
off by telling the overseer he would think about it.

Something else had changed during his absence. Jacob's bear cub had grown. The animal now stood three feet at the shoulder, and spent most of his time chained to a post behind the main house.

Apart from the fact that the crops had been harvested and the leaves were turning with the advent of autumn, Barlow found the plantation much as he had left it. Rose and Jacob were well, and beside themselves with joy at his safe return. Barlow was alarmed on the first occasion that he saw his son approach the animal, but the bear appeared completely tame, at least in Jacob's presence. Jacob fed him honey and acorns and sometimes took his fishing pole to the creek and returned with a catfish or bass for the animal; the bear ate leftovers from the dinner table as well. Rose had resigned herself to its presence. Carter didn't like the beast and didn't go anywhere near it; in fact, he approached Barlow one day and offered to take the bear off into the woods and kill it. Barlow declined the offer. He blamed himself for the current situation. He'd left home without having resolved it, even though he'd known that it needed to be resolved sooner rather than later. So he wasn't about to leave the unpleasant task of dealing with the bear to someone else. As for the hands, only Jericho would approach the bear. The others were deathly afraid of it.

"Thing is, Cap'n," Jericho told Barlow, "that bear there is tamer than the cats we got in the barn. He won't live long if we turn him out into the wild. Wouldn't be right to do it. Nossuh, it'd be better if you just kilt him. But killin' that bear would sure break Jacob's heart."

Barlow didn't need to be told this—he could see it was true. Every day Jacob would let the bear loose and walk it down the lane and back again. The bear always trailed obediently behind the boy, and paid the field hands no mind as they stopped work and warily watched the odd procession. Barlow decided it was necessary for him to take action. One morning, before dawn—before Jacob awoke—he took the bear, which had become accustomed to him, by its chain and led it across the fields into the woods. He had a shotgun with him, and intended to stake the bear and shoot it. Jacob would be grief-stricken, and would hate him, but Barlow thought that was better than to have the bear maul his son to death, which was what he fully expected would happen eventually, and without warning.

Only he couldn't do it. Not because of the bear— he had no particular fondness for the beast—but because of Jacob. It had something to do, he suspected, with his being absent so much of late. A feeling of guilt that he did not wish to exacerbate by snuffing out the life of an animal—a pet—that had become his son's boon companion during Barlow's recent long absences.

When he returned to the house, Jacob was up. The boy saw the shotgun on his father's shoulder, looked at the bear—and understood what had transpired. He came running and, with tears of gratitude in his eyes, hugged his father.

Nearly every day thereafter, Barlow walked with his son when Jacob went up and down the lane with the bear. He always carried a pistol under his coat, and he armed Jericho as well, telling the crippled slave who spent so much time looking out for Jacob that if the bear displayed any aggression, he was to shoot it in the brainpan. Jericho had never handled a weapon before, and he reminded Barlow of this, and of the fact that if the authorities discovered that Barlow had given a firearm to one of his slaves he might face prosecution under state law. Barlow wasn't worried

about that, or about Jericho's lack of experience with
a pistol; he knew that the slave loved Jacob as though
the boy were his own, and if the situation ever arose
that he needed to kill the bear to protect the boy, he
would do a good job of it. He showed Jericho how to
load the pistol and left it at that.

Throughout that autumn and the following winter,
a war fervor swept the country. Barlow kept up on
events with the help of the newspapers. Immediately
upon confirmation that the Texas Congress had accepted the United States plan for annexation, and that
a Mexican army had been positioned along the Rio
Grande, President Polk dispatched General Zachary
Taylor, and an army consisting of two thousand regulars, to the Texas coast—at Corpus Christi Bay. Simultaneously, the president sent an "envoy extraordinary
and minister plenipotentiary," John Slidell, to Mexico.
But the Mexican government refused to recognize
Slidell, and his trip south was for naught. Worse, the
rejection of Slidell was widely viewed by the hawkish
press as an intentional slight to the United States.

Shortly after Christmas, Polk ordered General Taylor to advance to the Rio Grande and to take up a
defensive position along the northern bank. He was
not to seek a fight with the Mexicans, but if they insti-
gated hostilities he was to take appropriate action. By
this time Taylor had an army of slightly less than four
thousand men, his regular army units augmented by a
flood of volunteers, most of them Texans.

Barlow saw Taylor's move to the Rio Grande as
nothing short of a declaration of war. As far as Mexico
was concerned, Taylor was the invader as soon as he
crossed the Nueces river into the disputed territory.

Taylor arrived within fifty miles of Matamoros, at
the mouth of the Rio Grande, and the location of the
greatest concentration of Mexican troops. There he

was challenged by the Mexican forces and took up a defensive position along the Arroyo Colorado, a shallow stream just north of the Rio Grande. The Mexican general, Francisco Mejia, issued a warning: any further advance on the part of the Americans would be viewed as an act of open hostility. It was a challenge Taylor knew he had to accept. In early March 1846, he marched across the arroyo. The Mexicans withdrew without firing a shot. Taylor occupied two strong positions on the north bank of the Rio Grande; at one, he began the construction of Fort Polk, and at the other work was begun on Fort Brown.

Less than a month later, the cautious General Mejia was replaced by a more aggressive commander, General Pedro Ampudia, who issued an ultimatum to Taylor: either he withdrew to Corpus Christi, back across the Nueces, within twenty-four hours, or hostilities would begin. Ampudia was a veteran of the Texas Revolution, and had fought at both the Alamo and San Jacinto. And he had brought three thousand veteran troops with him. Taylor was gravely outnumbered. But *Old Rough 'n' Ready,* as those under his command were fond of calling him, wasn't worried about the odds, or afraid of a fight. He replied that he'd been ordered to his present position and intended to stay put, and if a fight came his way he would not try to avoid it.

For some reason unknown to the American press— though some editorials speculated on the innate cowardice of Mexican soldiery in the face of the dauntless American troops, which Barlow took for complete nonsense—Ampudia did not carry out his threat. He was immediately replaced by General Mariano Arista, who brought more reinforcements to Matamoros, bringing the number of Mexican troops there to more than eight thousand. Arista promptly sent his cavalry across the river. Taylor responded by sending a squadron of dragoons under Captain S. B. Thornton to challenge the crossing. Thornton's command was surrounded and, after a brief fight, surrendered. Taylor wrote to President Polk that "hostilities may now be considered as commenced."

It was Barlow's friend, Captain Martin Broward, who brought word that war had been officially declared. Winter was over, spring had come and gone, and the heat of a Southern summer was beginning to be the norm when the captain rode up the long lane to the main house one sunny afternoon. Barlow was working on the plantation's records at a table on the porch, as he was wont to do when weather permitted; Rose sat in a chair nearby, sewing quilt pieces. When she saw Broward, her face fell. Barlow knew what she was thinking, and tried to reassure her.

"Don't worry, I'm not going," he said, with a smile.

"Even if the president himself orders you to?"

Barlow shook his head, adamant. "I would rather give up my commission than leave your side again."

Rose made no response to that, but she didn't appear entirely convinced.

When Broward had dismounted and Jericho had taken charge of his horse, Rose sent Jez inside for some mint juleps, and invited the captain to take a chair in the shade of the porch—an offer Broward gratefully accepted. He handed Barlow a newspaper

"Have you heard?" he asked, his voice pitched high with excitement. "Congress has approved a war bill that authorizes the president to accept fifty thousand volunteers. Appropriations of ten million dollars have been earmarked for the struggle. We're at war with Mexico, Timothy."

"I'm not surprised," said Barlow, taking the newspaper and bleakly scanning the bold headlines.

"I'm afraid you'll have to find someone else with whom to play cards," said Broward. "I and my command have been ordered to Texas."

"And Camp Gordon?"

"Abandoned. At least for the time being."

"You'll write us, I hope," said Rose.

Broward assured her that he would.

"And come back safe," added Barlow.

Jez arrived with a tray of mint juleps, which she distributed to the three of them.

"Of course," said Broward. "I doubt it will take long to whip the Mexicans. I just hope it isn't all over by the time I get there. We're to march to Prattville and descend the Alabama River by keelboat to Mobile, where we'll find passage aboard ship to Texas."

"There'll be plenty of fighting left to do when you get there, Martin."

"I don't know. They're butchers—we know that much from the atrocities they committed to put down the revolution in Texas. They slaughtered the garrison at Alamo, but it took an entire army thirteen days to take a makeshift fortress held by a hundred and thirty men. And then Goliad." Broward shook his head and glanced at Rose, assuming she was unaware of the event to which he referred. "Several hundred Texans under James Fannin surrendered to the Mexican army at Goliad. They were massacred. Cut down to the last man. It was cold-blooded murder." He looked at Barlow. "But when taken on face-to-face—the way your friend Sam Houston and his men did at San Jacinto—what happened?" He turned his attention once again to Rose. "The Mexicans turned and ran. And don't forget the Mier Expedition, Timothy."

Barlow nodded wearily. In retaliation for a raid by a Mexican force on San Antonio in 1842, a band of Texans had marched into Mexico and attacked the town of Mier. They were surrounded by Mexican troops but fought valiantly, causing their enemy to suffer high casualties, before running out of ammunition and surrendering. They raised the white flag on the understanding that they would be treated as prisoners of war. Instead, orders came to put them to death. It was Santa Anna who changed the order so that it applied only to every tenth man. The victims were chosen by drawing beans from a jar; those who drew a black bean were executed by firing squad. The treatment of the prisoners elicited a tremendous outrage among Americans, spurred on by sensationalized accounts of their suffering by the newspapers.

"So I think it's safe to say this war will be of short duration," continued Broward confidently. "One big battle and the Mexican government will sue for peace. We'll end up with Texas and California and all the land in between."

"Well, I hope you're right," said Barlow.

Broward leaned forward. "What about you, Timothy?"

"I've been to Texas, and have no intention of returning. I'm quite content to stay right here, and let you young bucks take on Santa Anna."

"Really." Broward was skeptical, but wise enough to forgo pressing the issue further in the presence of Rose Barlow.

They invited him to stay for supper and to spend the night, but Broward insisted that he was needed back at Camp Gordon; there were a hundred details to attend to before the garrison could set out for Texas. Barlow was sorry to see his friend go. He stood on the porch and watched Broward ride down the lane to the road, until he was out of sight. Rose watched him.

"You've never lied to me, Timothy," she said, "so

don't start now. A part of you wants to be going to war with him, doesn't it?"

Barlow turned and took her by the shoulders and looked her straight in the eye and said, "No, not even a part of me."

Reassured, she smiled and kissed him.

Chapter 16

In the weeks to come, newspaper accounts kept Barlow updated on the progress of the war. Not long after the capture of Thornton's cavalry detachment, the emboldened Mexicans crossed the Rio Grande in force. General Zachary Taylor, realizing that his Mexican counterpart, Arista, was now in a position to cut his lines of supply with Port Isabel on the coast, moved the majority of his troops to Fort Polk, leaving five hundred men to garrison Fort Brown. Arista immediately turned his attention to Fort Brown, and Mexican artillery engaged in a relentless bombardment of the American fortifications there. Taylor was compelled to come to the rescue.

This was Arista's hope all along. He led his army, six thousand strong, to meet Taylor at Palo Alto. Following an artillery duel, the Americans attacked. Arista's counterattack on the American right flank was repulsed. Summer, and its attendant drought conditions, had come early to the Rio Grande valley, and the dry, brittle grass on the field of battle caught fire. Taylor used the smoke from the grass fire to concentrate his forces on the Mexican left flank, hoping that with the element of surprise, he could bend the Mexican line to the breaking point and win the day. But

Arista was no fool. He became aware of the American troop movements and immediately launched an assault on Taylor's left flank. The Mexicans nearly succeeded in routing the Americans, breaching their line in several places, but the deadly accurate Yankee artillery turned them back. Night fell with neither side having gained a decisive advantage.

Early the next morning Arista withdrew to a stronger defensive position, a dry riverbed called the Resaca de Guerrero, which was sheltered by a heavy growth of chaparral—an effective shield against the American cannon. Taylor wasn't deterred. He decided on a frontal assault. His dragoons were first into action, smashing into the Mexican right flank. Taylor then dispatched his infantry. The struggle disintegrated into a melee of hand-to-hand fighting. Pistols, swords, bayonets and bare hands were used to maim and kill. After hours of intense combat, the Mexicans were finally routed. They fled to the Rio Grande and swam across, seeking the protection of the fortifications at Matamoros, and were constantly harassed by the victorious Americans. By the end of the day, twelve hundred Mexican troops had been killed or wounded. Taylor's loss was limited to one hundred and fifty men.

The newspapers hailed the Battles of Palo Alto and the Resaca as great triumphs of superior American arms. Zachary Taylor became an overnight sensation, the darling of the American public. He had defeated a Mexican army three times the size of his own. Barlow noted, with disapproval, that some overenthusiastic editorials went so far as to compare Old Rough 'n' Ready to General Andrew Jackson. That, he thought, was hardly appropriate. For one thing, Taylor had let Arista's army slip away. Rather than press the advantage gained at the Resaca, and continuing on to take

Matamoros, Taylor was lulled into inaction by an old ruse resorted to by Arista, who sent emissaries to the American commander to engage in prolonged discussions regarding possible truce terms. Meanwhile, Arista moved his cannon and supplies out of Matamoros, followed by—largely under cover of darkness— his entire army. In Arista's opinion, the troops under his command were too demoralized to hold the city. He was promptly sacked. But Barlow had to admire the Mexican general's good sense, not to mention his cunning. Had Taylor been more aggressive, he might have crushed the entire enemy army.

But nobody was saying that kind of thing. The entire country was jubilant. The American army had met a superior Mexican force and defeated it. They had occupied Matamoros by forcing a numerically superior enemy to abandon strong fortifications without a fight.

The city of Monterrey was the next prize. With about fifteen thousand inhabitants, it was the most important city in northern Mexico, situated on a road that passed through the mountains at Rinconada Pass. General Mejia, Arista's successor, was ordered to concentrate his forces there and prepare to defend the city to the last man. President Polk and his military advisers had decided that Monterrey's capture was essential to provide the necessary security for the Rio Grande area. That was the official reasoning, at least. But Barlow had to wonder if there wasn't an ulterior motive. Was there a feeling among the political and military leaders of the country that it might be possible to conquer all of Mexico? In the past there had been talk of doing just that, but the advocates of such a course of action had been dismissed as radical expansionists. But Barlow was convinced that lurking beneath the surface of American brass and bluster lay a pervasive sense of insecurity bordering on paranoia.

For that reason, war hawks in Congress had long advocated driving the British out of Canada. It was, they claimed, the destiny of the United States to possess the entire continent: in doing so, they would remove any future threat of invasion by a neighboring country. Perhaps, mused Barlow, that same reasoning lay behind the decision to carry the war deeper into Mexico.

It was at this point that his son came to him one day, and spoke to him for the first time about the war.

"Are you going away to fight the Mexicans, Father?" asked Jacob gravely, as they walked along the lane with the bear trundling obediently along behind them.

"No, son. I'm not going to war. I'm staying right here with you and your mother."

Jacob pondered this news for a moment. He seemed troubled rather than relieved. "They're raising a company of men in Athens to go off to war," he said at last.

Barlow nodded. "So I've heard. I suspect the same sort of thing is going on in many towns across the country."

"Why don't you command the company from here? You have more experience than anyone else."

"I can't, Jacob. For one thing, I still hold a commission in the United States Army. If I go off to war it will have to be with regulars."

"Then why don't you?"

Barlow stopped walking. He took Jacob by the shoulders. "So why don't you tell me what's bothering you? You talk like you *want* me to leave."

Jacob's expression was sheepish. "No, it's not that. It's just that, well . . . some of the other children at school say you're a coward."

"Oh, I see." Barlow sighed. He knew that Jacob was having a hard time at the one-room schoolhouse down the road. It wasn't easy being the son of a Yankee, much less a Yankee officer who had slain one of the heroes of Georgia, the renegade John Claybourne. When Jacob had turned ten, Barlow had tried to explain the circumstances that led to his having to kill the boy's uncle. He'd told how he and Claybourne had clashed first in Charleston, when Claybourne had led a mob of nullifiers in an attempt to seize a federal arsenal that Barlow held with a handful of troops. After that, Claybourne had been a wanted man, a fugitive from the United States government, fleeing charges of treason. He'd reappeared as the leader of a band of raiders attacking the Cherokees. Once again he and Barlow had clashed. And once again Barlow had prevailed. With no place left to run, Claybourne had come home to the plantation for a final confrontation. Standing there with Jacob, Barlow realized that John Claybourne had died not a stone's throw away. In fact, he had come here to die, to martyr himself on the altar of states' rights and Southern honor. *He knew,* mused Barlow, *that it was the only way to beat me in the long run. Knew that by forcing me to kill him, he could guarantee that I would never be accepted by many of the inhabitants of this state.*

He wasn't sure that Jacob fully understood the reasons why he'd had to kill John Claybourne. But the boy was all too aware of the consequences of being the son of an interloper. It didn't surprise Barlow that some of the other children were taunting Jacob because his father wasn't marching off to war. They looked for any excuse to torment him. Rose had talked about finding a private tutor, but both Barlow and Jacob had opposed the idea. Jacob stood up to his tormentors, and Barlow thought that it was right and proper for him to do so. It wouldn't do to run away from that kind of trouble. And staying home to be schooled by a private tutor was akin to running away.

"I don't believe them, of course," said Jacob gravely. "I know you're not a coward, Father."

"And neither are you," said Barlow proudly. "I wouldn't worry too much about what others say, especially when it's contrary to what you know to be the truth. They're just displaying their ignorance."

Rose was troubled, too. Barlow wasn't sure why. He had assured her and reassured her regarding his intentions. It wasn't that she didn't believe that he was sincere. He concluded that it had to be that she feared something would happen to change his mind. Barlow wanted very much to put her mind at ease. But, obviously, words were insufficient to that task. Only the passage of time would assuage her anxieties.

One night, after she had made love to him, Rose quietly slipped out of bed and went to a chest of drawers. Only a candle was lighted, and its soft, warm glow caressed her body. Barlow marveled at how firm and slender that body was—unchanged in all the years that had come and gone since first they'd met and loved. His attention quickly shifted to the letter in her hand as she returned to the bed. She sat there, not trying to cover herself, completely comfortable with him in her nakedness, and handed him the letter. He studied her face by the flickering candlelight, and saw resignation there behind a sad smile. She hadn't opened the letter, of course; it was addressed to him in a very neat, masculine hand. But she seemed to know what it contained. His eyes strayed from the proffered letter along her arm, to her shoulder, across her proud breasts, to the graceful curve of her neck, her full lips, and he was struck by the contrast of the choice he had a feeling he was about to make. A choice between his duty to his country, with all its attendant hardship and dangers—and perhaps even death on some dusty, remote field of battle—or his lovely, sensuous wife— the warmth of her flesh, the heat of her passion, the caress of her fingers and of her lips, leading him to paradise. He had an urge to take the letter and tear it up and then grab her and make love to her again. But he didn't. With resignation of his own, he took the letter, turned it over. On the back of the envelope was an imprint of the seal of the president in a dollop of crimson wax.

He opened the envelope and found two sheets of expensive vellum within. The top letter was signed by President Polk himself. It was addressed to Timothy Barlow, Major, United States Army, and it read:

Sir:

Numerous times in the past you have demonstrated an unwavering and selfless willingness to answer the call of duty when your country was in need of your services. That situation has arisen once again. As you know, the United States is engaged in a just and noble struggle to rescue Texas from Mexican tyranny. On the outcome of that struggle rests the future security and prosperity of the republic. Our brave army has met the enemy on the banks of the Rio Grande and won a great victory. But this is not enough. We must strike deep into Mexico and demonstrate once and for all to General Santa Anna the futility of prolonging these hostilities. Only when Santa Anna himself is defeated on the field of battle will he sue for peace. To that end, General Taylor is preparing to march on Monterrey, confident that this will draw Santa Anna into a battle as crucial as any ever entered into by American arms. Now is the time for all true patriots to rally to the flag

*and demonstrate their allegiance to their country
and all it stands for.*

*I have instructed the Secretary of War, and he
has written a letter of commission, which I have
included with this letter, to confer upon you the
rank of Colonel, effective forthwith. Upon acceptance of this commission, you are ordered to proceed with all haste to Matamoros, where you will
be charged with the vital task of establishing and
commanding a company of scouts, recruited from
any source you see fit. Said company will provide
General Taylor with the one thing he most sorely
needs at this juncture: reliable intelligence on the
activities of Santa Anna and his army. General
Taylor will be operating under severe disadvan-
tages in enemy country until such time as he re-
ceives this information.*

*You have been selected for this important task
because of the skill and resourcefulness you displayed in completing the mission which took you
to Texas some months ago. I trust you will answer
your country's call this time as well.*

*I hope this finds you and yours in the best of
health.*

*Yr. obt. svt.,
James K. Polk
President of the United States*

Barlow glanced at the accompanying letter of commission. Then he looked at Rose, at her slender body
aglow in the candlelight, at her eyes, which were fastened upon him.

"I won't go," he said. "I will decline the promotion.
In fact, I will give up my commission."

Slowly she shook her head. "No, I don't want you

to do that, Timothy. Because you'll regret doing it. You might even come to resent me because of it."

"I would never do that. This is my decision, and mine alone."

"It's a decision that affects us all. So shouldn't I have a say in it as well?"

Puzzled, he peered at her, trying to read her mind. "What are you saying? Surely you don't want me to go to war."

"My heart wants you to stay, of course. But my head tells me that you should go."

Barlow was startled. "I don't understand."

She rose from the bed and went to the window, parting the draperies slightly to look out at the moon-lit May night.

"I would go anywhere you wanted to live, Timothy. You know that. I would follow you to the ends of the earth just to be with you. But you never asked me. I know how difficult it has been for you to adjust to life here. You've not complained, ever, but I know what you've been through, and I know why you did it, and I love you even more for doing it—if it's possible that I could love you any more than I did when we first met. There are so many people around here who resent you, for several reasons. We both know what those are, so there's no need to go into them now. If you avoid this war, they'll resent you even more. But if you go and fight in this war, many of them will be appeased."

"Because it's a war that will benefit the South—and slavery—most of all," said Barlow bitterly. "You want me to fight for something I don't believe in."

She turned to look at him. "Yes. That's exactly what I am asking you to do. But not for the South, and not for slavery. But for us. For Jacob and I. I realize you don't care what others think of you. But you do care what they think of me. And how they treat our son, don't you?"

Barlow nodded. "Yes, I care very much. And I know it hasn't been easy for you, either, being married to a Yankee, and worse still, the Yankee officer who killed your brother."

"No, it hasn't," she said bluntly, turning to look out the window at the night again. "But it's a small price to pay to be with the man I love more than life itself."

Leaving the letters on the rumpled bedcovers, Barlow rose and joined her at the window, putting her arms around her. Rose leaned her body back against his, resting her head on his shoulder. The moonlight made her skin almost translucent, marbled with the blue veins in her neck. He kissed them, a kiss that lingered, and he could feel the blood coursing through those veins, pumped by a heart that was strong and steady.

"I guess she was right," he murmured.

"Who?"

"Churacho's sister. You remember. I told you all about them."

Rose nodded. She raised an arm, reaching behind her, running her fingers through his thick, tousled hair. "I remember. The woman who fell in love with you."

"I never told you that."

Rose laughed softly. "No, you left that part out. But she did, didn't she? What woman wouldn't fall in love with a man like you?"

"There are plenty who wouldn't, believe me."

"There are plenty of foolish women in the world, too."

"Are you jealous, then? Of Churacho's sister?"

"Should I be?"

"No."

She turned to face him, curled her arms around his

neck, her firm breasts pressed against his broad chest. "I think you'd better come back to bed and let me give you something to remember while you're gone," she whispered, her breath hot against his skin.

It was an offer Barlow wasn't about to refuse.

Chapter 17

When Timothy Barlow trudged down the gangplank from the deck of the merchant brig *Clementine,* just arrived at Port Isabel, he cast a look about him and saw nothing but a miserable row of shacks and shanties stretching the length of a wharf, surrounded by sand dunes and a few scrawny palm trees, the fronds of which were being thrashed by a prevailing wind, salty and humid, blowing in off the sea. The sun hammered the back of his shoulders, and he felt a bit light-headed, but he put that down to his long bout of seasickness, which he'd suffered almost from the moment the brig had set sail from Pensacola, bound for the mouth of the Rio Grande with a cargo of supplies for General Taylor's army and about seventy volunteers. Regardless of Port Isabel's disreputable appearance, it looked like Heaven to Barlow, who for the past week had seen nothing but endless vistas of choppy seas.

An officer—wearing the shoulder tabs of a captain on his dusty blue coatee—approached him. Barlow glanced at him, then did a double take; he knew this man. It took a moment to place him. He smiled, extended a hand, and the captain, grinning, gave him a salute before the hearty handshake.

"Colonel Barlow, it's good to see you again, sir."

"Captain Armstrong. It's been . . . what? Nearly ten years."

"Yes, sir. A lot of water under the bridge."

"How have you been?"

"Fine, sir. I'm with the 21st Infantry now, Colonel Kaufman commanding, but I've been seconded to General Taylor's staff."

"Watch out. That's how it starts."

"Sir?"

"The special duty."

Armstrong laughed. "Oh. Yes, sir. But this is one special duty I don't mind, sir. They told me to be here waiting for you when you arrived. But we weren't sure when that would be." He looked around. "I've been stuck in this one-horse town for the better part of a week. Needless to say, I'm thrilled to death to see you, Colonel."

"Well, we had some bad weather in the gulf that slowed us down." Thinking about it made Barlow's stomach do a slow roll. Those two days when the *Clementine* had lurched up one side of the steep sea swells and then tumbled down the other, tilting sharply as she was hammered by the gale-force winds, would forever live in his memory as the closest equivalent to Hell on Earth that there could ever be.

"Do you have luggage?" asked Armstrong.

"Just this," said Barlow, lifting the valise he had in one hand and the Colt Paterson rifle in a scabbard that he held in the other. "Where can I find the general?"

"Matamoros."

"When is he planning to march on Monterrey?"

"Ah, well," said Armstrong, with a rueful smile, "that's the question foremost on the mind of every man jack in the army, sir." He noticed that a couple of laborers were struggling under the burden of a very large trunk as they came down the gangplank behind Barlow. As it appeared to him that they weren't paying attention to where they were going, he barked a command at them in Spanish.

"You've picked up the lingo pretty handily, I see," said Barlow.

"I guess it's a gift," said Armstrong, with a self-effacing smile.

They left the dock, and Barlow discovered that the captain had two horses waiting for them near one of the Port Isabel shanties, watched over by a Mexican, who Armstrong paid off with a few pesos. They mounted up and rode to a ferry that carried them across a small bay, after which they struck a road that was soon running parallel to a wide brown turgid river—the Rio Grande. The terrain was rugged, with low bluffs at places along the river, and a rolling, arid plain beyond covered with sagebrush and sand and rocks and cactus and some stunted mesquite trees. The heat was oppressive—the air was seared, as though it had come straight out of a furnace, and seemed to burn the lining of Barlow's lungs.

Armstrong read his mind. "If there is such a thing as Godforsaken country, this is it, don't you think, Colonel? Makes you sit back and wonder, sometimes, why men are so ready to fight and die for it. It's not good for much of anything, except the rattlesnakes and scorpions and wild cattle that live in the brush, mean as Hell with the hide off."

"You might be surprised," said Barlow. "There's the answer right there." He motioned to the river. "With the proper irrigation, this entire valley could be made fertile."

Armstrong looked at him, amused. "I forgot, sir. You're a planter now. You've learned to notice such things."

Barlow laughed, somewhat embarrassed. "Yes, I suppose I have."

The ride to Matamoros took a couple of hours. They passed two cavalry patrols along the way. Armstrong told Barlow that even though they had occupied Matamoros and driven the Mexican army southward, the countryside still was not safe. The brush was full of cutthroats and spies and even small units of Mexican cavalry that would waylay a small detail or an American soldier traveling alone. Scarcely a day went by when there wasn't a killing or a skirmish somewhere along the river.

"Then I guess we make a prime target, don't we?" asked Barlow. "A couple of Americans with a lot of brass on their tunics."

"Absolutely, sir!" said Armstrong cheerfully.

Barlow smiled. He liked the captain. He'd liked him when they'd first met, at Camp Gordon ten years earlier, when Armstrong had been a lieutenant in command of a small detachment assigned to help Barlow in his task of overseeing the removal of the Cherokees from their homeland. Back then, Armstrong had been aching to see action. And he'd gotten his wish, in the clash with John Claybourne's raiders, who were preying on the Cherokee caravans bound for the west. It seemed to Barlow that Armstrong had seen a lot more action since. It was evident in the way he carried himself. As they made their way across the perilous countryside, Armstrong was alert but unafraid, secure in the knowledge that he was capable of handling whatever came his way, and without the burden of having to prove anything, to himself or to others.

They crossed the river—it was shallow enough to safely ford in numerous places—and approached Matamoros. The town had been heavily fortified, work begun by the Mexican army and continued by the

Americans. But Taylor had concentrated his efforts on the south side of town, and when Barlow and Armstrong approached from the north they found but a single detail of sentries manning a post on the road that rose up from the river to pass between several redoubts. Armstrong identified himself, and the two soldiers waved them through with hardly a glance, returning to a game of cards they were playing on top of a low adobe wall.

"I take it General Taylor isn't worried about an enemy attack," said Barlow.

Armstrong smiled. "The general doesn't care if the enemy attacks or not, if you ask me, Colonel. Like just about everyone else in the army, he has a very low opinion of the enemy's abilities."

Barlow watched several women from the town pass the sentry post, heading down to the river with empty *ollas* balanced on their heads, off to gather water. The sentries let them pass with little more than a lewd comment or two. It occurred to Barlow that Matamoros was probably full of enemy spies; it would be a fairly easy matter to smuggle agents in and information out.

Matamoros itself was a relatively large town, with one main plaza and several smaller squares, a half-dozen churches and dozens of adobe houses packed together along narrow, dusty streets. Those streets were filled with the inhabitants going about their business, children playing, dogs and pigs and chickens— and American soldiers, usually in groups of two or more. Barlow and Armstrong rode past an open market that was packed with people, Mexican citizens and American soldiers shoulder to shoulder. It seemed at first glance that the people of Matamoros were skilled at adapting to changing circumstances.

General Taylor's headquarters were located in the

cabildo, a long adobe structure on the east side of the main plaza, which was filled with soldiers. This, apparently, was the one part of town where the citizenry was not welcomed. There were guards arrayed along the front portico of the building, and several lookouts on the rooftop. The Stars and Stripes hung limply in the breathless heat from a flagpole in front of the building.

Armstrong informed a lieutenant—the officer of the day—that Barlow had arrived, and that General Taylor would want to see him immediately. The lieutenant went inside. Barlow dismounted, loosened the saddle cinch for the sake of his horse, and took a careful look around. There were probably four thousand officers and men in the plaza, many of them gathered in small cliques, talking, smoking pipes or cheroots. But there were also several two-man details patrolling the perimeter, and Barlow watched as one of these barred the way of an old Mexican leading a mule burdened with large straw baskets. The old man apparently wanted to cross the plaza, perhaps as the most direct route to the open market, but the detail would not let him proceed. Several main thoroughfares radiated off the plaza, and Barlow could see straight down one of them from where he stood. Several Mexican men lounged against an adobe wall in a ribbon of shade, their faces hidden beneath the brims of their sombreros. But it was clear they were watching the Americans in the plaza. Was it just idle curiosity on their part, or something more? Barlow told himself he was just being paranoid, but—considering the task that had been set for him—he wasn't sure but that paranoia might be an asset.

The lieutenant returned to inform Armstrong that the general would see Colonel Barlow at once. They entered the building, and waited in a short hallway furnished with nothing but several plain benches, upon which sat several other officers. Barlow knew none of them, and he was reminded of just how long he had been out of active service. A dozen years ago the army had been his home, these men his brothers. Not one for introspection, Barlow had never tried very hard to figure out why he'd not been close to his own family in Philadelphia. But after leaving for the military academy at West Point his visits home had been quite infrequent, and the letters he penned to his parents and younger brother and sister few and far between. At this moment, rather than feeling like the prodigal son, relieved to be back among his brethren, and having missed the rough camaraderie of army life, he experienced instead a keen attack of homesickness, a longing to see Rose and Jacob again. God help him, he even missed the Claybourne plantation—and that was something he hadn't dreamed would ever happen.

The officer of the day emerged from a room and beckoned for Barlow, who turned to Armstrong.

"Do you know why I'm here, Captain?"

"Well, no, sir, not really."

Barlow preferred not to speak of his mission in any great detail in front of these other officers. "I have a particular job to do. A pretty important job, I suppose. And I need your help. Care to sign on?"

Armstrong looked intrigued—and slightly amused. "Can't tell me a little more about the job you want me to sign on for, Colonel?"

"Not at the moment, no. But it will be a very dangerous job, I suspect."

Armstrong leaned in, pitching his voice low so as not to be overheard. "That suits me, sir. To be honest, being a staff officer is too dull for my taste."

"You don't want to keep the general waiting, sir," said the lieutenant.

"Come with me," Barlow told Armstrong, and led the way.

They found themselves in a small room with a single window covered with ornate iron grillwork. There was hardly space enough for a desk and a table, both of which were strewn with maps. Zachary Taylor was a tall, stocky man with a craggy, weathered face. His uniform was plain and rather unkempt. His voice was in keeping with his looks—gruff and brisk in tone.

"So you're Barlow?" he said. "I have a very difficult job that needs to be done. I'm told you're the man who can do it. I hope that's right, because whether we win or lose down here may depend on it."

Chapter 18

Taylor circled the desk and strode to the table littered with maps, making a curt motion for Barlow to join him. Then he spared Armstrong a glance. "You can go, Captain."

"I'd like for him to stay, sir," said Barlow.

"And why is that?"

"Captain Armstrong speaks Spanish, General. I don't. Considering what I've been sent down here to do, that's a big disadvantage. One that the captain's help could offset."

Taylor narrowed his eyes as he gazed at Barlow. "Just what the Hell are you trying to say, Colonel?"

Barlow was taken aback. "I mean I'd like for you to assign the captain to work with me, sir."

Taylor shrugged. "Very well; consider it done. Now look here." He pointed at the map. "This is Matamoros—where we are. This is Monterrey—where the Mexican army is. My orders are to engage the Mexican army and capture Monterrey. But I need to know what I'm up against. The Mexican cavalry has thrown up a screen between us and Monterrey. I can't punch through that screen unless I advance in force—and I don't want to do that until I know what's *behind* that screen. Do you follow me?"

"Of course," said Barlow. "You want me to find out all I can about the enemy, sir. His numbers, his movements, the strength of his fortifications."

Taylor nodded vigorously. "That's it. And just how do you intend to do that?"

"I have an idea. But it hinges on finding a man named Churacho. He's a *mesteñero.*" The puzzled look on the general's face caused Barlow to quickly add, "A mustanger, sir."

"What do you want with him?"

"If I can, I'll talk him into helping me get through that screen of Mexican cavalry and into Monterrey itself."

"He's a Mexican, I take it. Why would he help you?"

"We're friends. And he hates Santa Anna. I think he'll agree. The bigger problem lies in finding him."

"Maybe not," said Armstrong. "If I'm not mistaken, the man you're looking for is at Fort Brown."

Taylor's brow furrowed. "What is he doing at Fort Brown?"

"About to be executed, I should think, sir," replied Armstrong. "I'm surprised you don't remember. You appointed the officers to the military tribunal that tried him."

"I did?" Taylor seemed befuddled. "What was the charge against this man?"

"He killed a soldier, sir. A sergeant by the name of Farrow. It happened two months ago, right around the time you ordered the horses this man Churacho and his crew had brought to Matamoros confiscated."

"Wait a minute," said Barlow, turning his gaze from Armstrong to Taylor as his disbelief was transformed into anger. "You stole Churacho's mustangs?"

Taylor bristled. "Watch your tongue, Barlow—or you'll find yourself in front of a tribunal, as well."

Armstrong intervened. "We lost many horses at Palo Alto and the Resaca, sir. The General's standing orders were to confiscate all suitable mounts. This friend of yours was trying to escape across the river when he was caught. It was assumed that he meant the mustangs for the enemy."

"It's more likely that he just didn't want the horses taken from him without being paid for them," said Barlow dryly. "Is that when he killed the sergeant?"

"No, sir. Apparently that happened a little later. The talk is that Sergeant Farrow made some comment about a woman who was riding with Churacho. And that's when Churacho drew a pistol and killed him. Shot him right through the heart."

"That woman is Churacho's sister. And I can imagine what kind of comment this Farrow made about her."

"That doesn't matter," said Taylor sharply. "The man killed one of my men. He must be punished."

Barlow ignored him. "When is the execution set to take place, Captain?"

Armstrong shook his head. "I can't say that I know for certain, sir."

Barlow headed for the door. "We have to stop it. I'm going to Fort Brown."

"Excuse me, Colonel," roared Taylor. "You don't have the authority to stop anything."

"Then you'd better do it, sir," said Barlow. "I need Churacho's help for the job I've been given."

"He's a Mexican, for God's sake," said Taylor. "How could you trust him?"

"I trust him. And without him I doubt I'll be able to get anywhere near Monterrey. And I have to get near it, or better yet, in it, to find out what you want to know."

"What makes you think he'll help you, though, Colonel?" asked Armstrong. "I wouldn't be surprised if right about now he wants us all to go straight to Hell."

"I'll have to talk him into it," said Barlow. "It would help if the general will overturn the verdict of the tribunal and set him free."

"I'll do no such thing," barked Taylor. "You seem to forget, Colonel. This man killed a soldier. I will not let that go unpunished."

"Then you'll have to find some other way to get the information you need," replied Barlow.

Armstrong glanced at Taylor, then Barlow, and shook his head. These were two very stubborn men, and neither one was going to back down. "May I make a suggestion, General?" he asked.

Taylor didn't take his eyes off Barlow. "Go ahead, Armstrong."

"Sign the order that overturns the verdict, if it will get Churacho to help us. It's likely he'll be killed during the mission anyway. And if he isn't—I'll kill him."

Both Taylor and Barlow stared at him. Then the general turned to his desk. He bent over, angrily dipping pen into its inkwell and scribbling a brief order on a piece of paper. When he was finished, he handed the paper to Armstrong.

"I'll hold you to that, Captain," said Taylor.

Armstrong nodded, took the paper, and glanced at Barlow. "We had better be going, sir."

As they left the *cabildo* and reached their horses, Barlow finally spoke. "You know I won't let you do that, don't you?"

"I know it was the only way the general would sign such an order. And besides, I may very well be killed. Maybe Churacho will be. Or, maybe we all will be. Then we won't have to worry about it, will we?"

Barlow had to smile. He'd been right about Armstrong. The young captain was a quick and innovative thinker, someone who would do whatever it took to get the job done. He was just the kind of man this business called for.

They crossed the Rio Grande again, and reached Fort Brown in less than an hour. Even now, weeks after the Mexican bombardment of the fort, work details were laboring to repair the damage, and there were still considerable debris. Armstrong told him that the Mexican attempt to take the fort had been fierce and sustained, with almost constant artillery barrage and several major assaults. Many lives had been lost, including that of Colonel Brown, the garrison's beloved commanding officer. He warned Barlow that this was the worst possible place for Churacho to be incarcerated, and to be prepared for obstinacy and animosity.

As timber was in short supply in this arid country, the fort itself consisted primarily of adobe walls, built on bluffs overlooking the river. Upon arrival they were taken immediately to the officer in command, a Major Flagler. He read the order from General Taylor and then read it again, and Barlow, watching the man's features, could see the transformation of disbelief into stark fury. He looked at Armstrong and Barlow, his eyes like daggers.

"What the Hell is the meaning of this? That damned greaser killed one of my men. His execution is scheduled for dawn tomorrow. Every man in this command is looking forward to the occasion."

"Then I'm afraid every man in this command is going to be disappointed," said Barlow coldly. "Unless, of course, you intend to disobey a direct order. In which case *you* might be the one facing a firing squad."

"The Hell you say. I should walk over to the brig

right now and put a bullet in the greaser's brainpan. They'd pin a medal on me."

Barlow shook his head. "You're not going to do that, Major. What you're going to do is obey that order and turn Churacho over to me. Now."

Flagler stared at him, cheeks reddening. Then he turned to his aide. "Do it," he snapped, and went back inside his quarters.

The aide led the way across the dusty parade ground to a structure made of stone, with a heavy timber door braced with strap iron. There was a soldier on guard at the door. The aide took the key from the guard and removed a padlock, swinging the door open. Standing on the threshold, it took Barlow's eyes a moment to adjust to the darkness inside. He saw a shadow, denser than the rest of the shadows, in one back corner.

"Churacho?"

He heard a shuffling noise. The shadow moved slightly. Barlow stepped into the cell. His foot brushed against something. He picked up a wooden bowl filled with a gray mush. Sniffing at the contents, he flinched.

"What is this?" he asked the aide, who stood in the doorway.

"That would be his breakfast. And his dinner, too. He hasn't eaten much."

"Would you eat much of this slop?" Barlow tossed the bowl away, turned back to the shadow. "Churacho? It's me. Barlow."

The prisoner slowly raised his head. Barlow saw the cuts and bruises, and tried to keep his temper in check. Some of the injuries were old and healing; others were fresh.

"What have you been doing to him, Lieutenant?" he asked, his voice like ice.

"Early on he was attacking the guards when they came in to give him his food. They had to defend themselves."

Barlow looked around the cell. There was no floor, no window, no blanket, no bed. There wasn't even a pot to piss in. Nothing but cold stone walls. And, when the door was closed, there would be no light. He could scarcely imagine how Churacho—a man accustomed to the freedom of a mustanger's life on the open plains—could have kept his sanity in such a hellhole for so long.

"Churacho? Can you hear me?"

"I hear you." The voice was a croaking travesty.

"Can you stand?"

Barlow offered a helping hand. Churacho brushed him away. Relying heavily on the wall for support, he got slowly, stiffly to his feet. What little light was coming through the door—most of it blocked by the lieutenant and the guard and Armstrong—seemed almost too much for the prisoner to bear. Eyes narrowed to slits, he tried to focus on Barlow's face.

"What are you doing here, amigo?" asked Churacho.

"I came to get you out."

"I killed one of theirs. Now they want to kill me. I understand that. I am not afraid to die. But I am glad you came. I want you to find Therese. I want you . . . to make sure she is well. To take care of her as best you can. You must do this for me, my friend."

"You're not listening. You're getting out of here. You're being set free. You can take care of her yourself."

"Set free?" Churacho was slow to comprehend. Barlow could sense that the man had long given up hope of ever getting out of this hole alive. *"Por qué?"*

"We'll talk about that later. Come on, let's go."

Churacho looked down at himself. His trousers were filthy and torn, his *chaquetilla* black with grime. His beard was a tangled mat. He made a few ineffectual swipes at the dirt on his clothing, then straightened and walked to the door with as much dignity as he could muster. The lieutenant and the guard stepped aside to let him pass. The brightness of the outside world was too much for Churacho. He closed his eyes, began to sway. Barlow was there to steady him. His attention was focused on the mustanger, so much so that he didn't notice what was going on around him. But Armstrong did.

"Uh, Colonel, we might have some trouble coming," said the latter.

Barlow looked up. Word had spread quickly. A dozen soldiers were converging from various points of the compass, crossing the parade ground with resolute strides. Barlow had a hunch this was Flagler's doing—that the major had been sure to spread the word, hoping for some sort of confrontation from which he could absolve himself from responsibility later on, blaming whatever damage was done on the purely understandable outrage of the soldiers under his command, who could not bear to think of the man who had slain one of their own simply walking away. Barlow glanced at the lieutenant. The aide looked concerned, but he also looked like a man who had no intention of getting in the middle of what was about to happen.

"Stick close to Churacho," Barlow murmured to Armstrong. "I'll handle this."

He stepped forward, meeting the oncoming soldiers halfway. Though they outnumbered him, there was something about his approach that gave them pause, and stopped them all in their tracks. He scanned their faces, trying to identify the ringleader, and concluded

that it was a burly, balding man with corporal stripes
and a square-jawed face with its most prominent fea-
ture being a nose that had been broken on more than
one occasion. Barlow went straight up to him, stopping only when he was toe-to-toe and virtually nose-
to-nose with the two-striper.

"What do you think you're doing, Corporal?" he
asked.

"I'm gonna see justice done, that's what," snarled
the corporal. "Me and the boys have decided that
damned greaser ain't leaving here alive."

"How bad do you want him?"

"What do you mean?"

"Bad enough to die?"

The corporal looked down—and saw that Barlow
had a pistol aimed about an inch away from his
belly button.

"Ever been gut-shot, Corporal?" asked Barlow. His
tone was pleasant enough, but if one listened closely
they might have heard an icy edge to it. "It's a real
slow and painful way to die, or so I'm told. Why don't
I just pull this trigger, and then I'll wait around for
however long it is that you're able to talk without
screaming in agony too much, so you can tell me how
it feels."

The corporal dragged his eyes off the gun and
looked at Barlow, trying to judge whether the man
was serious, whether he would really pull the trigger.
What he saw in Barlow's eyes convinced him that he
would.

"So what you've got to decide now," continued Barlow, "is just how bad you want the greaser dead. You
want it bad enough to go to Hell with him? Then take
one more step."

The corporal looked at the men who had accompanied him. They were watching him, waiting for their

cue. Barlow knew he stood no chance against all of them, that they would take him down if a brawl commenced, and they might even kill him in the melee. But no one was going to make a move until the corporal made his, because none of them wanted to bear the responsibility for the two-striper's death.

"Whose side are you on?" asked the corporal, his expression one of utter contempt. "You Goddamned Mex lover."

Barlow didn't respond. He held the pistol rock-steady. The corporal looked down at it again and the conviction bled out of him. Barlow could almost see it fade away. The corporal heaved a deep sigh, then backed down, moving away from the pistol.

"I ain't gonna get gut-shot by some Mex-lovin' Yankee. I got me a bunch of greasers to kill yet. But you mark my words. That one yonder"—he nodded in the direction of Churacho—"he'll get what's coming to him. Come on, boys."

The soldiers dispersed. Barlow belted his pistol, and started breathing again. Then he returned to Armstrong and Churacho. They crossed the parade ground, the object of unfriendly interest by dozens of soldiers, standing in groups here and there. Reaching their horses, Barlow told Churacho to get into the saddle, and led the horse out of Fort Brown, with Armstrong riding along behind, keeping a careful eye peeled for more trouble. But there wasn't any. They negotiated a trail down off the bluffs and arrived at the river. There Barlow helped Churacho out of the saddle and the mustanger sprawled in the shallows, drinking his fill, letting the warm water soothe his battered body and rinse some of the grime off. Barlow and Armstrong waited, the latter sitting on a rock and taking a cheroot from under his tunic and lighting it. Barlow thought maybe it was the smell of the harsh

Mexican tobacco that brought Churacho out of the water. Armstrong provided the mustanger with a cheroot without having to be asked, and lit it for him. Churacho drew the smoke deep into his lungs, closed his eyes in ecstasy. Then he looked up at the fort, still visible above them on the bluffs.

"The bastards stole my horses," he muttered. "I will get them back. But first I must find Therese."

"Where is she?"

"When I was arrested I had one of my men take her to a safe place. If there is such a thing anymore."

"I'll ride with you. Meanwhile, Captain Armstrong will see about recovering your horses."

Armstrong smiled wryly. "Oh, sure. No problem. I'll just go back to my old friend General Taylor. You know he'll be glad to see me, especially when I tell him, again, what to do."

Barlow had to laugh. Armstrong joined in. Churacho looked at both of them. He didn't seem amused. But Barlow figured it was unrealistic to expect a man who had spent weeks in a stone cell—being beaten on a daily basis and being fed slop that even pigs would avoid—to have a sense of humor.

Churacho turned to Barlow. "I should thank you. You saved my life."

"Before you thank me, maybe you'd better hear the request I have to make of you. I need your help, Churacho."

Sitting on a rock to let the hot sun dry him, Churacho looked impassively at Barlow. "You need my help? To fight your war against Mexico. You want me to help your General Taylor, the man who was going to kill me. You want me to help this army"—he made an angry gesture at the fort above them—"that stole my horses. You want me to help your country conquer mine. Give me one good reason why I should help you?"

"For vengeance," replied Barlow. "To avenge your family, who died at the hands of Santa Anna's soldiers."

Churacho gazed at the sun shimmering on the surface of the river for some time. Barlow didn't say more, didn't try to sell the mustanger on the idea. He just waited, having already decided that if Churacho decided not to help him, he would drop the whole matter. He would let the man ride away, and face the wrath of General Taylor. He owed Churacho that much, if not more.

Finally Churacho looked back at him and nodded. "I will listen to what you have to say."

Chapter 19

When Zeke Fuller rode into Fort Brown at the head of a band of fifteen men armed to the teeth, he told the sentries that blocked his passage that he and his boys had come to volunteer. They were directed to the adobe that served as the garrison's command post, and were confronted there by Major Flagler. One of the riders had to dismount and help Fuller down off his horse. The major watched the old man grimace in pain and shook his head as Fuller unlashed a cane from his saddle and used it to balance himself.

"You boys are Texans, I take it," said Flagler.

"That's right," said Fuller. "We come to help you kill Mexicans."

"You're a little long in the tooth to go to war, aren't you?"

Fuller's smile was about as warm as a blue norther. "I may be long in the tooth, but I could whittle you down to a nub in two shakes of a lamb's tail."

Some of the horsemen laughed. Flagler wasn't amused, because there was suddenly something about this old man that scared him.

"Maybe you should cross over to Matamoros. See General Taylor. He may have some use for volunteers. That's where you'll want to be anyway—with the army that marches on Monterrey—if your desire is to kill Mexicans. This is just a garrison command."

Zeke Fuller nodded. "Maybe you're right there, Major. Matamoros—might that be where I'll find an officer named Barlow?"

"Colonel Barlow?" Flagler was startled. "You know him?"

"Yep. And I can see that you do, too."

Flagler grimaced. "I met him just yesterday. He showed up here, all high and mighty, with an order, signed by General Taylor himself, for the release of a prisoner."

"Is that so," murmured Fuller. "And who was this prisoner?"

"A murderer by the name of Churacho."

Zeke Fuller smiled broadly. "You don't say. Who did Churacho put on the wrong side of grass?"

"He killed a sergeant. A good man. All because the sergeant looked at his sister." Flagler shook his head. "You a friend of Colonel Barlow?"

"Wouldn't say a friend exactly. But he's the reason we're here."

"I see." Flagler assumed—as Fuller thought he would—that Barlow had recruited this gang of Texans for the war. "Well, you might find him in Matamoros. I don't know where he went after he collected Churacho."

Fuller touched the brim of his kossuth hat. "My thanks to you, Major."

The other man helped Fuller back into the saddle. Flagler didn't wait to see the Texans ride out of the fort. He turned and went back inside the adobe, glad to have rid himself of a gang of Texican ruffians.

When Fuller and his men arrived in Matamoros, he told the others to spread out and find Barlow. Though there were only two men riding with him that had actually seen the colonel, Fuller had described the man they were after, and he told them not to be shy about asking around. He didn't care if word spread that a band of Texans were looking for Barlow. No one, with the possible exception of Barlow himself, would know why—until it was too late.

Fuller himself, accompanied by one other man, his cousin Buell from up Nacogdoches way, located the *cabildo* where General Taylor had set up his head-quarters. Once again he had to be helped from his horse; using his cane, he hobbled up to the door—and found his way blocked by the sentry.

"I'm here to see the general," Zeke told the soldier. He was tired and in pain and in no mood for obstructions. "So get out of my way."

"What's your business?"

"Whatever it is, it ain't none of *your* business."

A young lieutenant emerged. The soldier started to relay to the officer what was transpiring, but Fuller interrupted him.

"I'm here to see a Colonel Barlow," he said gruffly. "Now stop wasting my time and get him."

The lieutenant gave him a frosty look. "And what do you want the colonel for?"

"We come to sign up for the war. But we won't fight except with the colonel."

"Then you have come a long way for nothing, sir," replied the lieutenant, "because Colonel Barlow has come and gone."

"Where did he go?"

"I'm not at liberty to say. And even if I were, I don't know that I would tell you."

Scowling, Buell clenched his fists and took a menac-ing step in the lieutenant's direction. Zeke Fuller threw out an arm and stopped him. The old man squinted at the shavetail. Then he forced a wolfish grin.

"You'll have to excuse my cousin Buell. He doesn't tolerate bad manners in folks. He can't talk—Comanches cut his tongue out back about fifteen summers ago up on the Llano Estacado. So all he can do when he gets riled now is throw a punch."

"You had better advise him not to," said the lieutenant, keeping a wary eye on Buell, who seemed oblivious to the fact that the sentry was aiming a rifle at his chest. Buell was such a brawny fellow that the lieutenant wasn't too sure that a bullet in the chest, even one fired at such close range, would be enough to stop him.

"Don't you worry," said Fuller. "We'll be on our way. Sorry to bother you. Come on, Buell." He turned and hobbled back out into the hot sunlight, and Buell, with one last scowl at the lieutenant and the sentry, lumbered after him. Buell helped Zeke back onto his horse, and Fuller—casting a look around the plaza, crowded with soldiers—spotted a cantina across the way, and directed Buell there. Buell walked along behind Zeke's horse, leading his own. At the cantina, Buell once more helped the old man to the ground. They went inside. It wasn't any different than a hundred other cantinas Zeke Fuller had been inside in his time—fly-specked walls, ramshackle furniture, dirt floor, the stench of stale beer and unwashed men. Zeke went to the nearest unoccupied table and sat down. The proprietor, an elderly Mexican, came over to take his order of a bottle of mescal. The bottle was promptly produced, along with two fairly clean glasses. Zeke filled them both. Buell knocked his drink back. It seemed to have no visible effect on him. Zeke just shook his head and took a sip to clear the dust, his shifty gaze flicking across the room at the other patrons. They were all soldiers.

"I reckon we'll just sit here and keep our ears open for a spell," he told Buell.

Buell just looked at him, uncomprehendingly. Zeke didn't bother trying to explain it to his cousin.

Zeke Fuller sat there for more than an hour, watching Buell put away the mescal like it was water, nursing his own drink, and listening to all the conversation around him. The soldiers came and the soldiers went, and none of them paid much attention to the two Texans. It wasn't long before Zeke discovered that the chief topic of conversation among the troops in General Taylor's army was the anticipated march on Monterrey. The question on everyone's mind was when that march would take place. Why were they lingering for so long? The consensus seemed to be that the general was waiting for his scouts to give him more information about the Mexican army and its preparations around Monterrey.

Eventually Zeke's nephew, Del Taggart, wandered into the cantina. When he spotted Zeke and Buell he came to the table, and his eyes lit up when he saw the bottle of mescal. But before he could take a drink, Zeke told him to go round up the others.

"You found Barlow?" asked Taggart.

"I think I know *where* to find him," replied Zeke. "Now do what I told you."

Taggart mournfully eyed the bottle, then wandered back outside.

Thinking back on it later, Barlow figured that finding Churacho alive had been nothing short of a small miracle. There were two more miracles in store for him. Churacho agreed to help him spy on the Mexican army. And Captain Armstrong produced a band of wild horses.

Churacho identified some of the mustangs as the ones that had been taken from him. But there were a half-dozen others in the bunch that he had not seen before. Armstrong assured the mustanger that he had done the best he could do. Taylor's army was requisitioning horses from any and all sources, and immediately dispersing them to cavalry units—wild or greenbroke, it didn't matter. But the stallion was among the bunch, which went a long way, thought Barlow, towards ameliorating the situation as far as Churacho was concerned.

Barlow wasn't too happy, however, with Churacho's decision to recruit four Mexicans in Matamoros. He claimed he needed help with the mustangs until he could reach his regular outfit, which was located a long day's ride to the west. He could not, he said, keep the bunch together by himself, and he didn't think Barlow and Armstrong had the wherewithal to help him. Barlow had to confess that this was true. Though he'd spent a few days with the mustangers during his first trip to Texas, and had learned a little about the trade, he recognized that there was a great deal he didn't know about it. Besides, he wasn't nearly the horseman that Churacho and the other mustangers were. But he was concerned about the *caballeros* Churacho recruited. Could they be trusted? Churacho said they could be trusted to help with the horses, but that was all. He advised Barlow to say nothing about his mission in their presence. Once they were reunited with Churacho's outfit, the Matamoros *caballeros* would be sent on their way. Barlow wasn't happy with the arrangement, convinced as he was that Matamoros was brimming with spies for Santa Anna. But he realized that there was nothing for it, so he went along.

Early in the afternoon of the next day, they reached a small adobe hut backed up against a low curving ridge, facing south across an arid plain of sand and cactus that danced in the shimmering heat. As far as Barlow could tell, they were many miles away from the nearest habitation. There was a large pen into which the mustangers drove the *mesteñas*. It was built against a rock face at the base of the ridge. The other three sides were comprised of limbs and brush packed down between pairs of cedar posts, two feet apart and tied together at the top with rawhide.

As this was done by the Mexicans he had picked up in Matamoros; Churacho headed toward the hut. Barlow and Armstrong followed, leading their tired horses and hanging back as Therese and several other men emerged, all of whom Barlow recognized as members of Churacho's outfit. Therese, crying out with joy, flung herself into her brother's arms. All grins, the men gathered round and pounded Churacho on the back. Two more came down off the ridge with rifles racked on their shoulders—presumably lookouts. Churacho greeted them, and sent them back to their posts. After a while, Therese separated herself from the group and came toward Barlow, her smile as warm as the sun that hung high in the summer sky.

"Did I not tell you?" she asked, with a quiet triumph.

"You were right after all. I did come back."

"And you saved my brother's life. All our lives."

"All? How do you figure?"

"Even though he had made them all swear not to, the *mesteñeros* were going to Matamoros in the morning. They were going to free Churacho or die trying. And even though they said I could not go with them, I was going to follow."

Barlow didn't bother telling her that it would have been too late for Churacho. His execution had been scheduled for the morning just past. And if the mustangers had made trouble, they would have been killed on the spot. He wasn't at all sure that Taylor's soldiers would have made an exception in Therese's case, either.

"We would have gone sooner," continued Therese, looking back at her brother, still being mobbed by the *mesteñeros,* who were cutting up like playful boys, so relieved were they to have their leader back in their midst. "But it took them a long time to decide to break their word to Churacho." She turned back to Barlow and before he could react had thrown her arms around his neck and kissed the corner of his mouth. "That is for saving my brother." She kissed him again, full on the mouth this time, and the kiss lingered. "And that," she said, when she was done, a little breathless, "is because I missed you. I have never stopped thinking about you. Even in my dreams, you . . ."

"Uh, Therese," said Barlow, so embarrassed that his cheeks were burning. "This is Captain Armstrong. A friend of mine."

She beamed at Armstrong, sticking out a hand. "*Mucho gusto,* Captain."

"The pleasure's all mine, ma'am," murmured Armstrong, taking the proffered hand.

She whirled away and returned to Churacho, jumping on his back, and the mustangers laughed as he spun around, mimicking a wild horse trying to buck a rider, but not trying *too* hard.

"I wish you'd mentioned that I had a little something to do with rescuing her brother," sighed Armstrong.

"Why is that?"

"Well, I might have gotten a kiss out of the deal like you did."

Barlow laughed. He noticed that Armstrong couldn't seem to take his eyes off Therese. "I'll be sure to mention that to her, first chance I get."

"Probably no point," said Armstrong. "She seems awfully fond of you, Colonel."

"Thanks for reminding me."

Chapter 20

Churacho paid the Matamoros *caballeros* with hard
money from a sack that had been kept somewhere in
the hut, and invited them to stay the night. But the
Matamoros men were eager to return home and spend
the pesos they had earned. Though none of them had
seemed unduly interested in what he and Armstrong
were doing, Barlow was glad to see them go nonetheless. He trusted Churacho's men, not because he knew
them very much better than he knew the riders from
Matamoros, but because Churacho trusted them. He
doubted they would betray Churacho, and if the mustanger committed to their enterprise, then neither
would they betray him or Captain Armstrong. He had
to operate on that assumption, anyway.

That evening Therese and the old cook roasted wild
pig over an open fire. This everyone ate with bread
made fresh that day in a mud oven, and washed down
with strong coffee or *mescal,* depending on one's pref-
erence. Then one of the *mesteñeros* began to play a
guitar; he was joined by another on a harmonica. They
played slow ballads and quicker tunes. Therese danced
to nearly every one, and with different members of
the outfit—under the watchful eye of her brother. Her
first choice for dance partner was Barlow, of course,

but he begged off, claiming he had two left feet. Armstrong, however, wasn't about to pass up his opportunity. But for the problem with Therese and her feelings for him—he was more than a little dismayed that time, apparently, had not diluted them at all—Barlow was content. He discovered that he'd missed the camaraderie of these mustangers. And he was glad to be sitting around a campfire out in the middle of nowhere, a sky bright with stars over his head, and in the far distance coyotes yip-yip-yipping a chorus to the music the *mesteñeros* made.

Later that night, he at last got his chance to talk to Churacho. The mustanger had said he would listen to Barlow's proposal, and Barlow was anxious to have his decision. They walked out to the pen where the horses were held. Their approach stirred the mustangs; the horses began to trot back and forth, throwing their heads and stamping the ground hard. The stallion turned chaos into order with a whinny. At the sound, the other horses gathered on the far side of the pen, with the stallion pacing back and forth in front of them, like an officer moving along a line of soldiers in battle, calming them by his defiance of danger.

"You said you needed my help," remarked Churacho, puffing on a cheroot and gazing at the horses. "What is it that you want of me?"

"I have a job to do. I have to learn the disposition of the enemy in and around Monterrey. General Taylor intends to march against the Mexican army there. But he doesn't know what he's up against."

"As far as I am concerned," said Churacho gruffly, "the best possible outcome would be if the armies fought until all the soldiers on both sides were dead."

"I understand why you'd feel that way."

"Do you?" Churacho peered at him. "I do not say this because one army killed my parents, and the other army almost killed me. No, I say it because all I want to do—all those men back there want to do—is live free, to chase the *mesteños*. What do we care about politics and boundaries? We follow no flag. We owe no allegiance except to one another. We just want to be left alone."

"I know," sighed Barlow, "and believe me, I *do* understand, my friend. But there are many people who love war because of what it can bring them. Glory, profit, vengeance."

"I am not one of those. Neither are my *compañeros*. And you are not one of those, either. So why are you here?"

Barlow's smile was rueful. "When I said good-bye to you months ago, I swore I would never return. That I had played my part in this war, and would play no more. But here I am. Because my country needs my services. I've spent my entire adult life answering the call to duty. It is a part of my nature that I cannot resist, no matter how much I may want to. That's one reason. The other . . . well, the other is far more practical. I'm here to help win this war because by doing so I will make life back home easier my wife and son."

"How can that be so?"

"I'm a Yankee, a Northerner. I live in the South. My wife is a Southerner. That's where her roots are, and I will not take her away from there. But most Southerners look on me as the enemy, because I have opposed slavery and secession—and I have killed one of their heroes. The South wants to win this war and expand slavery. That expansion will guarantee its survival, and the survival of a way of life that Southerners want to hold on to."

Churacho shook his head. "You hate slavery and yet you fight to protect it."

"Ah, well, there's the supreme irony of it all," said Barlow.

Churacho shrugged. "I will help you. But not because of what Santa Anna did to my family. No, I do this because we are friends, and that is the only reason."

Barlow looked at the mustanger, surprised—and honored. He also began to have second thoughts. What was he thinking? Putting not only Churacho's life but the lives of his fellow *mesteñeros* in peril just because he was fool enough to be here in the middle of a war?

"Thank you," he said, and it was from the heart. "The thing is, I don't think we could succeed in sneaking into Monterrey. . . ."

"No," said Churacho firmly. "Many of the soldiers in your army, they think the Mexican soldier is lazy, stupid and a coward. This is not true."

"I'm thinking that if my army is in such dire need of horses, the same may be true of the Mexican army. So maybe we should go in as mustangers, openly. We tell them that we want to sell these horses. If we're lucky, they might just invite us in through the front door."

Churacho nodded. "It is the only way. But you, my friend, you cannot pass as a Mexican. So what do we do about you and the captain?"

"The captain and I will say we're deserters. Northerners who are opposed to the war because we see it as a fight to expand slavery." Barlow smiled ruefully. "I think I can be pretty convincing when telling that tale. If they believe us, I'll give them some false information about General Taylor's forces."

"And if they don't believe you, you will face a firing squad."

"I know. That's why we'll go in as your prisoners.

You can tell them that you found us in the desert. And you know nothing more about us. That way, if things go badly for the captain and me, they won't suspect you and your men of duplicity."

"I cannot say this is a good plan," confessed Churacho, with a rakish grin. "But it is the only one that might work, I think. You will have to be rid of the uniform, or they will simply shoot you on sight—and us along with you. Now I will go talk to my men. I will not try to make them do this. They must choose for themselves whether to go or stay behind."

Barlow and Armstrong stood at the edge of the firelight while Churacho talked to his *mesteñeros*. When all of the mustangers agreed without hesitation to accompany them to Monterrey, Barlow wasn't surprised. Their loyalty to Churacho was one reason. It was unshakable. Where he went, they would go. Another reason was that the task, as Churacho spelled it out for them, was fraught with peril, and so appealed to their appetite for adventure. These men needed excitement the way other people needed air. It was in their blood—it was why they were *mesteñeros*. And finally they were brothers; not by blood but by ties just as strong as blood. Not one of them was inclined to stay behind while the rest rode away to risk their lives. The only reason they had not cheerfully ridden to their deaths in an attempt to free Churacho from the brig at Fort Brown was that they had given him their solemn promise, and he had charged them with taking care of Therese.

As for Therese, though, one man would have to stay behind just the same, said Churacho. They would have to draw straws—it was the only fair way to decide. It was at that point that Therese stood up and defiantly confronted her brother.

"No one will have to stay behind with me. Because I am going with you."

Churacho scowled. "You will stay. That is my last word on the subject."

"Maybe it's *your* last word, but not mine. You can't make me stay. If you leave me, I will follow. If you tie me up, I will get loose somehow and follow. If you take all the horses, I will follow on foot. There is no way you can stop me from coming with you—unless you kill me."

Barlow warily watched Churacho; he could see the anger rising up in the man, and wondered just how far the mustanger would go to appease his sister. By his own admission he was, sometimes, too lenient where she was concerned. Surely, thought Barlow, he would put his foot down in this case; surely he wouldn't let Therese ride with them to Monterrey. It was too dangerous.

But Churacho *did* back down.

"You are right," he told his sister. "I cannot stop you."

He turned away, and found himself face to face with Barlow.

"You can't be serious," said Barlow. "You can't let her come with us."

Before Churacho could speak, one of the lookouts from the ridge behind the adobe hut arrived at the campfire. He spoke rapidly to Churacho in Spanish. Whatever he said galvanized the other mustangers. They were all on their feet simultaneously. Barlow fired a querulous look at Armstrong.

"He's spotted a campfire about a mile east of here," explained Armstrong. "He thinks maybe somebody followed us from Matamoros. He says maybe the American general changed his mind about letting

Churacho go free, and sent some soldiers to bring him back."

Barlow shook his head. He didn't hold a very high opinion of Zachary Taylor, but neither did he think the man a fool. He needed Barlow's mission to Monterrey to succeed, and he wouldn't do something to jeopardize that. Barlow turned back to Churacho.

"If they are soldiers, Taylor didn't send them," he said.

"How do you know this?" asked the mustanger.

"Because he has no reason to."

"I killed one of his soldiers."

"Yes, but he's not worried about you escaping justice. You see, Captain Armstrong and I promised that if you managed to survive our ride to Monterrey we would kill you ourselves."

It had always been Barlow's impression that Churacho's *mesteñeros* understood very little English—but somehow they seemed to understand his words now, and they froze, watching him warily. Churacho stared at him for a moment. Then he threw back his head and laughed. He clapped Barlow on the shoulder. The mustangers relaxed, smiled, nodded to one another. Everything was all right. It was a joke.

"If it is not soldiers, we must find out who it is," said Churacho. "You and I will go."

Barlow nodded. "Good idea."

Chapter 21

Barlow and Churacho rode out immediately. Within a quarter-mile of the strangers' camp, they dismounted, left their horses, and proceeded the rest of the way on foot. They found some high ground less than a hundred and fifty yards away from the camp, from which vantage point they could see it clearly. Barlow counted fifteen men around the big campfire, then counted the horses on the nearby picket line. There were sixteen horses. He pointed this out to Churacho, even though he assumed the mustanger had already made note of it. One man unaccounted for meant there was a lookout somewhere in the darkness. They could only hope that, wherever he was, he hadn't spotted them. Belly-down on the crest of the high ground, surrounded by rocks and cactus and greasewood, Barlow figured they were pretty well concealed.

"Do you know them?" Churacho asked.

"No, I don't think so," replied Barlow.

Then he saw a man who had been seated on a rock stand up with the aid of a cane. The way he was gesturing, it was clear that he was addressing the others, though at this distance Barlow couldn't make out the words. Still, he knew immediately who the man was.

"Wait a minute," he said. "That's—"

"Zeke Fuller," said Churacho grimly.

They exchanged glances, and without another word, slipped down the back side of the high ground and headed back to their horses, searching the night shadows for any sign of the lookout. They saw nothing, heard nothing. But Barlow felt the hairs stand up on the nape of his neck. He wasn't sure if it was because he knew there was an enemy lurking out there somewhere, or just the fact that Zeke Fuller was in the vicinity. He and Churacho had come out here to identify the strangers and, if possible, discover their purpose. The sighting of Zeke Fuller had accomplished all of that. There was only one reason that Fuller would be out here. It was no unhappy coincidence.

Mounting up, they rode back to the adobe by a circuitous route, wanting to make sure they hadn't been followed, doubling back suddenly on their trail. It occurred to Barlow how lucky they'd been that Fuller and his outfit had decided to stop and make camp when and where they did. If they had come just a little further, they would probably have discovered the adobe, or at the very least seen the big fire the *mesteñeros* had built earlier that evening.

Only when the adobe was in sight did Churacho speak again. "I knew he would seek revenge. Such men always do. It is blood for blood with them."

"You think all those other men are kinfolk?"

Churacho shrugged. "Probably. Zeke Fuller could not afford to pay so many if they were hired killers."

"Well, whoever they are, we're outnumbered three to one. Worse odds than the last time—and we were lucky to get away with our lives then."

"What do you want to do about it?"

Barlow gave the question a few moments of careful

consideration before answering. "Fuller's presence complicates things, but it doesn't change them. I'm still going to Monterrey."

"Now we will have an enemy in front of us, and another one behind us," said Churacho.

"Maybe we'll get lucky and Santa Anna's dragoons will take care of them for us." He glanced at the mustanger. "One thing *has* changed, come to think of it. Therese."

"Yes, I know. We cannot leave her behind now."

"Right." Now Therese would be in as much danger if they left her as she would be if she accompanied them.

"The presence of a woman might give us an edge," remarked Barlow, trying to find the bright side. "The Mexican soldiers might be less likely to suspect us. If we were looking for trouble we wouldn't bring a woman along."

He could tell that Churacho wasn't convinced.

They left the adobe two hours before dawn the next morning. It was Churacho's idea to split into two groups. Therese, accompanied by Barlow and two of the *mesteñeros,* would proceed west about five miles before turning due south. Soon they would come to a river, and a crossing that all three of the mustangers were familiar with. Meanwhile, Churacho, Armstrong and the other four mustangers, with the entire *manada* of wild horses, would head directly south from the adobe and cross the river further downstream. They could not separate the horses—if they did, the band without the stallion would become unmanageable. The two parties would meet at a village called Salinas that was located on the other side of the river. Though it flew in the face of logic to split up when faced with a superior foe, Barlow accepted the plan, understanding that once Fuller found the adobe, as he surely would, he would hasten onward, thinking himself hot on their trail. His progress might be slowed if his prey took two separate routes; he might split up his own crew, or might proceed with caution, suspecting a trap. What Churacho was really hoping for was that Fuller would elect to follow him—the larger group, and the one with the horses. If that turned out to be the case, one mustanger would take Therese and ride to a town called Hidalgo, seventy miles to the west, while Barlow and the other *mesteñero* rejoined Churacho's group. In that event, Churacho made Barlow swear that he would make sure Therese went to Hidalgo. Barlow swore he would, even though he had no idea how he would go about keeping that promise. Therese was determined to go with him, and her brother, to Monterrey.

It wasn't hard figuring out how Fuller had come to the border country. He knew that Barlow was an officer in the army, and had assumed that he would be in the campaign against the Mexicans. So he had come to where the war was being waged. Arriving in Matamoros, he had asked around about Barlow, and had, no doubt, learned of the business with Churacho and the wild horses. Then, once he'd determined that Barlow wasn't in Matamoros, it had simply been a matter of swinging a wide loop around the town, looking for a trail made distinctive by the passage of so many unshod horses. That trail had led Fuller to within a mile of Churacho's adobe.

Before leaving the adobe, Barlow and Armstrong exchanged their uniforms for clothing donated by the mustangers. Barlow ended up with some buckskin trousers, a plain shirt of rough yellow muslin, and a *serape*. They carried their uniforms with them; it would make sense that deserters would shed them.

At midmorning of the first day away from the adobe, Barlow called a halt and found some high ground from which he could see twenty miles in any direction. It took but a moment to locate the telltale plume of dust. Riders were following them. Without getting too close for comfort, it would be impossible to tell whether the entire Fuller outfit was after them or if, indeed, Zeke had split his men into two groups. It really didn't matter—Barlow began to reconcile himself to the fact that they were stuck with Therese. He trudged back down to the where she and the other mustanger—whose name, Barlow had learned, was Ochoa—were waiting with the horses. Therese took one look at his expression and smiled triumphantly.

"They are coming after us," she said. "Good. Now you don't have to try to get rid of me. Which would have been impossible, in any case."

He just shook his head. "Those men will kill us all if they catch us," he said, "and yet you're happy that they're coming."

"I would rather die than be away from you anyway," she said.

Barlow groaned, and mounted up. "Let's ride."

And ride they did, all the rest of that long, hot day, pushing their horses—and themselves—to the limit of their endurance. The sun was setting when they reached the river. Ochoa's sense of direction had been unerring—they arrived right where a crossing could be made. This river—Ochoa said some people called it the Rio Verde—was different from the Rio Grande in several crucial respects. It was not as wide but it was much deeper and had a swift current as it ran between high, sandy bluffs. Barlow was worried that the horses, worn out from the day's exertions, might have trouble fighting the current. But there was no help for it. That plume of dust was still visible. Their pursuers had not gained on them, but neither had they fallen much behind.

As it turned out, they made the crossing without mishap—the distance the horses had to swim was actually short; they made it nearly halfway across the Rio Verde on a sandbar that marked a bend in the river, then had to swim for about twenty yards before reaching another sandbar that took them safely to the southern bank. There they dismounted and checked their saddles and cinch straps. They were all soaked to the skin, and Barlow noticed that Therese's shirt clung indecently to her breasts. She didn't seem to think anything of it—an indifference that was due, he supposed, to the fact that she had spent most of her life in the company of men, and under conditions that didn't permit much in the way of privacy. He didn't stare, but he noticed that Ochoa did—until Ochoa realized that Barlow was staring at *him*. Then Ochoa began paying close attention to the bluffs that loomed over them. He pointed upstream, and spoke to Therese in Spanish.

"He says there is a ravine not far in that direction, by which we can reach the top," she informed Barlow. "I myself have only been here once or twice, but I seem to remember that this is so."

"Good. Let's go find it."

It was as Ochoa said. They negotiated the ravine, leading their horses, for it was too steep to ride, and the sandy soil was treacherous, sometimes giving way beneath their feet. Arriving at last at the top, they paused to catch their breath. Barlow looked once more to the north, along their back-trail. He calculated that the riders following them were no more than four or five miles away.

"Is there another crossing nearby, either upriver or down?" he asked Therese.

"I don't think so." She posed the question to Ochoa, who answered quickly. No, the nearest crossing was nearly twenty miles downriver—the very crossing, in fact, that Churacho was planning to use to reach Salinas.

"What are you thinking?" Therese asked Barlow.

"I'm thinking about slowing them down," he said grimly. "This is the perfect place, a perfect opportunity. They'll reach this crossing at right about dusk. Up here with a rifle, I could pick off one, maybe two of them, before they could get out of range. And if some or all of them do manage to get across, I can be well away before they can climb these bluffs."

"It is a good plan," she said. "We all have rifles."

"No," snapped Barlow. "You and Ochoa proceed to Salinas. Your brother will be there tonight—if he isn't there already."

"I will not leave you to face those men alone."

"Yes, you will—if I have to tie you to the saddle, you will."

She looked hurt. "You would do that?"

"Don't play games with me. Churacho has entrusted me with your safety, and it's a trust I take very seriously."

"So it is not because you care for me, but because my brother does, that you wish to keep me out of danger," she said.

Barlow sighed, glanced at Ochoa, who was watching them uncomprehendingly. It was a shame, mused Barlow, that he didn't speak Spanish well enough to order Ochoa to take her to Salinas. And even if he could issue such an order, and be understood, there was no guarantee that the mustanger would obey him. These men had given their loyalty to Churacho because Churacho had earned it, probably many times over. The same could not be said for Barlow. And besides, they had to be careful how they dealt with Therese, precisely because she was the boss's sister.

"So what's it going to be?" Barlow asked her. "You either go to Salinas in the saddle, or across it."

"Fine," she said huffily. She climbed into the saddle and turned her horse around so quickly that Barlow had to step back to avoid it. Then she leaned down and grabbed the front of his *serape* and pulled him closer. "I'm warning you," she said—and then, suddenly, planted a kiss on his mouth—"that you had better come back to me."

She let him go, then dug her heels into the mount's belly, kicking it into a canter. Ochoa was already in the saddle, and took off after her. Barlow breathed a sigh of relief before turning his full attention to the task at hand.

He led his horse back from the rim, far enough so that it would not be seen from below, in case his calculations were off and the pursuers arrived before dusk. From the saddle he took the long gun that he had brought all the way from Georgia—it hadn't made much sense to be heading off to war without something that had a longer range than pistol or saber. The weapon was a Colt Paterson Model 1836 rifle that he had purchased several years earlier. It was a hammerless percussion rifle, .44 caliber, with an eight-shot fluted cylinder, and it had plenty of range to knock a man off his horse on the other side of the river.

Picking a good spot along the rim of the bluff, Barlow settled belly-down on the ground and waited. He spent the time checking the rifle, making sure the cylinder carried good loads, and that the barrel was clear of dust and debris. Then he watched the sun setting. He tried to do anything besides think about the fact that his intention was to kill. He'd done his share of killing, but it wasn't something you grew accustomed to. Not unless there was something wrong with you. It didn't help much to remember that the men he was about to shoot at were dead set on killing him. That wasn't really the point. The point was that he was preparing to take lives. It was what a soldier did when called upon. But this business with the Fullers wasn't really a war. It was a senseless vendetta. So whoever died today was going to die needlessly. Yes, he had taken Daniel Fuller's life, but that had been self-defense. He'd had no choice; it was kill or be killed. Which, of course, held no water where Zeke Fuller and his clan were concerned.

They arrived at the river as the light began to bleed from the sky and the first stars began to appear. The sun had set below the western skyline, but was still providing enough light for Barlow to see his targets. There were seven riders—he didn't bother straining to see if Zeke Fuller was one of them. This wasn't a case where killing the leader would cause the others to call the whole thing off, so it really didn't matter if Zeke was here or with the other group, which, presumably, was following Churacho and the mustangs.

The trail made earlier by Barlow, Therese and Ochoa led straight down to the river—the riders had no trouble seeing where they had crossed, and after a brief, from-the-saddle conference, they started across, single-file. Barlow nestled the walnut stock of the rifle to his shoulder and drew a bead on the first horseman. He knew the rifle well, and was a good enough shot to make the necessary adjustments, to take into account not only the range but the fact that he was shooting downward from at least a hundred feet above the river. He put it all together—range, height, velocity and the movement of the target—and lined up his sights on the head of the horse the first man was riding. Then he squeezed the trigger. The bullet hit the rider and not the horse, as Barlow had intended. The man catapulted off the back of his horse, which spooked and jumped sideways and tumbled with a splash off the sandbar into the deep water. The man Barlow had shot disappeared under the surface of the river, then came up standing in waist-deep water, clutching at his guts, then toppled again. One of his kinsmen leaped from the saddle and fished him out of the drink. That one's horse took the opportunity to hightail it back to dry land. The other horsemen were trying to get their mounts under control and figure out where the shot had come from. It didn't take them long. Before Barlow could line up another target, they were shooting at the top of the bluff. But they had two things working against them: they weren't sure of his exact location and they were doing their shooting from the saddle—and their horses were upset and hard to control, aware that one of their own was floundering in the strong current that was sweeping it downstream.

Barlow fired again. This time he hit his target a little high—it was because the man's horse was pivoting. Still, a .44-caliber bullet in the shoulder at such relatively close range was enough to knock the man sideways off the saddle. This time, though, the others were watching, and they saw Barlow's muzzle flash—and in seconds the air around him was scorched with hot lead. These were frontiersmen for the most part, and good shots all.

Barlow rolled away from the rim. Getting up, he moved at a running crouch to the right about sixty feet and plopped down again, crawling cautiously back up to the rim. The men down below were still shooting at the location he'd just vacated. Several of them had dismounted, knowing this made them more difficult targets. And some were heading back to dry land, where they could seek cover. But there were three still in the river—two on horseback and the one Barlow had winged. His first victim had been dragged ashore, then left there on the water's edge, his legs still in the river. He wasn't moving. Barlow figured he was dead—or else his rescuer had realized he was gutshot and, so, doomed, and had abandoned him to seek shelter.

Ignoring the man he had wounded, Barlow aimed for one of the two riders still in the river. But this time he missed his target and hit the man's horse instead. Man and horse went crashing into the shallows. The man came up and stumbled for the bank, while the horse floundered, drowning. Barlow would have shot it again, to put it out of its misery, but the three men who had found cover on the far bank were shooting at him, and Barlow had to withdraw from the rim as the bullets began to slam into the dirt entirely too close for comfort. Once more he pulled back far enough to be out of their line of sight. This time he ran to the left, about a hundred feet. Again on his belly, he crawled to the rim. The last of them was out of the water now. He watched for muzzle flash, then fired another shot into the brush that concealed his adversaries. He couldn't tell if he hit anything, but that didn't matter now. He had done what he'd set out to do. There wasn't much point in lingering any longer.

He crawled back from the rim for the last time and went to his horse. He slid the rifle in its scabbard and mounted up. The men down on the riverbank were still shooting. Barlow figured they'd stay under cover for quite some time, on the chance that whoever was shooting at them was still up on the bluff, waiting for one of them to show his face. In less than thirty minutes it would be fully dark. Only then, he figured, would they be emboldened to try a crossing. Then they had to find the ravine, and climb to the top of the bluff. Their progress would be slow, they would be cautious. And when they found he was gone, they still had one wounded man and one dying, if not already dead. And they were short a horse. If he was very lucky they wouldn't continue the pursuit until daylight, for fear of riding into another ambush.

Riding away, Barlow had no second thoughts. He had bushwhacked those men, but he'd learned a long time ago—in his first campaign, in fact, the one led by Andrew Jackson against the Red Sticks—that if you wanted to survive, you took advantage of any situation that allowed you to do maximum damage to the enemy while minimizing the risk to yourself. Honor and fair play had absolutely nothing to do with it. It was all about staying alive.

Chapter 22

Barlow traveled through the night. He knew it was risky—there was always the chance that his horse would step in a hole, and a man left afoot in this country was at serious risk even without a pack of vengeance-seeking gunmen on his trail. But he wanted to catch up with the others, wanted to make sure that Churacho and Armstrong had made it to Salinas. Wanted—he had to admit it to himself—to make sure that Therese was all right, and not entirely because Churacho had elicited a promise from him that he would guarantee her safety. His feelings for her were more as a brother feels towards a sister. He wasn't in love with her, and he was able to suppress the desire he felt for her—that any man would feel for her. So he pressed on through the night. If he was in the saddle he held the horse to a walk, letting it pick its way. Sometimes he dismounted and led the horse, but always he was moving; he never stopped, even though his body ached fiercely. He'd had very little rest since stepping off the *Clementine* at Port Isabel. He was, he thought ruefully, getting too old for this sort of thing. And he swore to himself—a hundred times if he swore it once—that this would be his last campaign. Were he in Georgia, he'd be asleep in his comfortable bed, with the warm, lithe body of his wife curled up against him. Being here instead of there made Barlow wonder about his sanity.

This was new country for him, but it wasn't difficult to reach Salinas—all he had to do was keep the Rio Verde near at hand. So it was that he reached the village shortly after dawn. The place was just awakening. Smoke curled out of the chimneys of the small adobes. Children romped with dogs, chickens and pigs in the rutted streets. Adults stopped what they were doing and stood in the doorways to watch him pass by, their features inscrutable. No one, mused Barlow, was more stoic than the Mexican peasant. It was a necessary condition, imbued with a stout dose of fatalism. What else could one expect of a people who lived in a lawless land that had for more than twenty years—ever since independence from Spain—endured political unrest, where yesterday's leader might be today's bandit, or vice versa, where *bandoleros* and *revolucionarios* and *federales* might sweep down upon the town and loot, pillage, and rape? These people lived, or tried to live, in a situation that offered no security, no guarantees. And when you lived every day with the knowledge that you and your entire family might be dead by sundown, you could scarcely be criticized for being a fatalist. The *campesinos* who watched him ride into Salinas revealed nothing in their faces—it did not pay to take sides in Mexico if you were a poor peasant. If any one of them was pleased by his arrival, or resented his presence, Barlow couldn't tell by looking.

As he arrived at the *zocalo*—the square that marked the center of town—he was relieved to see Armstrong and one of Churacho's mustangers at the well, giving their horses a drink from a bucket of water. When Armstrong saw Barlow, he waved and jogged towards him, a grin spread across his dusty, sun-dark face.

"I was about to come looking for you," said the captain. "What happened? Therese and one of the mustangers showed up late last night, said you'd stayed behind to slow down the bunch that was following."

"That's right." Barlow kept walking towards the well. His horse needed water—and so did he.

"So did you slow them down, or not?"

"We'll see." Barlow didn't care to revisit the events of the day before. He'd killed a man, and that wasn't something he liked to dwell on, much less talk about. "What about you? Only about half of Fuller's crew came after us."

Armstrong nodded. "The others are hot on our trail. Churacho said we'd have to leave within the hour to stay ahead of them. That's when I told him I was going back to find you."

Barlow stopped and leveled an earnest gaze at the young captain. "Listen. If anything happens to me, you have to keep one thing in mind. The reason we're out here is to provide General Taylor with intelligence about the Mexican army and fortifications in Monterrey. If I can't, you finish the job, understand?"

"Yes, sir," said Armstrong, looking a bit resentful. "I understand completely, Colonel. If you get into trouble I'm supposed to just write you off and go about my business."

"That's right."

"And is that what you'd do, if I was in trouble?"

"Without a second thought."

Barlow got some water from the well for his horse, and then the three of them rode out of Salinas. The *campesinos* watched them go with the same impassivity with which they had observed their coming. But

Barlow figured these people had to be inwardly delighted that at least three strangers had come to their
town and gone without taking anything that didn't belong to them.

Churacho's camp was only a mile or so out of town.
As Barlow and his two companions arrived, five *mesteñeros* were taking the *manada* of wild horses south,
leaving behind only Churacho, Therese and the old
cook who drove the wagon. The latter was climbing
aboard a mule, holding a rope that led to another
mule laden with a makeshift pack. Barlow wondered
what had become of the wagon.

"We lost the wagon crossing the river," Churacho
told him, as though reading his mind. "We lost many
of our supplies. But we have enough to get to Monterrey. It is but a two-day ride from here."

Barlow nodded. "I'll make sure you receive recom-
pense for the wagon." He figured that was only fair—
Churacho and his crew were undertaking the business
of the United States.

Churacho shrugged. "No matter. We will travel faster
without it. How many did you kill at the crossing?"

"Only one, I think. But I'm hoping it slowed the
others down some."

"The ones who follow us—they are not far behind."
He took a long, speculative look at both Barlow and
Barlow's horse. He could tell that both man and beast
were exhausted. "We should not stay here long."

"Then let's get moving," said Barlow.

Churacho nodded, and allowed himself a slight
smile. "*Mucho hombre,* eh?" he asked his sister, nodding at Barlow.

"Yes, he is," said Therese admiringly. She hadn't
taken her eyes off Barlow since his arrival.

"*Andale,*" said Churacho, and they started off in
the wake of the *manada*.

*   *   *

It was a given that every mile they made brought them that much closer to discovery by the effective screen of scouts watching the approaches to Monterrey. Barlow found himself hoping it would be sooner rather than later, considering that there was a fair chance that both he and Armstrong would be killed instantly. All too often in war it was simply a matter of shooting first and asking questions later. They were Americans, therefore they would be presumed enemies. But it was the uncertainty—and the mounting tension that accompanied that uncertainty—which made Barlow eager to arrive at the moment of truth.

It wasn't as though they were trying to avoid detection. Quite the opposite was the case. They rode as though fully expecting to be greeted with open arms by the Mexican soldiers. They had to *act* innocent if they were to have any hope of being *taken* as innocents.

And yet they traveled that entire day without seeing any sign of the Mexican army. Nor, looking behind them, did they see any telltale dust marking the progress of the Fuller clan. Armstrong was finally compelled to ask Barlow if he believed that Zeke Fuller and his gang had given up the chase. Maybe, suggested the captain, they didn't want to venture any deeper into Mexico, seeing as how there was a war going on. Barlow just shook his head. He didn't think Hell, high water or the prospect of running into Santa Anna himself would deter Zeke Fuller from pursuing vengeance. He wasn't the type to head back for the Rio Grande and bide his time, hoping that Barlow and Churacho would one day reappear. No, he wouldn't even want to take the chance that the Mexicans might kill the men he was after before he got a chance to skin them alive. If the lack of dust meant anything, it was just that the pursuers had fallen back. Maybe, mused Barlow grimly, they had stopped off in Salinas for a little pillaging along the way.

That night they made a cold camp, without a fire, and without any music or singing either. It wasn't that they were too tired—though they were all weary. It was, rather, the fact that all knew tomorrow would surely bring them into contact with the Mexican army. Barlow was more worried about Therese than his own skin, and he could sense that Churacho felt the same way. Few words were exchanged. Most of the mustangers took the time to carefully check or clean their weapons.

Barlow thought he could also sense an urgency in Therese, a desire to be near him. She seldom took her eyes off him. For his part, he studiously ignored her. He figured she wanted to spend some time alone with him, recognizing that this might be their final opportunity. But he had no such desire. It was a simple matter of resisting temptation—and that was something he could do much better in Churacho's presence. So he stretched out on the ground and rolled up in his blankets and within minutes was fast asleep.

The following morning they had been traveling but an hour when Churacho pulled his horse alongside Barlow's.

"They are close, I think," said the mustanger, intently scanning the terrain ahead of them. The country here was relatively flat, arid plains, crisscrossed with arroyos, and marked by an occasional butte standing in splendid isolation. One could see, Barlow guessed, for at least fifty miles in any direction. And yet, despite the fact that it seemed to be country ideal for spotting trouble well in advance of its arrival, he knew that to be a deception. There were many hiding places—an entire army could be concealed within ten miles of them and they would not know it.

When Churacho told him of his suspicions, Barlow took a long, careful look about him, and saw absolutely nothing of an alarming nature.

"What makes you think so?" he asked the mustanger.

"I just feel it. Here." Churacho placed a hand over his stomach. "You cannot see it or hear it, but you know it is out there. Something dangerous."

Barlow nodded. "I understand. And I trust your instincts. But there's nothing for it except to keep going." He glanced at Churacho, wanting to apologize for the hundredth time, for dragging the mustanger into such a perilous undertaking.

Moments later, the dragoons seemed to rise up out of the ground straight ahead of them.

Barlow realized that they had been concealed in an arroyo, but still, the effect was unnerving. The wild horses were certainly affected; the stallion whinnied a shrill warning and veered off, instinctively leading the mares away. Churacho's men were inclined to let the horses run, and follow. The dragoons were prepared for this; four of them set their mounts to a gallop, twirling ropes over their heads as they guided the responsive horses beneath them with their knees. All four succeeded in surrounding the stallion, so that it could run but one way, then neatly tossed the looped ends of their lariats over the animal's head. The stallion reared, hooves flailing, with magnificent defiance, but it was all for naught—the dragoons had him. The mares ran a little bit further, then slowed, then stopped, looking back at their stallion, unwilling to leave him. The mustangers drew their weapons, but Churacho had put spur to horse and was shouting at them not to shoot as he thundered up.

An officer rode up to Churacho and Barlow. Though he looked to have been on the trail for quite a long time, he still managed somehow to look resplendent in his uniform—a green and gold tunic with scarlet epaulets, gray trousers with a broad red stripe down the outside of the leg, and a helmet with a chin strap made of gold links, and adorned with a black plume and red cockade. His men were similarly dressed. Each was armed with an iron-hilted, straight-bladed saber and an *escopeta*—a cut-down Brown Bess musket. Their pistols, Barlow noticed, were old smooth-bored British flintlocks. The *escopeta* would be inaccurate at anything but very close range, and the pistols were muzzle-loading. But then, Barlow suspected that the saber was the weapon of choice among these men, as with all cavalry. They were professionals, veterans all—he could take one look at them and see that.

"*Señor,*" said the officer, addressing Churacho, "you and your men are under arrest, and we are confiscating your horses."

"I have come to sell these horses to the army," replied Churacho. "If you intend to take them, you will have a fight on your hands, Captain."

The captain looked about him, and appeared somewhat amused. "You are outnumbered, *Señor,* better than five to one."

"I didn't say we would win," answered Churacho firmly. "Only that we would fight. And before you kill us, we will kill many of your men."

The captain's steady gaze swept past Therese with only casual interest—then fastened on Barlow and Armstrong. Barlow thought he saw a glimmer of surprise in the officer's features.

"You are *norteamericanos?*" he asked, in passable English.

"They are deserters," said Churacho. "Or so they said when we found them."

"Deserters." The captain continued to stare at Barlow and Armstrong, and the former found himself wishing fervently that he could tell what the man was thinking. This was, after all, the moment of truth, and he needed every edge he could get. But the man was inscrutable. Not for the first time in his life, Barlow had the sensation of being at the very brink of death. One word from the captain, a brief order given, and the dragoons would kill him and Armstrong. It would be over in seconds. And they would leave the bullet-riddled bodies in the dust of the desert, and the scavengers would pick their bones clean—and he wondered, if it happened, how long it would take Rose to receive word that her husband had embarked on a special mission behind enemy lines and never returned? How long would she stand at the window of their bedroom—as he sometimes imagined that she did when he was away—to watch the lane that led down through the fields to the road beyond? How much time would pass before, finally, she gave up hope and tried to get on with her life? And how would Jacob fare, growing up without a father? Barlow silently cursed himself for a fool. He did not belong here. His responsibilities lay elsewhere. He should be home, in Georgia, with his family. This wasn't cowardice. He wasn't afraid of death in and of itself. He was only afraid of the impact his death would have on those he loved. He would be wrong to put them through the grief of losing him.

The captain made up his mind. "You will both surrender your weapons," he said to Barlow. "I will take you to my commanding officer and let him decide what to do with you."

Barlow nodded at Armstrong, and they quickly divested themselves of their weapons. The captain's decision was by no means a guarantee of survival beyond the time it took them to get to Monterrey, but at least it was a stay of execution. And, under the circumstances, Barlow was willing to settle for that.

Chapter 23

Churacho and his mustangers were allowed to keep their weapons, and to drive the wild horses, but they were closely watched by the dragoons. A detail of four dragoons was given the task of keeping a very close eye on Barlow and Armstrong. The rest of that day, Barlow threw an occasional glance over his shoulder, looking for that now-familiar plume of dust—and not seeing anything to indicate that Zeke Fuller and his gang were still in pursuit. But he had to assume that they were. And what would the old man do when the tracks he followed alerted him to the fact that Barlow and Churacho had fallen into the hands of the Mexican army? Barlow was fairly certain that Fuller would have little doubt this was what had transpired; the man was no fool, and since the trail would continue to lead straight to Monterrey, it was the only conclusion he could reasonably make. Would he be deterred from further pursuit? Barlow could only hope so; he had his hands full with the Mexicans. He didn't need anything else to worry about.

They arrived at their destination late in the day. Barlow could see immediately why Monterrey was so strategically important. The city stood in the foothills of the Sierra Madre range, on a main thoroughfare that crossed the high country by means of a pass. The city's setting made it easily defensible. It was located on the north bank of the Santa Catarina River. The main road approached from the west along the river, passing between two commanding heights, both of which were heavily fortified. Federation Hill rose just south of the river, while to the north rose Independence Hill. On the former stood a stone fort known as El Soldado. On the latter stood the Bishop's Palace, a ruin that had been turned into a stout stronghold. The batteries established on either height could sweep the road. To the north of the city the land was fairly level, and here the Mexicans had dug a labyrinth of trenches and breastworks. Closer to the outskirts was an unfinished structure that had been transformed into a bastion called the Citadel, surrounded by artillery. To the east, the approach was guarded by two more works bristling with heavy guns—one an old tannery, the other called Devil's Fort. Behind the city, in the foothills to the south, the fortifications were fairly light. The terrain was too rugged for an enemy to make an attack in any force from this direction.

They struck the road just west of the city and followed it in, with the river to their right and Independence Hill looming to their left. Barlow made mental notes of everything he saw. Armstrong noticed that he was openly exhibiting curiosity about the Mexican defenses, and pulled his horse up alongside Barlow's.

"Wonder why they didn't blindfold us," murmured the captain.

"Because they don't think .we'll get out of here alive," replied Barlow, matter-of-factly.

Armstrong glanced at him. "Will we, you think?"

"We have to. That's our job, isn't it?"

One of the dragoons detailed to guard them snapped a brisk order.

"What did he say?" asked Barlow.

Armstrong put a finger to his lips and turned his horse away from Barlow's.

At the dragoon captain's direction, Churacho and his mustangers drove the wild horses into a cedar pole and brush corral on the edge of the city. The *mesteñeros*—along with Therese—could do nothing but look on as Barlow and Armstrong were escorted away by the captain and the detail of guards. Barlow gave them a reassuring nod—and couldn't fail to notice the expression of distress on Therese's face. He knew what she was thinking. That she might never see him again. It was a very real possibility. But he tried to exude confidence; he didn't want her to do something reckless, like trying to rescue him. If any one of them made trouble, all of them would likely pay a terrible price. It appeared that the dragoon captain had accepted Churacho for a mustanger who had just happened upon a couple of American deserters—which meant there was a possibility that the mustangers would be paid for the horses and allowed to go on their way.

Monterrey was a city of considerable size—from what Barlow had learned of the place prior to his arrival at Port Isabel, it had a population of about fifteen thousand. That number had been greatly augmented by a concentration of Mexican infantry, cavalry and artillery units. The most difficult intelligence to gather, mused Barlow, would be an accurate number for the Mexican troops participating in the defense of the city. From the little that he saw that day, though, he knew it had to be in the thousands.

They were taken to an encampment on the northwest edge of the city—the bivouac of a regiment of dragoons. From this location Barlow could look west and see the forbidding stronghold of the Bishop's Palace atop Independence Hill, and to the east to the Citadel, with its numerous breastworks and redoubts. Then he had to turn his attention to matters closer at hand—namely a tall, lean gentleman who sat at a camp table in the shade of a canvas awning, surrounded by younger officers. Barlow knew right away that this was the regimental commander—and the man in whose hands his fate now lay.

As the dragoons drew near with their captives, the commander looked up, idly curious at first, then fully intrigued. He rose and stepped out into the slanting, late-afternoon sunlight. His hair was close-cropped and the color of iron filings. He had long, carefully trimmed sideburns, and a thin mustache. He also had the piercing eyes of a hawk, which fastened on Barlow and Armstrong as the dragoon captain spoke rapidly, explaining who his prisoners were and how he had come by them. All Barlow could do was sit his horse and keep quiet and look the commander squarely in the eye, showing none of the fear that had been creeping through his bones ever since he'd first seen the dragoons. One word from the commander and they would be shot on the spot, their bodies deposited in shallow graves or perhaps even cast out beyond the perimeter of the encampment for the night scavengers to dispose of.

When the captain had concluded his narrative, the commander nodded curtly. He stepped closer to Barlow's horse.

"Step down," he said, in very precise English.

Barlow did as he was told, and Armstrong followed suit. Hands clasped behind his back, the commander walked past Barlow, sized Armstrong up, then turned back.

"You," he said to Barlow. "Identify yourself."

"Timothy Barlow, sir."

"Your rank?"

Barlow didn't hesitate. He had already decided that it would be pointless—not to mention foolhardy—to try to deceive this man about his background. Like himself, the commander was a career military man, and he had not acquired the position of responsibility he now held by being a poor judge of men. It was likely that he had pegged Barlow and Armstrong as fellow officers of the regular army.

"I am—I *was* a colonel in the United States Army."

"A colonel. Indeed. And your colleague?"

"His name is Armstrong, and he held the rank of captain."

"A colonel and a captain, both deserters." The dragoon commander smiled, but there was no warmth in it. "How extraordinary. Why did you desert?"

"It was a matter of conscience," said Barlow stiffly, as though offended by the commander's tone. "I won't speak for the captain, but only for myself when I say I could no longer countenance participation in an unjust war."

"And why, in your opinion, is this war unjust? Because it involves the invasion of a sovereign nation, perhaps?"

"No. Because it is being fought for the purpose of expanding slavery."

The commander studied Barlow for a moment, the smile gone—his expression more serious now, more contemplative. It was the one argument, thought Barlow, that a Mexican officer might buy. Because such a man would be one of the educated elite in Mexico. He would know that in the United States there was growing sectional strife with respect to the existence of slavery. It was the great moral argument of the day among the *norteamericanos,* and already men had died on both sides in skirmishing over the peculiar institution and its future. It was the only issue that might possibly account for the desertion of an officer in the United States Army.

"Were you intending to offer your services to us, then?" asked the dragoon commander.

"No," said Barlow firmly. "I will not fight for slavery, but neither will I fight against the Stars and Stripes."

The commander turned to the dragoon captain who had brought the two Americans in. "What do you think, Captain Rodriguez? Is he telling the truth?"

"I do not know, sir," responded Rodriguez. "I don't think it matters. They are the enemy. They should be executed."

"They might be spies, Colonel," said one of the younger officers, who was venturing from the shade of the canvas awning, and staring truculently at Barlow. "I agree with the captain. They should be killed at once."

"Spies," murmured the commander. "If that is so, it would be, I think, an amateurish attempt to infiltrate the city. Especially when you consider, Lieutenant, that there are some Mexicans who would betray their own country and work for the *norteamericanos* as spies. Such traitors would be much better suited for the task of getting past our defenses than these two."

"With all due respect, Colonel, why take the chance?" asked the lieutenant. "Whatever they are, or are not, they will pose no threat to us dead."

"That is inescapable logic, Lieutenant. Except for one thing. Men of such rank might be able to tell us a great deal about the enemy's disposition."

A dragoon arrived on a lathered horse, which he checked sharply, leaping from the saddle as dust drifted among the men who stood before the regimental commander's tent. The dragoon crisply saluted.

"Colonel, our scouts have spotted a small detachment of *norteamericanos* a few miles to the north."

"Who are they?"

"We do not know for certain, Colonel."

"I know," said Barlow.

All eyes turned to him.

"They're Rangers," he said flatly. "About fifteen, sixteen of them, by my count. They've been chasing the captain and myself since we left Fort Brown."

"Texas Rangers," murmured the colonel. "Yes. Only Texas Rangers would be foolhardy enough to ride, in such small numbers, so deeply into Mexico."

"They're manhunters," said Barlow, "and they don't quit until they get their man. I suppose that's why they were given the task of bringing us back. Dead or alive."

The colonel nodded—and made up his mind. He turned briskly to the young lieutenant. "Have Captain Montero come and see me at once. I want two companies on their way within a quarter of an hour. By nightfall I want all the Rangers killed—or captured."

The lieutenant saluted. *"Sí, mi coronel."* He took off running into the encampment. The regimental commander turned to Rodriguez.

"Captain, you will escort these two over to Malveux. The Frenchman has a talent for interrogation. He is to learn all that he can from these two men."

"Yes, Colonel!"

The commander nodded and, with one last, dismissive glance at Barlow, returned to the shade of the awning.

"Who is Malveux?" Barlow asked the dragoon captain.

"The last man you would ever want to meet," said Rodriguez. "It would be more merciful to execute you than to turn you over to Malveux."

Chapter 24

"Being stubborn will avail you nothing, Colonel Barlow."

Barlow heard the voice as though it came from deep within a well, distorted by the pounding of his own pulse. He opened his eyes, tried to focus, had to blink away the blood that was obscuring his view. He could dimly make out the man named Malveux. He was a short, stout, balding man with a pleasant expression on a moon-shaped face. But if one looked closely enough, there was something distinctly unpleasant lurking in the Frenchman's eyes. He enjoyed watching the men he called his "two Indians" inflict pain. At the moment they stood on either side of the chair to which Barlow had been tied. It was a very stout wooden chair, secured to the floor with iron braces, located in the center of a windowless stone room. Torches burned in wall sconces, providing a flickering light. Barlow knew where he was—in a room below the El Soldado fortress. This room, and several others, had been carved out of the guts of the hill upon which the fortress stood—originally, assumed Barlow, for the safe storage of munitions, which, down here, would be impervious to enemy cannon fire. But this room had become Malveux's torture chamber.

The torture had been dispensed for the past hour by the big, hard fists of the two Indians—solidly built and completely impassive men in the plain attire of peasants. But they weren't peasants. They were very skilled at what they did: inflicting severe pain without causing permanent damage. Barlow was pretty certain that no bones had been broken, no organs ruptured. But there were great raw, open wounds on his face where the flesh had been gouged away. His midsection ached from constant pummeling, so that even drawing a breath was almost more than he could bear. The clothes of the two Indians were splattered with his blood. There was more blood staining Barlow's trousers, for he'd been spitting it up for some time now. It had reached the point where the pain was the only reality in Barlow's life. Several times he had passed out, and each time they had roused him with a bucket of cold, brackish water hurled into his face. They had just done that again—and he'd slowly come to, with Malveux's voice echoing in his ears.

"You can put an end to this right now, Colonel," said Malveux. "Simply tell us what we want to know. How many men in General Taylor's command? When does the general intend to march on Monterrey? Two simple questions requiring two simple answers. And then you will die swiftly, and with a minimum of pain. This I will guarantee."

"Who are you?" asked Barlow, and he was startled by his voice—a croaking travesty. He desperately wanted water. He licked drops of it from his cracked and swollen and bleeding lips. "You're not Mexican."

Malveux smiled. He glanced at one of his Indians, who produced a stool, placing it in front of Barlow's chair. Malveux settled himself upon it, and smiled beneficently.

"No, I am a French officer. I have been sent here

to provide advice and assistance in any way I deem fit to the Mexican army. I have a great deal of expertise that my king thought might be of some use to our Mexican friends. And besides, we would prefer to see your country's war of aggression fail."

"Well, I can't help you. I don't know how many men Taylor has or what his plans are. He never saw fit to make me privy to his plans. And even if I did know, I wouldn't tell you."

"More's the pity." Malveux looked again at his two Indians—and gave a slight nod. Then he sat there and watched, with a sort of clinical detachment, as the men began to strike Barlow again and again, methodically trying to break him down. Barlow had thought that after an hour of excruciating pain he would be better able to handle it. Instead, it was just getting worse. The blows that rained down on his wounds made his nerve endings scream in agony. A voice inside his head—the voice of self-preservation—screamed at him to tell them something, anything, to make the pain stop. But there was another part of him, stronger still than the urge to save himself, that compelled him to keep his mouth shut. It was pride. And it was all he had left to cling to.

The two Indians stepped forward and Barlow closed his eyes, tried to brace himself for what he knew was coming. It didn't do any good. When those fists came slamming into him, his entire world exploded into fresh pain. He had no idea how long the beating went on—time meant nothing to him now. He passed out. They brought him to with another dose of foul-smelling water, and then the fists came at him again, pummeling him without mercy.

"Enough," said Malveux.

The beating ceased. Barlow had sagged forward in the chair, drooling blood. When he opened his eyes, the floor was spinning, tilted crazily to one side, so he closed them again.

"Monsieur," said Malveux, his tone one of gentle admonition. "You are being foolish. Your comrade has already told us everything we wanted to know. All you must do is corroborate what he has said. There is no shame in this. After all, you are not the one who betrayed his country."

By sheer willpower Barlow raised his head and looked at Malveux. "Go to Hell," he said, the words muffled as his mouth filled up with blood again.

Malveux sighed and shook his head. "This one will not talk," he told the two Indians. "So there is no point in continuing. Cut his throat, and then dispose of the body."

As Malveux turned away, Barlow spat out the blood and leaned back in the chair, heaving a sigh of relief. At least the pain would be over soon. Where Armstrong was concerned he felt only regret—and guilt. If what Malveux had said was true—if Armstrong had, indeed, broken under torture—Barlow did not hold him at fault. If anyone was to blame it would be himself, for bringing the young captain on this misbegotten mission in the first place. He could only hope that Churacho and Therese and the mustangers were able to get away from Monterrey with their lives.

Malveux reached the door—a portal of heavy timbers braced with iron straps—just as it swung open and a Mexican officer Barlow was pretty sure he hadn't seen before entered. The officer looked at Barlow, tried to conceal his revulsion for what had been done to the prisoner, and spoke to Malveux in French. Malveux replied in what Barlow thought was an angry tone. The officer answered curtly, with authority. Malveux looked none too pleased as he turned back toward Barlow—just as one of the Indians stepped closer, brandishing a knife.

"Stop," said Malveux.

The Indian froze, the blade scant inches from Barlow's throat.

"Put it away," said Malveux brusquely. "Apparently, the general thinks this one might be of more value to him alive than dead."

Clearly disappointed that he would not have the pleasure of cutting Barlow's throat, the Indian put the knife away.

Barlow wasn't entirely pleased by this turn of events. Now the pain would continue. Perhaps there would be more torture. He didn't consider this a reprieve, but rather a mere postponement.

The officer spoke again to Malveux, then gave Barlow a final glance before departing.

"Clean him up," Malveux told the Indians. "The general wishes to see him. He is not to bleed all over the general's floor."

When Barlow was brought before General Ampudia, he could barely walk. The Indians had stripped him of his blood-soaked clothing and dressed him in the plain garb of a *campesino*. There were no shoes on his feet. They had washed the blood off his face, and even used a needle and catgut to sew up two large gashes. One of his eyes had swollen shut. Every joint in his body was stiff, every muscle complained.

The general's quarters were located within the city of Monterrey, in a villa that had obviously once been the property of a very well-to-do individual, located on the slope of a hill and overlooking the heart of the city. The room to which the guards delivered Barlow was a spacious chamber, with tall windows along one wall, open to allow a breeze that ruffled damask curtains. The floor was oak, polished to a high sheen. A chandelier hung from the coffered ceiling, and there were ornately framed paintings on the walls. General Ampudia sat behind an elegantly carved mahogany desk. He apparently had no concept of its intrinsic value—he had propped his booted feet up on one corner, and his silver spurs had scarred the wood. He was smoking a cigar and leafing through some papers when Barlow was escorted in. When he looked up, Barlow saw a man with a lot of Indian blood in him—a swarthy man with coarse features, small black eyes set close together, a thick, barrel-chested body. Barlow decided that this was a man with little formal education, the son of peasants, but a man with great cunning. A survivor. A fighter.

Ampudia was not alone. Two cuirassiers, resplendent in their brass cuirasses adorned with silver national coats of arms. Their helmets were also brass with silver ornamentation. They wore sky-blue jackets with crimson collars and cuffs beneath the brass breastplates, and sky-blue trousers with broad crimson stripes, tucked into tall, black riding boots. Each was armed with a saber and an *escopeta*. In addition, another man, clad in the yellow and blue tunic of an infantryman, was sitting in a chair beside the desk. Ampudia spoke to this man in Spanish. The man turned to Barlow.

"The general wishes for you to sit down," he said, in English.

Barlow looked at a single wooden chair facing the desk. It was not unlike the one in the underground chamber at El Soldado, and he felt a sudden powerful aversion to it. The guards, noting his hesitation, shoved him forward, and pushed him down into the chair.

Ampudia again spoke to the infantry officer, who translated for him.

"The general wishes to inform you that he admires your courage. It is a shame that you fight for the enemy."

"I'm not fighting in this war," said Barlow, having to work at enunciating his words so that they could be understood.

The translator relayed his reply to Ampudia, who smiled and nodded and spoke.

"The general says if you were really a deserter, you would have spared yourself so much pain, and told us what we wanted to know about the Yankee army."

"I'm not going to betray my country. I just choose not to fight an unjust war."

"The general wishes to know, then, why you came to Monterrey, if all you want to do is stay out of the war."

"I didn't *come* here," said Barlow. "I was *brought* here, by those damned mustangers."

"The general says you should fight with us. We are only defending our country against the Yankee invaders. Surely you find that to be a just cause?"

"Maybe," allowed Barlow. "But I won't take up arms against the army I once served."

"Even though the men they sent after you would have killed you, if they'd had the chance?"

"The Rangers."

"Yes. Most of them are dead now. Three were captured, and brought here."

Barlow was silent for a moment. He wondered if Zeke Fuller was one of the survivors. At least he had one thing to thank the Mexican army for: it had effectively dispensed with the threat posed to him by the vengeful Fuller clan. Not that it mattered now; Barlow didn't have much hope of getting out of Monterrey alive. But what if the survivors, whoever they might be, were subjected to torture at the hands of the Frenchman, Malveux? Would they contradict Barlow's assertion that he was a deserter? And if they did, would they be believed? It would have made matters much simpler had all of the Fuller clan be killed. Barlow had been certain they would put up a fight when the dragoons showed up. In fact, he'd been counting on it.

"I don't care about them," said Barlow. "But what about Captain Armstrong? What have you done with him?"

"He is still alive," said the young officer, translating Ampudia's response. He paused to listen as the general continued to talk. "The general has decided that both of you might be worth more to him alive than dead. Several of our officers were taken prisoner at the Resaca and at Palo Alto. It is our intention to arrange an exchange. The general is confident that your army will want the two of you returned alive, so that an example might be made of you."

Ampudia continued to speak, and then burst into laughter.

The officer said, "The general asks why he should go to the trouble of executing you when your own army will want to do the thing for him?"

Barlow felt like laughing, too. Of course, it wouldn't do to reveal how delighted he was with this unexpected turn of events. He was, after all, supposed to be a deserter, who would not be happy to hear that he was going to be returned to the army that he had deserted. *I'll be damned,* he mused. *It looks like I might just survive this business after all.*

Ampudia spoke again.

"The general says that if you change your mind about cooperating with us, and telling us what we want to know about Taylor's army, he might reconsider the exchange."

Barlow shook his head. "No, he wouldn't. He'd let me spill my guts—and then he'd make the exchange anyway."

The young officer looked surprised, and hesitated. "You would do well not to impugn the honor and integrity of the general, *señor.*"

"Just do your job," said Barlow curtly.

The officer shrugged, and translated his last remark for Ampudia's sake. The general stared at Barlow a moment—and then burst into laughter once more. He laughed so hard that he had some trouble catching his breath, and a moment passed before he was able to speak again.

The officer, translating, said, "The general says you are very clever—and you are right. He would not consider a promise made to a *gringo* something that should not be broken."

Ampudia spoke brusquely to the guards who had delivered Barlow, and made a dismissive gesture. Barlow was lifted out of the chair and placed on his feet. He jerked his arms free.

"I can walk on my own," he growled.

Ampudia chuckled. "*Mucho hombre,* eh?" he asked the young officer.

Barlow knew that it was a sarcastic comment—not a compliment. He turned and, with as much dignity as he could muster, left the room with his guards in tow.

Chapter 25

Barlow was taken back to El Soldado, and tossed into an underground chamber not far removed from the one in which he had suffered so much pain. This one, while considerably smaller than the other, bore certain familiar characteristics—the walls were stone, there was no window, and the door was made of heavy timbers secured by iron straps. As he was shoved roughly into the cell, he noticed that a man who looked vaguely like Armstrong was huddled in a corner. He caught barely a glimpse before the door was slammed shut—then all the light in the room, save for a sliver leaking under the door, was gone. On hands and knees, Barlow crawled across the chamber and reached out to touch Armstrong's leg. Armstrong moaned, jerked the leg away reflexively.

"How are you holding up, Captain?" asked Barlow.

"What did you tell them?" mumbled Armstrong.

"Nothing."

"They told me . . . that you did. I didn't believe them. . . ."

"They told me the same thing about you."

Armstrong was silent for so long that Barlow began to wonder if he had slipped out of consciousness. Finally, though, the captain spoke. "Did you . . . believe them?"

"No. I knew you wouldn't talk. That's one of the reasons I recruited you. For which, by the way, I am truly sorry."

"It was my decision. So you . . . thought something like this might happen."

"I knew it was a possibility. I guess I should have told you."

"Wouldn't have made any difference." Armstrong's speech was slurred in places, so much so that Barlow could scarcely distinguish the words, and he worried that perhaps the captain had sustained serious head injuries.

"You're a brave man, Captain," said Barlow. "I'm proud to serve with you."

"Thank you," murmured Armstrong. "Now how do we get out of here?"

Barlow eased his aching body against the wall beside Armstrong. Leaning his head back against the rough stone, he closed his eyes.

"Well, therein lies the irony, Captain. It looks as though the Mexicans have decided to exchange us for some of their officers that Taylor is holding prisoner."

"Really?" There was a hint of hope in that single word—hope where, only seconds earlier, there had been none.

"Yes. And I have more good news."

"I'm not sure I can handle any more good news, Colonel."

Barlow laughed, but cut it short, because laughing hurt entirely too much. "The Mexican dragoons took care of the Fuller clan. Or at least most of them. They brought back a few prisoners. Killed the rest."

"The ones left alive," whispered Armstrong. "Do they know the truth about us?"

Barlow shrugged, then realized the gesture could not be seen in the pitch black hole in which they were imprisoned. "Who knows? They may turn out to be as tough as we are—and won't talk."

"I'm afraid I don't feel very tough, Colonel."

"If somebody hit me with a feather I'd probably pass out from the pain."

"Hopefully there won't be any more hitting," Armstrong wheezed. "But who the Hell is that Malveux character? Where did he come from? I mean, I know he's a damned Frenchman. But what is he doing here?"

"I don't know. But I would like to get my hands on him."

"Thee and me, sir," said Armstrong. He sounded better—stronger—than he had just moments before. Good news, thought Barlow, was sometimes the best medicine.

"Try to get some sleep," suggested Barlow.

"Guess I will. Not much else to do around here."

Barlow said nothing more, heard Armstrong's back sliding along the wall as he lay down on the cold dirt floor. He listened carefully to the captain's breathing, and after awhile was pretty certain that Armstrong had, indeed, gone to sleep. Though he realized it would be wise to take his own advice, Barlow stayed awake, thinking his way through everything that had happened since their capture by the dragoons. He was most concerned about Churacho and Therese. He couldn't bear to think of either one of them suffering as he and the captain had suffered. He hadn't dared ask Ampudia what had become of them—any demonstration of concern on his part would have spelled their doom. In all likelihood, he would have to wait until he had been exchanged, and was back with Taylor's army, before he could learn of their fate. He prayed they would be there, safe and sound, when he got back.

One worry kept nagging him. What if Taylor refused an exchange? There was no valid reason for him to do so—the exchange of officers during war was accepted practice. Except that Barlow did not consider Zachary Taylor a professional soldier—and he hated Mexicans, that was clear. But if the Mexicans gave the identities of their prisoners, then Taylor would surely jump at the chance. He needed any intelligence Barlow and Armstrong might have obtained.

They spent ten days in the black, windowless cell. Barlow kept rough track of the time by the number of meals he and Armstrong were given. They were fed twice a day—once in the morning and once in the evening. Their meals were always the same—a thin, pasty gruel and a piece of stale black bread. They were never allowed out of the cell. Barlow was sure that he would have gone insane had he been alone. But he and Armstrong whiled away the time talking. They talked about anything and everything. They told each other their life stories, down to the smallest detail. By the end of it, Barlow felt as though Armstrong was like a brother to him.

On the tenth day, they had two visitors.

The first was Churacho. The guards locked him inside the cell. He had a small candle with him, which he placed on the floor in front of Barlow and Armstrong before sitting cross-legged, facing them. He grimly studied their damaged faces.

"How bad was it?" he asked.

"Bad enough," was Barlow's rueful supply. "How goes it with you?"

Churacho shrugged. "No trouble. They believed my story. They bought the horses. Paid me well for them.

And now, as part of the bargain, we are breaking the *mesteñas.*"

"You should have gotten out of here as soon as they paid you," said Barlow.

"There was no point in even trying to get Therese to leave this place," sighed Churacho. "Not so long as the two of you were imprisoned here."

"How is she?" asked Armstrong anxiously.

"She is worried about you and the colonel. Otherwise she is well. She has been nagging me to help you escape from this place." Churacho took a look at the stone walls that surrounded them. "I told her it was impossible, but she did not want to hear that. Like all women, she refuses to hear bad news."

"There was talk of an exchange," said Barlow.

Churacho nodded. "Yes, I have heard that talk. In a day or two you will be taken to the village of Salinas. You remember it?"

"Yes. We passed through there on the way down here."

"It is halfway between Monterrey and Matamoros, more or less. That is where the exchange is to take place. It would seem your General Taylor was very eager to secure your release."

"I admit, I had some doubts as to whether he would," said Barlow.

Churacho leaned forward and pitched his voice very low, in case the guards were standing right outside the door. "Have you learned all that you came here to learn?"

"I have a pretty good idea of the fortifications. But I still need an accurate number of troops that Ampudia has under his command. The identity of the units themselves would be nice. How many cannon does he have in place? That sort of thing."

Churacho allowed himself a slight smile. "We already know many of these things. Every night, after our work is done, my *muchachos* and I go into the city and visit the *cantinas* where the soldiers drink. We can come and go as we please, and no one bothers us. We have seen much, and heard much. What we do not yet know, we will find out before it is time for us to leave."

"And when will that be?" asked Barlow.

"As soon as Therese knows you are safely away from here," replied Churacho, with a soft chuckle.

"I have a question," said Armstrong. "How come they let you in here?"

"You would be surprised what these guards would do for a jug of *aguardiente*," said Churacho. "But now I must go." He pushed the candle a little closer to them. "Keep this. The guards will say nothing about it." He rose and went to the door, knocking on it. A guard opened it immediately. Churacho turned, gave them a reassuring nod, and walked out. The guard looked at the prisoners sitting against the back wall of the stone cell, glanced at the burning candle—and shut the door.

"I wonder why," murmured Armstrong.

"Why what?"

"Why is he helping us? Against the country of his birth?"

"He has no allegiance to flag or nation," replied Barlow. "To him, such things are illusions. But friendship—for a man like Churacho, friendship is everything."

Armstrong was silent for a moment, mulling it over. Then he said, "Maybe he's right. Maybe that's all that really does matter, at the end of the day. That, and love." He spared Barlow a sidelong glance. "I know this sounds foolish, but I'm . . . I'm in love with her, you know. At least, I think I am. It's foolish, because she hardly knows I exist. She only has eyes for you. I tell myself I should be jealous of you. For some reason, though, I can't be. Maybe a little envious." He laughed. "As though any of that matters. The most foolish part of it all is that I'm still thinking about the future. About how it could be. When chances are I won't even see next week."

"You'll survive—and you'll go home. We both will. And as for Therese—well, don't throw your cards away just yet."

Their second visitor came an hour or so later. It was the officer in charge of the guard detail at El Soldado. He carried Barlow's and Armstrong's uniforms, and gruffly told them to change their clothing. He saw the candle, but made no comment. An old man in *campesino* garb came in, carrying a bowl of water and shaving accoutrements. He knelt before the prisoners and whipped up some lather in a cup. His hands were shaking. As he prepared to apply the foam to Barlow's face with a brush, Barlow caught his arm at the wrist, and shook his head. The officer, standing by the door watching, spoke brusquely.

"He says we are to be shaved," translated Armstrong. "General Ampudia doesn't want General Taylor to think he did not treat his prisoners fairly."

Barlow had to laugh. "Right. We were beaten half to death, and it will be a while before the wounds fully heal. I don't mind a shave, but I'll do it myself."

Armstrong spoke to the officer in Spanish. The officer in turn spoke to the guards, and left the cell. The old man followed him, leaving the shaving gear. One of the two guards stepped inside and stood beside the door, rifle at the ready, watching Barlow as the latter picked up the brush and dabbed the lathered soap on his face. When he put the brush down and picked up the straight razor, the guard stiffened, raising the rifle

slightly. Barlow scraped the beard from his face,
flinching now and then as the razor aggravated partially healed wounds. When he was done, he rinsed
his face with water from the bowl, and washed off the
razor before handing it to Armstrong.

"How do I look?" he asked.

"To be honest, sir, you looked better with the
beard."

Barlow laughed. Armstrong joined him. For some
reason they found it difficult to stop laughing. The
guard standing inside the cell peered at them, puzzled
and wary, then glanced at his *compadre,* who
shrugged, thoroughly mystified, as the laughter of the
gringos rang through the subterranean labyrinth of
El Soldado.

Chapter 26

They arrived in Salinas two days later, escorted by the
dragoon captain, Rodriguez, who had commanded the
detachment responsible for their capture nearly a fortnight earlier. He had twenty men under his command
this time. Barlow noticed that the American detail,
which had already arrived in the village, also numbered twenty. The Americans had three captured
Mexican officers with them, and had gathered in the
village square. Rodriguez stopped his column a few
hundred yards away and rode forward with only a
corporal who did double duty as bugler and flag-
bearer. The captain in charge of the American detail
mounted his horse and rode out alone to meet Rodriguez. They met, talked briefly, then returned to their
respective commands.

Barlow was indifferent to these goings-on. He had
little doubt that the exchange would take place as
planned. And if something happened to spoil the
arrangement . . . well, he and Armstrong had already
agreed that they weren't going to be taken back to El
Soldado. Not alive, anyway. Instead, Barlow surveyed
the village, noting that the people who, two weeks
earlier, had stood in their doorways and watched his
passage through their community, were nowhere to be

seen. He smiled grimly. All these people had to go on was past experience, and this was no doubt the first time that two groups of armed men had ever met in Salinas without the result of bloodshed. He imagined that this particular meeting would be a topic of discussion for a long time to come.

Rodriguez and the American officer exchanged salutes, and then the dragoon captain returned to his command.

"You will dismount, and walk forward only when the Mexican officers have begun walking this way," he told Barlow and Armstrong.

They did as they were told. As they passed the three Mexican officers walking the other way, Armstrong glanced at them, then at Barlow.

"They don't appear to have gotten the same sort of attention we received," he remarked sardonically.

When they reached him, the American captain saluted them, then shook their hands vigorously.

"Glad to have you back, gentlemen. I see those sons of bitches worked you over."

"I don't know about Mr. Armstrong," said Barlow, "but I'm not feeling much pain right at the moment."

"That's good," said the captain, "because General Taylor instructed me personally to bring you to him with the utmost haste. I take it the both of you are up to a long ride?"

"Don't worry about us," said Armstrong. "We've gotten this far, the rest will be easy."

"Then take your pick." The captain motioned to the three horses recently abandoned by the Mexican officers. Climbing into one of the saddles, Barlow chanced to look across the square at the Mexican dragoons. Rodriguez was watching them, and when Barlow's eyes met his, he nodded. It was, thought Barlow, an acknowledgement of professionalism between two hostiles—and perhaps an acknowledgement, as well, of the possibility that they would meet again.

The dragoons departed Salinas. A few moments later, Barlow and Armstrong were on their way north in the company of the American mounted rifles.

They arrived in Matamoros late the next day and were taken almost immediately to see General Taylor. As before, Old Rough 'n' Ready was in his headquarters in the *cabildo* on the east side of the town's main square.

"Gentlemen," said Taylor, coming forward to greet them with a warm enthusiasm that had been notably lacking, mused Barlow, during his previous visit. "I see they gave you a bad time. Believe me, the sacrifices that both of you made for your country will not go unnoticed. I trust you were successful in getting the intelligence we require." He headed back to his desk, picked up a letter and waved it at them. "The president is, shall we say, *anxious* that we move on Monterrey as soon as possible. Campaigns are under way in other theaters of the war. Since you've been gone, I have received several important dispatches. Colonel Stephen Kearny, who is an extremely able officer, has marched from Fort Leavenworth with fifteen hundred men, His orders are to invade the province of New Mexico, with his chief goal being the city of Santa Fe. And by this letter I am informed that the president plans a second prong to our advance into Mexico proper. That army will be transferred by sea to some point, probably Veracruz, on the eastern coast, and from there will march on the capital, Mexico City. It has been decided that to reach Mexico City from here might prove impossible, due to the immense desert that lies between. This, of course, hinges on the outcome of our struggle at Monterrey.

If the Mexican government capitulates following our victory there, then all is well and good. But, frankly, the president and his advisors think that is unlikely. So do I. Tell me, then, what you saw in Monterrey."

Taylor called in an aide to put down on paper everything that was said from that point on, and Barlow proceeded to go into great detail regarding the defenses thrown up around Monterrey. General Taylor settled wearily into a chair behind his desk, folded his hands over his belly, and listened. Barlow thought that the general's expression grew ever more grave as he continued with his remarks about the Mexican fortifications—El Soldado, the Citadel, Independence Hill, Bishop's Palace, Devil's Fort. Taylor produced a map of Monterrey that was several years old—Barlow was asked to mark on it the locations of the artillery batteries, the redoubts, the barricades and anything else he could remember. He remembered quite a lot, and the process took more than two hours. Taylor then asked Armstrong if he had anything to add. The captain shook his head.

"Not really, sir. Colonel Barlow has been exceedingly thorough in his report. I will only say that the Mexican troops that I saw were regular army. Veterans, well-armed, well-provisioned, and, most importantly, committed to defending Monterrey."

"No conscripts? No irregulars? Surely there must be. I am told that Ampudia has between eight and ten thousand men under his command. They could not all be regular troops. Santa Anna is holding the majority of his regiments in and around Mexico City, anticipating, I think, just the sort of undertaking the president has decided to pursue—an invasion from the direction of the Gulf Coast."

"I don't know how many men Ampudia has in his command, General," admitted Barlow. "We were incarcerated before we had a chance to look into that. However, the mustanger, Churacho, was able to acquire that information in my stead. He will be better able to tell you what you want to know in that regard."

"Churacho!" Taylor's craggy face darkened. "I had forgotten all about that scoundrel." He fixed his piercing gaze on Armstrong. "As I recall, you gave me your word that murderous villain would not survive the mission."

"As it turned out," said Armstrong casually, "he proved to be of tremendous service to our cause. Worth a great deal more to us alive than dead, I should say."

"And where is he, then?"

Armstrong glanced at Barlow, brows raised.

"We're not exactly sure," confessed Barlow. "But I expect him to arrive any day. I would suggest that you alert all your commanders to make sure their pickets do not fire upon the *mesteñeros* when they come in."

"And I am supposed to rely on the information given me by a man like Churacho?" asked Taylor. The prospect seemed to offend him.

"I'll vouch for it," said Barlow.

"As will I," Armstrong chimed in.

Taylor mulled it over, clearly displeased. But Barlow wasn't worried. He knew that, in spite of the man's prejudices, the general had no choice but to depend on Churacho.

"I will inform my regimental commanders," said Taylor, and the words were bitter in his mouth. "They will, in turn, inform their pickets to keep an eye out for these mustangers. Captain Armstrong, you will return to your regiment. Colonel Barlow, as you are not attached to a regiment, I would have you on my staff, if you have no objections."

"None, sir," said Barlow. "Thank you."

"See the officer of the day. He will find you quarters nearby."

A moment later, Barlow and Armstrong were outside in the slanting sunlight of the late afternoon. The square, as had been the case before, was filled with soldiers and civilians attached to the army. Barlow looked around and, oddly, felt at loose ends. He'd done the job he had come down here to do. Now he had another mission in mind—a very personal one. He intended to make sure that the fortress of El Soldado ceased to exist, and that the Frenchman named Malveux never again had an opportunity to do to a prisoner what he had done to Barlow. Hatred for his torturer and the site of his recent ordeal ran deep— too deep to be denied. To achieve this goal he had to accompany the army to Monterrey and fight the Mexicans. That suited him just fine. But it would take days, perhaps weeks, before Taylor's men were ready to march. What was he to do until then?

"Well, I suppose I'd better get back to my messmates," said Armstrong, and there was reluctance in his tone. He saluted Barlow. "It was an honor to serve with you, Colonel."

"Stop that." Barlow extended a hand. Armstrong shook it. "I'll be seeing you around."

Armstrong nodded, smiled, and walked away.

Barlow turned to locate the officer of the day, and passed Taylor's message on. He was escorted to the end of the *cabildo* and through a side door into a narrow hallway with doors on either side. The first door on the right led into a small room that contained three narrow beds, and room for little else. Barlow learned that he would be rooming with two more of Taylor's staff officers, a Captain Stevens and a Captain Tibbett.

"Do you have any gear, Colonel?" asked the officer of the day. "Any personal effects?"

"No." All that he'd had was now in the possession of the Mexicans, including the sword he'd carried since his first campaign, with Andrew Jackson against the Red Stick Creeks. He supposed he would never see it again.

"I'll see what I can round up for you, sir."

"Right now I need a fresh horse, Lieutenant, and a pistol."

"Yes, sir. I'll bring them around at once."

Barlow thanked him. When the officer of the day was gone, Barlow looked longingly at the beds. He was bone-tired, and would have liked nothing better than to get a few hours sleep. A few days would be even better. But he couldn't rest until he was sure Churacho and Therese and the other mustangers were safe.

Ten minutes later, the officer of the day returned to inform him that there was a horse waiting outside. He handed Barlow a No. 2 Colt Paterson belt pistol. The .31-caliber percussion pistol had a five-shot cylinder, and had been altered to include a loading lever. Barlow made sure it was fully loaded.

"Very nice," he said, nodding approval. "Where did you find it?"

"It's mine, sir. You can have the loan of it. I have another."

"Thanks, Lieutenant."

"Begging your pardon, sir, but are you going somewhere?"

Barlow smiled. "Yes, I am. And now I have one more favor to ask of you. If anyone asks you where I am, tell them you don't know."

"Is that an order, sir?"

"Would it make it easier for you if it were?"

"Yes, sir. Just in case somebody asks. Then I'll just be following orders when I lie to them."

"Very well, then. Consider it an order, Lieutenant."

The officer of the day saluted. "Yes, sir. Thank you, sir. Will that be all, sir?"

"Yes."

The lieutenant pivoted briskly on his heel and walked out. Barlow shoved the pistol under his belt, waited a few minutes, then walked out to find a blaze-faced sorrel waiting for him at the side of the *cabildo*. He climbed into the saddle and, avoiding the main square, rode out of Matamoros.

Chapter 27

Barlow arrived in the town of Salinas—for the third time in little more than a fortnight—the following day. He hadn't seen a soul since leaving Matamoros, and found that somewhat odd, considering that this country lay between two opposing armies, and he knew there were scouting patrols from both sides all around him. He didn't expect anyone to come after him—it was unlikely that anyone would even notice he was gone, unless General Taylor requested to see him specifically on some matter. As for a Mexican patrol, he was prepared to hide if he spotted one, and to run if he was spotted *by* one; if his luck went bad and he was captured again, at least he had carried the information on the Monterrey defenses to Taylor. He had done his job, he had served God and country and all of that. Now he was on a personal mission. And he just hoped he wouldn't have to go all the way to Monterrey to find Churacho and Therese, but if that was what it took, he was prepared to do it.

His arrival in Salinas drew the expected response—silent, impassive observation by the denizens of that remote village on the Rio Verde. Even though he was no longer a total stranger, they treated him like one. Barlow thought the fact that he had passed through twice before without bringing harm to anyone who lived here—and without taking anything save for a little water for himself and for his horse—would have warranted at least a slightly warmer reception. But they avoided him as he went to the community well in the little square at the center of the town, and brought up some water in the bucket for the sorrel. Then he splashed some water on his sunburned face and sat on the edge of the well and looked around him. He figured there was a better-than-fair chance that Churacho would pass through here on his way north—this was the location, after all, of one of the few safe crossings of the Rio Verde. But he had to acknowledge to himself that he was grasping at straws. There really was no way of knowing what route Churacho might take to return to Matamoros, if indeed he were free to return at all. Barlow needed to ask someone here if they had seen the mustangers, even though his Spanish was very poor, and he doubted that anyone in Salinas spoke English.

Three women, two of them young and nubile, the other old and stout, approached the well, chattering away, carrying empty *ollas*, which they intended to fill with water. When they saw Barlow they stopped and stared, as though they had seen a ghost—or, thought Barlow ruefully, the devil himself. They debated among themselves for a moment, and then two of them—the old woman and one of the young ones—turned away. The third stood where she was, watching Barlow with hooded eyes. He realized his mistake—by his very presence he was preventing the people from partaking of the well's contents. He touched the brim of his hat and led his horse away, heading for a crumbling adobe wall where a dusty, wind-twisted oak tree stood. He sat on the wall in the shade of the tree, took off his hat, and wiped sweat from his brow.

Now that he was gone from the well, the young woman approached it, still watching him warily. She drew water, filled the *olla,* and went on her way. She was not, decided Barlow, much more than a child, but he imagined that she was already married, and possibly had a child or two herself. Life for the *campesinos* of Mexico was short, hard and often brutal. One grew up quickly, married early, and died early, too. He didn't think President Polk's grand design for the outcome of the war included taking over the province of Coahuila and bringing it into the Union, but Barlow speculated on whether these people would fare any better under American rule. He decided that they would not. Too many Americans considered the Mexicans as somewhere down the evolutionary chain from their exalted position; perhaps not so far down as the Africans—and descendants of Africans—enslaved to work on Southern plantations, but certainly not much better. Barlow had seen this prejudice, and knew it was prevalent.

Her task completed, the young woman spared him one final glance, then hurried away. A few moments later, several men—all clad in their plain white shirts and trousers, and all wearing sandals—appeared in the square. They stopped, talked together for a moment—Barlow sensed that he was the topic of conversation—then approached him, shoulder to shoulder. Two of the men carried crude scythes, tools they used to harvest the maize grown in irrigated fields along the banks of the nearby river. The third had a knife beneath the rope he'd tied around his waist to keep his baggy britches up. Barlow felt his pulse quicken. The scythes and the knife might be the tools of farmers, but in this situation they were being carried as weapons. The people of Salinas had decided to ignore him no longer—though this wasn't exactly the kind of reception he had hoped for.

Barlow stayed where he was, making no move for the Colt Paterson tucked under his belt. He could kill all three of these men if they made a hostile move, but that was the last thing he wanted. If they wanted him to leave—and he assumed that was the purpose behind this visitation—he would go, and not make trouble.

The three men stopped ten paces away, and the one in the center spoke to Barlow in Spanish. Barlow shook his head.

"No habla español," he said.

The three men consulted one another again, speaking rapidly and with much gesticulating. Then the man on the right stepped forward.

"I speak a little English," he said haltingly. "What you do here?"

"I'm looking for a man named Churacho. The *mesteñero*. I met him here about two weeks ago. Do you remember?"

The man nodded. "We know Churacho. You are . . . friend?"

"Yes. I'm a friend of his. Have you seen him this past day or two?"

The man looked at his companions. They shook their heads, and he turned back to Barlow, and shook his. "No. We not see the *mesteñeros*. You give us *pistola,* you can wait here for him. You keep *pistola,* you must go."

"Will I get the pistol back when I leave?"

The man once more consulted with his companions. Then he nodded to Barlow. *"Sí."*

Barlow stood, slowly removed the Paterson from his belt, and approached the trio, holding the pistol by the barrel as he held it out to them. The man who had spoken took the pistol. The three men were visibly relieved. They had approached Barlow with all the caution they might exhibit to corner and kill a rattlesnake. But now they had pulled the rattler's fangs.

Barlow was about to return to his place on the wall when the man spoke again.

"You have food?"

"No," said Barlow. "I haven't eaten in . . ." He thought back, and was astonished by the realization that he had not eaten for nearly two days. "I have not eaten in a long time."

"You will have food," said the *campesino*. And with that, he and his companions turned and walked away.

A little while later, a young woman arrived with a bowl of beans and several thick tortillas in a small basket. She was scared of Barlow, but she mastered her fear and put the food on the wall beside him, then turned and walked quickly away. He was without his fangs, but he was still a rattlesnake. Barlow sighed, called after her to say thank you, and dug in. Once he started eating he couldn't stop until it was all gone. Then he went to the well and drank some water. Returning to the wall, he sat down in the shade with his back to the adobe and pulled his hat down over his eyes to block out the slanting sun of the late afternoon that slipped through the dusty branches overhead. His belly full, he went to sleep.

He was awakened by the sound of horses. Opening his eyes, he saw Churacho and Therese riding into the Salinas square.

When she saw him, Therese let out a cry of joy and leaped from the saddle to run to him. She threw her arms around him, and Barlow glanced warily at Churacho. The mustanger seemed nearly as overjoyed as his sister. At least he was willing to overlook this open display of affection on Therese's part.

"I told him you would come to find us," she said, sounding vindicated.

Churacho, still in the saddle, nodded confirmation. "*Es verdad.* That is what she said. I don't know how she knew."

"Where is the captain?" asked Therese. "Is he all right?"

"He's fine. Back at Matamoros."

"We should talk later," said Churacho grimly. "There is not much time."

"What do you mean?" asked Barlow.

"The soldiers are after us," said Therese, matter-of-factly.

"What for?"

"I took back the horses," said the mustanger.

"You *what?*" Barlow could scarcely believe his ears. "Why did you do a thing like that?"

"Do you think I would really sell horses to the army of Santa Anna?" Churacho shook his head. "No. So we took back the *mesteñaros.* At least they are easier to handle now. Most of the mares are greenbroke. Not the stallion, though. He will take more time. They will be here soon—Therese and I have come to make sure there were no soldiers in the village or at the crossing."

"There aren't any. How far back are the ones who are chasing you?"

"Not far enough. They are lancers."

"With orders to kill all of you, no doubt," said Barlow, "and to bring the horses back."

"*Sí.* But you and me, we will slow them down, just as you did to the Fullers. What do you say?"

Barlow looked at Therese. He had no doubts, either, as to what the lancers would do to her—before they killed her. That meant there was no choice but to participate in Churacho's plan, even though he couldn't be sure that vengeance wasn't motivating the mustanger.

"I say let's get to it," he replied, disentangling himself from Therese's embrace and turning to his horse.

They left Salinas and headed for the river crossing. There they waited for the rest of Churacho's crew, with the horses, who arrived a few moments later. They crossed the Rio Verde and, as per Churacho's orders, the other mustangers, save one—the man named Ochoa—continued to run the horses northward. Churacho appropriated Ochoa's rifle and cartridge pouch and tossed them to Barlow. Then he told Ochoa to take Therese and rejoin the others.

"The colonel and I will slow the lancers down and catch up with you later," he said.

"I will stay with the two of you," said Therese. "I can shoot as well as you can, my brother. You know this."

"I know you will do what I say," snapped Churacho. "Your stubbornness is tiresome, Therese. Go with Ochoa."

Therese hesitated, looking at Barlow.

"Don't worry," said Churacho dryly. "I'll try not to let anything happen to him."

"Get going, Therese," said Barlow, casting an anxious look back across the river, expecting at any instant to see the lancers appear on the opposite bank.

She rode away, Ochoa in tow. Dubious, Barlow studied the terrain. On either side of the crossing the ground rose to high, cutbanks that stood fifteen to twenty feet above the level of the river. There wasn't much cover along the rims of these, but they would prevent the lancers from reaching this side of the river except at the crossing. The question was whether he and Churacho could discourage them sufficiently to prevent them from getting across. Because if they *did* cross, it would be all over; there would be no chance of escape. It was an-all-or-nothing proposition.

"I'll take this side," said Churacho, and headed for the cutbank to the west of the crossing. He was, thought Barlow, just a little too eager to start killing Mexican soldiers.

"Fine," said Barlow. "Just one thing."

Churacho stopped and turned and looked at him.

"If they get halfway across the river, we go," said Barlow. "If we wait any longer than that, it may be too late. I want your word on it, *amigo*. The lancers reach the halfway mark, and you see me riding out, you leave, too."

Churacho nodded. "You have my word. But they will not reach the halfway mark."

Barlow left his horse tied to a fallen tree about fifteen yards from the rim of the cutbank, to the east of the crossing. He settled down a few feet from the edge of the embankment and checked Ochoa's rifle. It was an old .51-caliber percussion rifle with a browned, half-octagonal barrel of thirty-two inches. Barlow couldn't tell the maker—the plate had been removed or had fallen off—but he thought it was of American manufacture. It boasted a six-shot cylinder, so all Barlow had to do—at least for the first six shots—was to replace a spent cap with a new one. Ochoa's shot pouch had plenty of caps and about a dozen ready-made cartridges. What worried Barlow was that the rifle did not appear to have received the best of care over the years.

He looked to his right, and saw that Churacho was belly-down on the other cutbank, about ninety yards away. Barlow realized that it might just be his imagination, but he sensed that the mustanger couldn't wait

for the lancers to show themselves. He wasn't angry
with Churacho—though he knew he ought to be—for
stealing the horses back, and in so doing orchestrating
this confrontation with the Mexican army. He'd already figured out that Churacho was a man ruled by
powerful emotions; the kind of man who would remain loyal to a friend to the very end, but who also
let his hatred run deep. He blamed Santa Anna for
the death of his family, and he would wage his private
war against the Mexican dictator until he'd drawn his
last breath. Unfortunately for the lancers who were
about to arrive at the crossing of the Rio Verde, they
were Santa Anna's proxies. Churacho would never
have the chance to wreak vengeance on Santa Anna
himself. But he could bleed Santa Anna by killing as
many of his men as possible. Barlow was just glad to
know that Churacho was his friend, not his enemy.

He saw the dust first—kicked up by the iron-shod
hooves of many horses, coming from the south. He
was relieved to see that they seemed to be skirting the
village of Salinas and making straight for the crossing.
Barlow checked the sun, and calculated that there was
at least an hour's worth of daylight left. But he knew
that, in the heat of combat, an hour could seem like
a lifetime.

The first things he saw were the tips of the lances
gleaming in the late sun—a forest of lances, moving
in nice, neat rows. A moment later the head of the
column came into view. These were irregulars. Their
garb was homespun and buckskin, sombreros and pon-
chos—quite different from the splendid uniforms worn
by the dragoons Barlow had encountered two weeks
earlier—but that didn't mean Barlow could afford to
underestimate these men. They rode like they were
born to the saddle, and maintained a very military
order as they rode, in column, four abreast, down to

the riverside. Here they stopped as the officer who rode at the head of the column, accompanied by a bugler and two noncoms, one carrying the flag of the Mexican Republic with its golden eagle on a field of white, flanked by broad bands of red and green, the other bearing the regimental guidon. The commanding officer stopped his horse at the water's edge and brandished a spyglass. Barlow stopped trying to count how many men the detachment contained, and drew a bead on the officer with the glass. There wasn't enough cover atop the embankments to conceal his and Churacho's presence, or—more importantly perhaps, their number—from the opposing lancers. So, before the officer could fairly begin his survey of the Rio Verde's northern bank, Barlow had fired.

Flicking the spent percussion cap clear of the breech and fitting a new one in its place, Barlow squinted through a drift of powder-smoke and saw, to his dismay, that the commander was still on his horse. He had lost all interest in using the spyglass, however, because the horse was trying to buck him off—kicking and snorting and wreaking havoc among the other mounts at the head of the column as its rider struggled to regain control. Not having seen where the shot went, Barlow couldn't be sure whether he was shooting too high or too low. Such was the risk in using an unfamiliar weapon, one he'd not had a chance to test-fire before getting into action. Barlow heard Churacho's rifle boom—saw a horse and rider near the front of the column go down—and fired a second time, aiming right into the melee of lancers. A lancer somersaulted off the back of his horse.

"Now that's more like it," muttered Barlow, replacing the spent cap with a fresh one.

He and Churacho spent the next ninety seconds firing as quickly as they could into the lancers. Barlow didn't bother trying to aim, he simply attempted to place his shot in the midst of the enemy, leaving the rest to chance. Almost as important as bringing down lancers was creating the impression that there were more than just two riflemen contesting the enemy's crossing. Even so—and in spite of the initial confusion their ambush caused—the lancers were veterans. They had been under fire before. And, being lancers, they knew their job was to charge forward into their adversaries, regardless of the fire directed at them. They expected to suffer high losses in exchange for the chance to close with the enemy and do what they did best—kill at close range. Barlow figured it was just a matter of time—a matter of minutes, really—before the lancers recovered from their surprise and, almost by instinct, launched an assault across the river.

He was right. The commander regained control of his mount and immediately ordered the bugler to sound the charge. At the sound, his lancers surged forward as one. Barlow thanked his lucky stars that they had waited just long enough for him to shove new cartridges into the cylinder. He was able to fire three more times before the lancers had made it halfway across the river. Then, without hesitation, he left the embankment and ran to his horse. Leaping into the saddle, he turned the horse and looked across at Churacho's position. The mustanger was still shooting—and the lancers were now less than a hundred feet from the bank. Barlow shouted a warning, but of course that was futile, as Churacho would not be able to hear him over the sound of his rifle and the crashing of the lancers coming across the river, a battle cry in many of their throats. Barlow kicked his horse into a gallop, crossing open ground to the other embankment, getting closer to Churacho—close enough to be heard when he shouted again.

"Damn it, Churacho! Let's go!"

He brought rifle to shoulder and fired his last three rounds into the lancers, who were now less than sixty feet away—close enough that he could distinguish the features of those in the vanguard of the charge. The rifle empty, he drew the Colt Paterson and fired it until the hammer fell on an empty chamber. It was now virtually point-blank range. The lancers faltered in the face of the fusillade, earning the two men a few precious seconds. Barlow saw, out of the corner of his eye, that Churacho was running for his horse, and an instant later the mustanger was mounted. They rode north as fast as their horses could carry them, and before long they had outdistanced the weary mounts of the lancers. At sunset they paused on high ground to scan their back-trail, and could see no sign of pursuit.

"You think they've given up?" asked Barlow.

"Who knows? But they will not ride after dark, for fear of another ambush."

"We shaved the odds a bit."

Churacho grimly shook his head. "We did not kill enough of them."

He rode on. Barlow decided it would be fruitless to point out to his friend that he would *never* kill enough to rid himself of his grief.

Chapter 28

They rode late into the night, slept a few hours in a cold camp, then were in the saddle again before daybreak, rejoining the others early that morning. By midday they had reached the outermost pickets of Taylor's army, and before much longer, Barlow was presenting Churacho to the general himself. Taylor greeted the mustanger with a frosty cordiality, and listened without saying a word as Churacho took twenty minutes describing in detail all that he had seen and heard in Monterrey. He had identified all of the units in Ampudia's army by the time he was done. When at last he was finished, Barlow took the liberty of speaking up before Taylor could say a word.

"By my count, that would mean General Ampudia has at least seven thousand men in and around Monterrey, sir. And some of the finest units in the Mexican army, too."

Taylor gave him a sour look. "Yes, so it would seem—if we take everything this man has told us at face value."

Barlow bristled. "And why wouldn't we, General?"

"Has it occurred to you that perhaps he doesn't *want* us to attack Monterrey? That he is inflating the numbers intentionally, to discourage us from pressing on with our campaign?"

Barlow glanced at Churacho. The mustanger was gazing at Taylor with hooded eyes, lips clamped shut.

"I vouch for him, sir," said Barlow, keeping a tight lid on his temper. He had no desire to spend the rest of the war in the brig at Fort Brown. "I'm sure he is telling the truth."

"It doesn't matter how many men Ampudia has," growled Taylor. "We will advance, and we will take—" he said, slamming a fist on the desk to punctuate the statement—"Monterrey."

"Of course, sir," said Barlow.

"As for *you*," said Taylor, fastening a hostile gaze upon Churacho, "I still consider you a murderer, a thief and a cutthroat. And if I had my way, you would be hanging by your neck from the nearest tree before nightfall."

"Then you would have to hang me right alongside him," said Barlow.

Churacho looked at him, his expression unfathomable.

"Yes, I'm well aware of that," said Taylor acerbically. "Which is why I will not press the matter. It's not worth having to explain why one of my own officers was executed." He turned his attention back to Churacho. "But I would advise you not to linger long in Matamoros. The man you killed had many friends, and some of them may seek to take justice into their own hands. Not that I encourage that sort of thing, but I'm not certain that I can prevent it from happening."

"He has more than twenty green-broke horses for sale, General," said Barlow. "The same ones you . . . confiscated, before. Do you want them?"

"Yes. We need horses. A fair price will be paid for them."

"*Gracias,*" said Churacho, not without a touch of irony in his voice.

"As for you, Colonel," said Taylor, "I trust you will not undertake another adventure without my authority, since you are now on my staff."

"Yes, sir," said Barlow.

"There is much yet remaining to be done before we can march on Monterrey, which I want to do by the end of the week. But first, tonight, there is an officers' ball being held across the river, at Fort Brown. I trust you will attend."

"Yes, sir," said Barlow. He had no desire to do any such thing, but he could tell that this was more than simply a request on Taylor's part. And he decided that the least he could do for the general's display of forbearance where the execution of his friend was concerned, was to play at being the obedient staff officer.

Taylor nodded, rose from behind his desk. "Take him to the bursar, have him paid a fair price for the horses."

He did not go so far as to thank Churacho for the intelligence he had delivered regarding the Mexican army—but then, in Barlow's opinion, that would have been expecting too much from Old Rough 'n' Ready, so he stood, saluted, and left with Churacho.

The officer of the day—the same officer who had made Barlow the loan of his Colt Paterson—directed them to the bursar's office, located in an adobe building across the square. Barlow returned the pistol to him, with thanks, assuring him that it had come in handy.

"I hope you didn't get into any trouble on my account, Lieutenant."

The officer of the day flashed a boyish grin. "Oh, not too much, sir. I just told them you had given me

an order, and I was obligated to obey it." He looked
at the Colt Paterson—and handed it back to Barlow.
"I'd be honored if you'd keep this, Colonel."

Barlow was taken aback. He accepted the pistol
with heartfelt gratitude. "Thank you, Lieutenant. I'd
be honored to have it."

He and Churacho crossed the bustling square to the
adobe where the bursar had set up shop. There was
an armed guard at the door and another inside the
room. There was no haggling of price—Barlow simply
instructed the bursar to pay Churacho what he knew
to be the going price for top horseflesh. Then there
was the matter of paperwork. When that, finally, was
completed, the bursar wrote out a chit and handed it
to Barlow.

"What's this?" asked Barlow.

"A note," said the bursar.

"Pay him in hard money."

"Twenty horses at fifty dollars a head—that's one
thousand dollars, Colonel. We're going to have a hard
enough time paying officers if this campaign goes on
much longer—and it's my understanding that it will.
As it is, the enlisted men haven't been paid in two
months."

"That's not my concern," said Barlow. "I want you
to pay this man in coin. Understand? And don't tell
me you don't have it. If you didn't, you wouldn't have
this guard, either."

The bursar grimaced, then nodded. He opened a
small safe located behind his desk, and brought out
several bags of twenty-dollar gold pieces. He counted
out a thousand dollars worth, put this in a small
pouch, and handed it, begrudgingly, to Barlow. Barlow
handed the pouch to Churacho, nodded to the bursar,
and followed the mustanger outside.

Churacho brandished two cheroots, offering one to

Barlow and clenching the other in his teeth. He struck
a sulfur match to life on the buckle of his belt, lit both
cheroots. He took a long pull on his, drawing the
smoke deep into his lungs, then letting it trickle out
through his nostrils.

"Well, I guess that's it, then," said Barlow. "I think
you should take the general's advice, my friend, and
leave as soon as you can."

Leaning against an adobe wall, Churacho smoked
his cheroot and looked about him, smiling faintly. "I
will leave—when I am ready. And what about you,
amigo? You have done your duty. Why do you not
go home to your family?"

"I will—after we take Monterrey. After I make sure
that El Soldado is no longer standing. And after I'm
certain that Zeke Fuller is dead. I don't want to wake
up one morning to find him standing over me, a knife
to my throat. Or, worse yet, over my wife or son."

Churacho nodded. "Good idea. I will stay with you
until then. I need to make sure of these things, too."

"Don't be a fool, Churacho. You can't be part of
the battle that's coming. There's no place for you."

"Except at your side."

Barlow sighed. He considered Churacho a good
friend—one of the best he'd ever had—and he understood that the mustanger had certain ideas about
friendship and loyalty that were real attributes.

"General Taylor wouldn't like that," said Barlow.
"You're lucky you weren't tossed right back in the
brig when you got through with your report today.
There are just too many people who want you dead,
on both sides. Get out while you can. And don't forget
Therese. A battlefield is no place for her."

Churacho smoked his cheroot, thought it over,
and—much to Barlow's relief—nodded. "You are

right. It is no place for her. But she thinks her place is with you."

"Well, it isn't," said Barlow brusquely. "I'm married. I've told her that. She just needs to get over it."

"You have no feelings for my sister, then?"

"No. Not those kind of feelings. I think of her as friend—as I think of you. Nothing more. And, as far as I know, I haven't said or done anything to indicate otherwise. You've got to talk some sense into her, Churacho. Help her get over this . . . this infatuation of hers."

"Is that what it is." Churacho flicked the half-spent cheroot away, pushed off the wall. "I will try to do what you say."

Barlow stuck out a hand. "Then I guess this is good-bye." There was more he wanted to say, but he had no idea how to put his feelings into words.

Churacho shook his hand. He said nothing—merely gave a nod, then turned and walked away. Barlow soon lost sight of him in the crowded square. He figured that was the last he would see of the mustanger. Pensively, he headed back to the *cabildo,* and the small room he shared with two other officers, intent on getting some much-needed sleep.

Barlow was shaken out of a deep slumber by a man who introduced himself as Captain Tibbett, one of his roommates.

"I'm honored to meet you, Colonel," said Tibbett.

"Honored?" asked Barlow, still groggy. "Why honored?"

"I've heard about what you did. I guess by now just about everyone in the army has heard. That was a remarkable feat, sir. Into the den of lions, so to speak."

Barlow finally caught on. "Oh. You mean Monterrey."

"Yes, sir."

Barlow looked around. "Where is my uniform?" He remembered shedding his trail-grimed tunic before laying down to sleep.

"I took the liberty of getting it cleaned, sir. It should be back soon. I'm assuming your presence has been requested at the officers' ball."

Barlow grimaced. "Yes, unfortunately I'm having to attend."

Tibbett laughed. "Oh, it won't be too bad, sir. Females will be in short supply, though. They've rounded up about twenty pretty *señoritas* from Brownsville for dancing partners. Almost none of the married officers brought their wives on this campaign. Are you married, Colonel?"

"Yes."

"I'm not . . . yet. Engaged to be. Her name is Edith. Would you like to see a picture. She sent me a daguerreotype. Most amazing thing, really. . . ."

Barlow didn't particularly want to see a picture of Tibbett's fiancée, but there was no way around it without being rude, so he nodded. Tibbett happily produced the photograph, enclosed in a small, leather-bound case.

"She's a lovely girl," said Barlow. "I'm sure the two of you will be very happy."

"We were going to be married last December," said Tibbett, taking the daguerreotype back and gazing at it. "But then I requested to come here and, well, we decided it would be best to wait until I returned."

"You requested."

"Yes, sir. Didn't want to miss out on the war, you know, sir." Tibbett grinned. "Thought Edith might prefer to marry a real, honest-to-God hero."

"She didn't mind that you had to leave?"

"Oh, well, yes, sir, she minded, I'm sure. Though Edith isn't the sort of girl who would make a big scene. I've been in the army nine years, sir, and this was the first opportunity to come my way. I couldn't let it slip through my fingers, now could I, sir?"

"No, of course not."

Tibbett said he would go see about Barlow's uniform, and excused himself. Barlow sat on the edge of his narrow bunk and cradled his head in his hands, trying to wake up. The captain returned a few minutes later with Barlow's tunic. It was the cleanest it had been since his departure from Georgia. Barlow thanked Tibbett, donned the tunic, and accepted the captain's invitation to accompany him to the officers' mess. This turned out to be under a cedar-pole *ramada* a short walk from the *cabildo*. More than two dozen officers were eating at rough-hewn tables by lantern-light—the sun had just dropped below the horizon, and the sky was darkening from blue to indigo. Several Mexican women were providing the officers with tortillas and *frijoles* and meat that, when he tasted it, Barlow couldn't identify. Tibbett told him it was goat. Barlow found it tough and stringy, but he ate it anyway. He'd learned from experience that, on a campaign, one could never be sure when the next meal was coming.

When Tibbett introduced Barlow to the table, the other officers showed keen interest. It seemed that the captain was right—word of Barlow's exploits had spread throughout the ranks. For the next thirty minutes, he fielded questions regarding what he had seen and experienced in Monterrey. He tried to convey to them the strength of the enemy fortifications, expecting that they would be prone to underestimate the Mexican army. But he was wrong about that. It was

the general consensus that the battle they were about
to fight would be the most difficult of the campaign.
The Mexicans would be reluctant to give up the strategically important city, and it was fully expected that
they would contest every foot of ground. Even so,
the officers were confident that American might would
triumph. And they could only hope that the Battle of
Monterrey would go down in the history books as the
greatest struggle of the war. Barlow looked at the
faces of the officers at his table and realized that all
of them were ten to twenty years younger than he. It
was probably safe to assume that none of them had
seen action prior to this campaign. He could still remember when he had been a young and inexperienced
shavetail, fresh out of West Point, thinking only of
duty, honor and glory, and taking survival as a given.
He'd been fortunate to live long enough to realize his
mistake. Honor and glory were no longer sufficient
motivators in his case. He had to have something else
worth fighting, and perhaps dying, for. This time he
had something else—El Soldado, Malveux, Zeke Fuller. He had to make sure all of those were destroyed.
Once that was accomplished, he could go home. He
didn't particularly care about the strategic value of
Monterrey. The war had become a very personal matter for him.

Someone produced a bottle of brandy. Nearly all
the officers present emptied their cups of the bitter
black coffee that had been brewed by the Mexican
women, and had a splash of brandy instead. It was
Captain Tibbett who stood to give the toast—to victory. Barlow felt compelled to stand up after Tibbett
to make an addition—to survival, long enough to at
least enjoy the victory.

Chapter 29

Major Flagler and the garrison at Fort Brown had outdone themselves in preparing for the officers' ball. A platform one hundred feet square, made of timber that, Barlow learned, had been salvaged from a schooner hopelessly run aground some months ago just up the coast from Port Isabel, had been set out in the center of the parade ground. Posts had been erected at all four corners, and rope had been strung from post to post. From these ropes dangled gaily colored Japanese lanterns. A regimental band was stationed on a wagon-bed nearby. Tables had been placed all around the dance floor, and these were laden with refreshments. Best of all, the weather was cooperating—the night was cool but not too windy, and there wasn't a cloud in the sky, a fact testified to by the dazzling array of stars. All in all, thought Barlow upon arrival, it was a very romantic scene—considering that its setting was a fortress where, not too long ago, a life-and-death struggle had taken place between American and Mexican soldiers. Barlow felt a pang of longing for Rose stronger than that which usually afflicted him. He was suddenly impatient; why were they wasting time with a ball when the army could be marching on Monterrey, bringing the conclusion of the campaign that much closer?

Arriving with Captain Tibbett and several others from the mess, Barlow resolved to stay only as long as it took to be noticed by General Taylor. That way there would be no question that he had attended, as per the general's request. But Taylor had not yet made an appearance, so Barlow went to one of the tables and took a glass of watery punch that tasted like orange rind. He scanned the congregation of officers, and spotted Major Flagler, who was staring at him from the opposite side of the dance floor. It was clear that the commander of the Fort Brown garrison had not forgotten their last meeting. Barlow cordially raised his glass, but Flagler turned away.

It was then that Barlow happened to glance in the direction of the main gate—and what he saw stunned him.

It was Armstrong, with a beautiful young Mexican woman on his arm. Barlow had to take a second look to be sure that it was Therese, for she was dressed as he had never expected to see her, in a gown adorned with satin and lace. Churacho was with them, clad in a brand-new *chaquetilla* and doeskin trousers adorned with big silver *conchos*. Barlow looked for Major Flagler. As he'd feared, the garrison commander had already spotted Churacho, and was staring at the mustanger as though he couldn't believe his eyes. Barlow figured that the astonishment would wear off quickly, to be replaced by an emotion that would mean trouble for Churacho. He circled the dance floor, wending his way through the revelers, to reach Armstrong and the others.

"What are you doing here?" he asked Churacho.

"Pardon me, Colonel," said Armstrong. "I invited them. I was surprised to learn that you hadn't."

"No, I didn't. I was hoping they'd be miles away from here by now." He turned back to Churacho. "Don't you understand how dangerous it is here for you? For both of you?"

Churacho shrugged, grinning sheepishly—and Barlow caught a whiff of strong liquor emanating from him. The mustanger was drunk!

"I told her, I told her," said Churacho. "But she would not listen. And then the captain, he comes with the invitation. What am I to do?" He put an arm around Barlow's shoulder, brandished one of his cheroots, and tucked it away under Barlow's tunic. "I'll tell you. I buy her a new dress, that's what I do."

The regimental band had launched into a waltz. Armstrong bowed to Therese.

"May I have the pleasure of this dance?"

Therese glanced at Barlow, who simply shook his head in disbelief.

"I do not know this dance," she admitted to Armstrong.

"That isn't a problem. I can teach you. Just follow my lead."

He led her to the dance floor. Major Flagler passed them, coming towards Barlow and Churacho, with several junior officers in tow. Flagler had gotten over his astonishment. Now a cold fury was etched into his face.

"What's the meaning of this, Colonel?" asked Flagler. He was mad, but not quite mad enough to forget himself—or the fact that Barlow outranked him. "What is this man doing here?"

"He's not doing any harm, Major," said Barlow.

"That's a matter of opinion," said Flagler stiffly. "I must tell you, frankly, that his presence here is an affront to the entire garrison."

"This man risked his life for us in Monterrey."

"That does not mitigate against the cold-blooded murder he committed. . . ."

"You're right," said Barlow. "I'll take care of it, Major."

Flagler was stymied. He could not very well question Barlow's sincerity without affronting the superior officer's honor. "I will trust you to do just that, Colonel," he said icily, and turned away. His grim entourage of junior officers spared Barlow and the grinning Churacho hostile glances before following their commander.

"Well, that was pleasant," said Barlow.

"You need a drink," said Churacho. "And come to think of it, so do I."

"I think you've had enough to drink. Come on, we're getting out of here."

"Therese. . . ."

"Therese has the gallant Captain Armstrong to look after her," said Barlow wryly.

It was as he started to turn that he heard Armstrong's voice, raised in anger, over the music being played by the regimental band.

"Get your hands off her, mister!"

He turned back, just as the crowd on the dance floor began to spread out, leaving Armstrong, with Therese standing sheltered behind him, facing another officer in the center. Barlow didn't recognize the officer, but assumed it was another of Flagler's subordinates.

"Just wanted to dance with the lady, Captain," said the officer, with a thick Southern drawl.

"She doesn't want to dance with you, Lieutenant," replied Armstrong.

"I imagine she has danced with a great many men in her time," said the officer, leering. "I don't see why she would refuse me, when she has obviously accepted so many others in the past."

"Stay here," Barlow muttered to Churacho, and started forward—leaving the mustanger, swaying slightly, to his own devices.

"I don't like what you're implying," said Armstrong. Fists clenched, he took a menacing step towards the lieutenant. The officer wasn't the least bit intimidated; he stood his ground, a taunting smile curling the corners of his mouth.

"That's enough, Captain!"

Barlow's tone was stentorian—it provoked an immediate, involuntary response from both Armstrong and his tormentor: both men snapped to attention. That gave Barlow time enough to reach them.

"Captain Armstrong, you will escort the lady out of the fort at once."

"It isn't her fault that—"

"I gave you an order, Captain," rasped Barlow, his anger seeping into every word.

"Yes, sir." Armstrong turned stiffly, presented an arm to Therese. She took it, and Armstrong marched her off the dance floor.

Barlow turned his attention to the Southern officer. "I don't believe I know you."

"Lieutenant Bishop is one of my aides," said Major Flagler, emerging from the crowd that encircled the dance floor. "Surely, Colonel, you don't hold him in any way responsible for this unpleasantness."

"Certainly not," said Barlow. "We'll be going now."

"An excellent idea, Colonel."

Barlow turned—and just in time, too; he intercepted Churacho, who was coming across the dance floor with a scowl on his face.

"What did he say?" asked the mustanger. "What did he say about my sister?"

Barlow got in his path, put a hand on his chest. Churacho was focusing in on Bishop. He didn't even

glance at Barlow, just knocked the hand away. But
Barlow loosened the rein on his anger; he grabbed
Churacho and spun the man around and then knocked
him down. The mustanger sprawled on the dance
floor.

"Don't get up until I tell you to," rasped Barlow.

Churacho froze, detecting something in Barlow's
voice that he hadn't heard before. He looked around
at the dozens of faces. All eyes were on him now.
Some of the officers were smirking. They enjoyed
seeing him knocked down, and were hoping for a
chance to see more of the same. Churacho's face darkened with a rising anger. Barlow saw this, knew its
source; he had humiliated the mustanger. Churacho
was nothing if not proud, and his pride had just been
damaged by a man he had considered a friend. It was
a betrayal that he would not soon forget. Barlow understood that. But he could see no other way to keep
Churacho alive.

"Now," said Barlow, "when you get up, you're
going to turn around and leave the fort. If you don't,
I'll knock you down again. And this time you'll stay
down."

Churacho smiled coldly. "You think you can do
that, eh?"

"Yes. I can."

The mustanger gave him a long, unreadable look.
Then, with as much dignity as he could muster, he got
to his feet, brushed off his new trousers, straightened
his new *chaquetilla,* and turned to walk away.

Barlow glanced at Flagler. The major nodded, well-
satisfied with the treatment that had been meted out
to Churacho. Barlow had a few choice things he very
much wanted to say to Flagler. But he bit his tongue,
and without another word followed Churacho out of
the fort.

Armstrong and Therese were waiting for them outside the gate. They were mounted, and Armstrong was holding Churacho's horse. The mustanger climbed into the saddle, grimly silent. The captain could tell that something was very wrong, and he asked Barlow what had happened.

"He was about to get himself arrested and thrown into the brig—again," said Barlow, exasperated. "I guess some people just never learn their lesson."

"That lieutenant was wrong to say what he did," argued Armstrong hotly. "Somebody should have taught him some manners."

"I thought you were brighter than that, Captain. It was a fool's game to come here in the first place. You were just inviting trouble. And that's what the lieutenant—probably at Major Flagler's bidding—was trying to start. You should have just walked away."

"He insulted Therese," snapped Armstrong. "Doesn't that matter to you, Colonel? Because it certainly matters to me."

Barlow turned his attention to her. She was sitting her horse quietly, and he thought, by her expression, that she knew what she had done, and regretted it. He walked up to stand beside the horse and look up at her.

"Therese, if you keep this up, you're going to get your brother killed. Do right by him. Take him away from this place, before it's too late."

"But, what about—?"

"I'm going home to my wife and son, just as soon as I take care of some unfinished business in Monterrey. There's no chance for us. It just wasn't meant to happen. Accept that, and move on. The sooner you do, the better off you'll be."

She reached out to touch his face, then thought better of it and withdrew her hand. Nodding her acceptance of what he had said, she smiled bravely at him through her tears and turned her horse. Churacho followed her, studiously ignoring Barlow. The latter watched with regret as the mustanger rode away into the darkness.

"I'll make sure they get out of here safely," said Armstrong, and then he, too, was gone, leaving the impression that he wasn't any happier with Barlow than Churacho had been.

With a sigh, Barlow went back to the gate, intent on collecting his horse and returning to Monterrey. He was both saddened and relieved that Churacho and Therese were gone—saddened because he had become very close to both of them, and assumed that he would never see them again. But also relieved, because now he could concentrate on the all-important business at hand—namely, getting through the impending battle and returning to Georgia in one piece.

Chapter 30

Standing on a rise little more than a mile north of the city of Monterrey, scanning the Mexican defenses by means of a spyglass, Barlow felt the excitement stirring his blood. Zachary Taylor and his army had just today arrived on the scene. The usual skirmishing had taken place as the Mexican commander pulled back his pickets. Even now—across the vast, arid plain between the rise where Barlow stood and the beginning of the Mexican defensive works—came the sound of desultory musket fire. Off to the west, a Mexican battery on Independence Hill was firing a cannon. A pall of dust overhung the entire scene as—behind Barlow's position—elements of Taylor's army marched into position and—in front of him—units of Ampudia's army scurried hither and yon among the fortifications.

Seeing all of this through the spyglass, Barlow could not deny to himself that he was glad to be here. He'd been dragged—a reluctant participant—into this war, but now, at this moment, he had no remorse. Who could say but that—had he declined President Polk's request to serve his country in the struggle, and had returned to home and hearth—he would not have experienced keen regret for having missed what would probably turn out to be his last opportunity to fight.

He was a soldier, and this was what soldiers did. This was what they trained for—and lived for. It did not escape his notice that he had been hypocritical in condemning those who had agitated for this war with Mexico. For was he not, when you boiled it down, as much a war lover as they?

General Taylor and the rest of his staff—protected by a detachment of mounted riflemen—shared the rise with Barlow, and the general and several of his subordinates were also using spyglasses to survey the enemy's disposition. Eventually Taylor lowered his glass and looked about him.

"Well, gentlemen, I think we've seen what we needed to see. Let's get ourselves situated, and then we'll discuss how to take possession of the city."

As they vacated the rise, an artillery company charged up to its crest to aim their cannon at the Mexican fortifications. Elsewhere, other units were fanning out on either side of the Cerralvo Road. Taylor and his entourage took the road north to another piece of high ground where several abandoned adobes had been appropriated for the general's headquarters. This would be the hub of the army's main encampment. Here the supply wagons were beginning to arrive. The hospital tents were being erected. The units to be held in reserve began to pitch their tents as well, on the flats to either side of the adobes. As the general dismounted in front of the hovels, Barlow wondered how he would take to such miserable quarters—quite different from the comfortable Matamoros *cabildo*. To his credit, Taylor seemed little concerned with his own comfort or safety. He dispatched his staff officers to instruct regimental commanders to come to him within the hour, so that they might discuss the best way to launch an assault on the enemy. Barlow's orders were to find General Worth, who was supposedly some-

where out on the right flank. For his part, Barlow was
glad to get away from the general staff, if only for a
few hours. Every since Matamoros, the vast majority
of his labors had been concentrated on wagon invento-
ries and marching orders and casualty reports—various illnesses sweeping through the ranks during the
long sojourn at Matamoros had reached alarming pro-
portions. These were all very necessary tasks, and he
knew that. But knowing didn't make him like them
any more.

As he made for what be believed to be Worth's
position, Barlow happened to cross open ground some
eight or nine hundred yards from the Citadel. A cannon in one of the redoubts spoke. Barlow checked his
horse, and wondered what the Mexicans were shooting
at. He quickly got his answer. The cannonball struck
the earth about a hundred and fifty yards shy of him.
Even at that distance, the explosion was deafening,
and it nearly spooked Barlow's horse. Barlow figured
it wasn't personal—the Mexican artillerymen were just
using him for target practice, trying to nail down the
windage and range of their big gun. They fired again,
and then a third time. On the last occasion Barlow
actually heard the sinister whistling of the ball through
the air. It landed less than a hundred yards away,
marked by a geyser of flame and dirt and debris. Barlow kept a tight rein on his horse as he swept the hat
off his head and bowed tauntingly from the saddle. In
the distance he could hear the Mexican artillerymen
cheering. Barlow continued on his way, keeping to
an unhurried pace, just to show the enemy that he
wasn't rattled.

He found General William Jenkins Worth a short
while later. The general, accompanied by several
aides, was riding along his lines, making sure that
every man in his command was in position. Barlow

relayed the news to Worth that General Taylor requested his presence as soon as possible.

"Yes, of course," said Worth, with a trace of sarcasm in his voice. "Let me guess, Colonel. We're to have another powwow about how to conduct the war. We had a great many of those during the interminably long weeks we spent in Matamoros. I do believe that the general is still seeking some way to fight a battle without any loss of men, and without any chance of failure."

Barlow said, "I wouldn't know, sir."

Worth peered at him, then laughed. "No, of course you wouldn't. You're much too clever to get in the middle of it."

Barlow had heard that William Worth was a highly ambitious man—a character trait he shared with Zachary Taylor. Both men had hopes of being the real hero of the war, the conquering Caesar returning to Rome—or, in their case, Washington—in grand triumph, idolized by the people, and destined for high political office. What made matters worse, Worth had been considered by President Polk for the job Taylor currently held.

"Tell the general I'll be right along, Colonel," said Worth.

Barlow returned whence he had come, and by the same route, willing to play the part of target once more for the Mexican artillerymen. This time, though, they did not fire at him, but only cheered his passage. Barlow wasn't fooled by their apparent acclamation. He knew that if he gave them a chance, they would kill him without hesitation or regret.

Arriving back at the headquarters encampment, Barlow spent the remainder of the afternoon helping Captain Tibbett set up their small tent. Then he proceeded to clean his weapons. It had been a slow, hot and dusty trek from Matamoros; now that they were face-to-face with the enemy, it was time to make sure all of his weapons were in proper working order. As a staff officer to the commanding general, he was not likely to see hand-to-hand action, but one never knew. A battle was chaos, and no one was completely safe from violence.

An hour prior to sundown, Taylor held his meeting. As Barlow had come to expect, the general relied heavily on maps. Several were spread out on a folding camp table in the shade of a *ramada* alongside the adobe which served as his office-cum-quarters. The regimental commanders, with their own staffs, congregated there, and it occurred to Barlow that a couple of well-placed cannon shots on the part of the Mexicans could have wiped out most of the American army's officer corps.

"There is no practical way to outflank the enemy," said Taylor. "Therefore, our only recourse is to break through his defenses by brute force. We can expect casualties to be high. But I stress to you, gentlemen, that the benefits will be worth the sacrifice. Once we have Monterrey, the border will be secured. Texas will no longer have to fear an invasion from the south. We must prevail, regardless of the costs. Defeat is not an option."

He stabbed at the map on the table. "This is the Saltillo Road, which runs parallel to the Santa Catarina River, entering Monterrey from the west. It passes between two of the strongest points in the enemy's defensive works—Independence Hill and Federation Hill. Those two strongholds must be overrun if an assault on the northern fortifications is to succeed. Otherwise, our troops would be subjected to crossing fire from the Mexican artillery emplacements located on those heights. Therefore, General Worth, you will take two thousand men and circle to the west, arriving at the Saltillo Road and using it to guide your assault on those hills. Once you have gotten the attention of the Mexican soldiers there, we will commence our frontal assault, all along the line. Any questions?"

"I have a comment, General," said Barlow. "Ampudia has a large number of cavalry. Lancers and dragoons—even a battalion of curassiers. He will not use them in the trenches. We can expect him to mount counterattacks all along the line, using his cavalry as shock troops."

"That is a possibility," conceded Taylor. "If it comes to pass, what do you suggest we do to counter it?"

"Our cavalry doesn't match up," said Barlow. "You have mostly volunteer units—mounted rifles from Arkansas and Kentucky—and just a handful of regular mounted troops. The only other effective countermeasure against cavalry assault is artillery. We should keep our batteries mobile, sir—able to respond at a moment's notice to wherever it is on the field that the enemy's horse appears."

Taylor stared at Barlow for a moment, a scowl on his craggy face, and Barlow braced himself for a reprimand. He knew the general didn't like him, and so would be predisposed not to take his advice. But Taylor surprised him.

"An excellent plan," conceded the general. "Does anyone else wish to comment on this matter?"

"I think we should do exactly what the colonel suggests," said Worth. "But we should position some of our artillery to bombard the strong points along the Mexican line. The Citadel, the Bishop's Palace, Devil's Fort." He pointed out each of these locations on the map.

Taylor concurred. "Colonel Barlow, I will leave it

to you to organize these artillery detachments as you deem necessary. General Worth, you will begin your maneuver to the west in the morning. You will have twenty-four hours to prepare for an assault along the Saltillo Road, as I intend to engage the enemy in battle on Monday, the 21st."

"We'll be ready, sir," said Worth. He seemed well aware of the opportunity he was being given here, and eager to prove himself up to the task. "May I recommend, General, that, beginning tomorrow afternoon, you engage in one or more feints against the enemy's fortifications. In that way we might be able to keep Ampudia confused as to our real plans, and he may decide not to reinforce his left flank."

"Consider it done," said Taylor. "Good luck to all of you gentlemen. I know you will acquit yourselves with the courage and audacity I have come to expect from you. And I trust you will all survive to receive the praise of an adoring nation for the victory I am confident we will achieve here. That will be all."

Chapter 31

Taylor's army consisted of many volunteers, most of them from the South, though there was one entire brigade from New England. Barlow wasn't sure of the exact percentage, but he felt sure that well over half of the infantry were irregulars. That didn't bother him; he figured that would always be the case when the United States went to war, considering the fact that the American people would not tolerate a large standing army—a prejudice that could be traced all the way back to colonial days, when the hated British redcoats had patrolled the streets of town and village and even quartered themselves in private homes. The United States Army had numbered little more than ten thousand men of all ranks when the war with Mexico broke out, so volunteers were essential, especially since President Polk had decided on a two-pronged invasion of Mexico proper while sending yet another army—Kearny's so-called Army of the West—to take Santa Fe.

Barlow recalled the volunteers with whom he had fought nearly thirty years ago, in the campaign against the Red Stick Creeks and, subsequently, the Seminoles in Florida. Most of the men who marched for Andrew Jackson in those campaigns had been backwoodsmen and farmers, and Barlow could testify to the fact that whatever they might have lacked in discipline and training, they more than made up for with enthusiasm. Most Americans—be they farmers or clerks—could put down their plows and ledgers, pick up their rifles, and head off to war and acquit themselves quite well. It was the nature of the people—a people accustomed to fighting for what was theirs . . . and sometimes fighting for what they wanted that belonged to someone else.

In terms of Taylor's artillery, however, the units contained only regular troops, and Barlow was glad of that. He brought the battery commanders together and explained what he'd been authorized to do. It didn't take long to put together two autonomous groups. Each consisted of twelve guns, most of them twelve-pounders. There were some larger cannon available, but Barlow relegated them to fixed emplacements, where they could bombard the strong points of the Mexican defenses. The eight-pounders were heavy enough to do the job he envisioned. They were all loaded with grapeshot, and each caisson was assigned an extra team of horses, so that there would be replacements immediately on hand if one or more of the four horses that made up a caisson team was shot down during the action. The key to the success of Barlow's plan was mobility: the *flying batteries,* as he called them, had to be able to move at a moment's notice, and quickly arrive at a point from which they could meet head-on any cavalry charge launched by the enemy.

He found out during the course of the day that a number of regimental commanders were unhappy with the arrangement—they wanted as many cannon as possible amassed all along the line, directing their fire at the fortifications against which they would have to send their men. Barlow didn't blame them. But he was convinced that his plan was the right one; he knew that Ampudia had a large contingent of cavalry—dragoons and lancers both. He also knew that in most cases, infantry—particularly volunteer infantry—could not withstand a determined cavalry charge. The lancers especially were shock troops, and Ampudia would hurl them at any weak points he discerned in the American line. Of this Barlow was sure. Taylor didn't have enough cavalry to match Ampudia saber for saber. That meant artillery was the only answer.

Late that Sunday, word came from Worth that he was in place, about two miles west along the Saltillo Road from Independence Hill. He had two thousand men under his command, leaving Taylor with perhaps twenty-five hundred effectives. Barlow had to admit to himself that Taylor was showing he had plenty of nerve. There had been questions raised about his fighting spirit during the long weeks when his army dallied in Matamoros. But now, on the eve of battle, Taylor was putting to rest any doubts his soldiers might have had about his resolve. He was taking a great risk, dividing his army even though he was confronted by an enemy of superior numbers. But Barlow thought it was a risk worth taking, and said as much to his old friend Martin Broward, whom he had last seen on the eve of his departure from Georgia. Broward was with the Second Infantry Regiment, and they met quite by accident that Sunday afternoon, while Barlow was in search for additional supplies of powder and the lead necessary for the case-shot.

"I wouldn't worry about the Mexicans attacking us while we're divided," said Barlow. "Ampudia is going to stay behind his fortifications. It's an advantage he won't dare forsake."

"Unless he figures out that he outnumbers us by at least two to one."

Barlow laughed, and shook his head. "You've been listening to too many rumors, Martin. Ampudia doesn't have more than seven thousand men under his command."

"That's still more than we have."

"Haven't you heard? One American can whip at least three Mexicans."

"You believe that?"

"No. But there are a lot of men in this army who do believe it. I guess they're about to find out if it's true. But look on the bright side, Martin. The war waited for you, after all. You're going to see some action, just like you wanted."

Broward forced a smile. He was having a case of nerves, with battle so imminent. Barlow figured that probably two out of every three soldiers in Taylor's army was suffering in the same way. It was perfectly understandable, especially among those who had never seen action before. It was a time of second-guessing, and self-doubt. Men like Broward were asking themselves if they had the guts to advance under fire. Nine out of ten men would settle down and perform well in battle. But you had to wonder if you'd turn out to be the tenth man—the one who lost his nerve, who broke and ran, who shamed himself forever. Barlow could vividly recall wrestling with those very same doubts himself, on the eve of the Battle of Horseshoe Bend.

"I knew you were going to throw that back in my face," said Broward ruefully. "It isn't that I'm getting cold feet, because I'm not. I want to be here. It's just that . . . well, this might sound odd to you, but it's just that I wish I'd done some things before I came down here."

"What things?"

"Get married. Have a family. That kind of thing. The kind of thing that you've done."

Barlow shook his head. "You're right, that is an odd thing to say, Martin. I can't speak for all the other married men in this army, but as for me, I sometimes wish I didn't have a wife, or a child. Because if I didn't, and something happened to me, I wouldn't be leaving anyone behind, to fend for themselves. I wouldn't break anybody's heart by dying."

"Well, I guess it's pure selfishness on my part, then," confessed Broward. "I wish I'd done those things because I'm afraid I might never get the chance to experience them. I hadn't really considered the possibility of leaving a grieving widow behind. I'm sorry, Timothy—I shouldn't have brought it up. I mean, you *are* married, and now, thanks to me, you're probably thinking about your wife and son back in Georgia."

"I was thinking about them anyway, Martin. So don't worry about it."

"Are you . . . going to write them a letter? Before the battle, I mean. I've seen some of the men doing that. I've heard the veterans telling them to pin the letter to the front of their shirt. That way, if they fall, someone can come along and retrieve the letter and make sure it gets where it's suppose to go."

"I've also known some men who thought it was bad luck to write such a letter, on the eve of battle," said Barlow. "But to answer your question—no, I won't be writing a letter. Not until it's over. Then I can tell Rose that I'm coming home. My letter will be good news, not bad."

"I wish you the best of luck," said Broward fervently, and extended a hand. "And I'll hope to see you in the streets of Monterrey."

Barlow shook the proffered hand. "We'll have a

drink and celebrate our good fortune at remaining on the right side of the grass."

Broward smiled. "Sounds fine. Now I must be on my way. Good luck, my friend."

Barlow wished him good luck, and watched him walk away, rejecting a premonition that sent a chill down his spine—a sense that this would be the last time he'd see Martin Broward alive. Of course, that was patent nonsense, or perhaps just superstition. Broward had as good a chance as anyone else in the army to make it through alive. Barlow didn't believe in jinxes and he didn't believe in predestination, either; he refused to accept that Fate would befall a man regardless of what he did or did not do.

It was close to sunset that Sunday before Barlow arrived at the army headquarters on the Cerralvo Road to inform General Taylor of the completion of his task regarding the flying batteries. He had to wait awhile, though, because the general—along with most of his staff and officers from the units to be held in reserve—was participating in a religious service. A minister, a tall and gaunt man with the face of an ascetic, clad in dusty black, his voice grave, was standing before the uniformed congregation, a Bible open in one hand, the other raised above his head to punctuate with gestures the sermon he was preaching. Barlow was able to identify it at once as the first chapter of the Book of Joshua:

> There shall not any man be able to stand
>   before thee
> All the days of thy life:
> As I was with Moses, *so* I will be with thee:
> I will not fail thee, nor forsake thee . . .
> Be strong and of a good courage;
> be not afraid, neither be thou dismayed:

For the Lord thy God *is* with thee
  whithersoever thou goest.
Then Joshua commanded the officers of the
  people, saying,
Pass through the host and command the
  people, saying,
Prepare you victuals; for within three days ye
  shall pass over this Jordan,
to go in to possess the land, which the Lord
  your God giveth you to possess it . . .
Your wives, your little ones, and your cattle,
Shall remain in the land which Moses gave you
  on this side Jordan;
But ye shall pass before your brethren armed,
All the mighty men of valor, and help
  them. . . .
And they answered Joshua, saying,
All that thou commandest us we will do,
And whithersoever thou sendest us, we will go.

The minister finished reading and for a moment gazed
out upon the faces of the officers. "Soon you will go
forth," he said solemnly, "like the Christian soldiers
commanded by Joshua, and you will win a great victory for the Lord and for justice. Do not be anxious—
for if you are called to the Lord you will go before
him just as the great pagan warriors went unto Val-
halla, covered with glory, and blessed by your sacrifice
for God and country. And, as is said in Second Chron-
icles, chapter 20, verse 15, "Be not afraid nor dismayed by reason of this great multitude; for the battle
is not yours, but God's."

He then bade them bow their heads, and led them
in the Lord's Prayer. Barlow bowed his head along
with the rest, and murmured the words he knew by
rote. A chorus of *Amens* marked the conclusion of

the service. General Taylor rose from his field chair and shook the minister's hand. Barlow waited for his chance, and when Taylor started for the adobe in which he was housed, Barlow intercepted him. Taylor listened without interrupting while Barlow explained concisely the arrangements he had made. Then the general nodded his satisfaction.

"Well done, Colonel. You look tired. Go get something to eat, and then rest. It will be a long night—and a longer day tomorrow."

"Yes, sir."

Captain Tibbett, who had been in the congregation, spotted Barlow and came striding over. "I took the liberty of reserving you some space in that tent yonder, Colonel."

Barlow thanked him. He went to one of the nearby cook-fires, where he was provided a plate of beans laced with side-meat and some hard biscuits, washed down with a cup of bitter black coffee. One of Taylor's young lieutenants offered him a flask of whiskey, but Barlow declined. He didn't need whiskey to sleep. Listening for a few minutes to the conversation around the fire—conversation that never touched upon the subject of the Mexican army or the upcoming battle, but rather almost exclusively on people and places back home, Barlow finally rolled up in his blankets on the hard ground. Clouds were rolling in from the north, beginning to blot out the stars. His last thought was that tomorrow would probably bring rain—and that would be a significant factor. It might slow down the enemy's cavalry. But it would slow down the flying batteries as well.

Chapter 32

Watching the battle unfold from the high ground near the adobes that Taylor was utilizing as headquarters, Barlow had an uneasy feeling. He stood among several other staff officers, with Taylor sitting his white horse nearby. All of them were scanning the battlefield with spyglasses.

At dawn, Taylor had struck the first blow, sending several strong feints against the Mexican lines, particularly on the enemy's right flank, near the Tannery, and another straight down the Cerralvo Road, passing within range of the Citadel, perhaps the strongest point in Ampudia's defenses. Taylor was taking the advice of General Worth, and attempting to convince the Mexicans that he was attacking all along the line in earnest. This, it was hoped, would prevent Ampudia from rushing reinforcements to his left flank, where Worth was launching his assault.

Barlow could see it all from where he stood. The feint at the center of the Mexican line, the one on the Cerralvo Road, was being punished by withering fire from the cannon at the Citadel. The troops were falling back in disarray. The attack on the enemy's far-right flank was not faring much better. The pall of

smoke that drifted over the field of battle was so thick
now that Barlow couldn't make out much as far as
Worth's advance was concerned; he could tell that the
guns atop Federation and Independence Hills were
being fired at a furious rate.

The rain wasn't helping visibility any, either. It was
an unceasing drizzle, buffeted by gusts of cold wind
out of the north that cut right through to the bone.
The clouds hung low over the battlefield, trapped
against the heights of the Sierra Madre behind Monterrey. Wisps of gray cloud scudded so low to the
earth that at times Barlow thought he could have
reached up and grabbed a handful. All in all, it was
miserable weather for fighting. Barlow could only
imagine the difficulty the soldiers down there were
having, with poor footing and wet powder.

That, of course, was the problem—those men down
there were fighting, and some of them were dying,
while he was standing up here out of harm's way,
watching it all through a spyglass. It didn't feel right.
He wasn't a hero, or a glory-seeker, and he wasn't
aching to get himself killed, but he felt as though it
was his duty to be *down there* and he was embarrassed
that he wasn't.

He heard Taylor mutter a curse, and lowered his
glass to glance at the general.

"What the Hell is Worth up to?" asked Taylor, his
tone reflecting utter exasperation. He wasn't directing
the question to anyone in particular. "He should have
taken Independence Hill by now, and turned those
guns on Federation Hill. I cannot keep sending my
men against the Mexican defenses, to be slaughtered
for naught."

"Let me find out, sir," said Barlow, trudging
through the muck underfoot to reach Taylor's horse.

Taylor looked down at him and smiled faintly. "You can't stand it, can you? Well, you'll get your chance. Look there." He pointed.

Barlow used the spyglass again. He could see a mass of horsemen organizing just to the east of Independence Hill, in the shadow of Bishop's Palace. He knew right where they were, for he'd been in that exact spot some weeks earlier—in the encampment of the dragoon regiment.

"So what do you imagine they're up to, Colonel?" asked Taylor.

"They're going to launch an attack," replied Barlow. "Now that we've been turned back at the center, Ampudia is going to test our mettle, and try to drive a wedge between us and General Worth."

"My thoughts exactly. It's time to put your flying batteries to the test, Colonel. I suggest you go make certain that they work as you've promised they would. And when you've turned the enemy aside, you may proceed to General Worth and, with my compliments, ask him what the Hell is taking him so long!"

Barlow suppressed a smile. He was beginning to change his opinion of Old Rough 'n' Ready, who seemed an entirely different man on the battlefield than the one Barlow had crossed swords with, figuratively speaking, in his Matamoros headquarters.

"Yes, sir!" he exclaimed, and hurried to his horse.

The flying batteries were being held in reserve near the adobe huts on the Cerralvo Road. Barlow was there in a matter of minutes. The horses were hitched to their caissons, and the gun crews were huddled around fires that they were trying to keep alive despite the rain.

"Gentlemen!" he called, remaining in the saddle, "It's time to go to work."

They needed to hear nothing more than that. The drivers clambered aboard the caissons while the rest mounted their horses. There were eight guns in the battery, six of them twelve-pounders, the rest eight-pounders. Barlow led them at a gallop across rough terrain, but the limbers and caissons were sturdy conveyances, and they reached the spot Barlow had selected without mishap. This was a low ridge located about a mile and a quarter from the Cerralvo Road. They arrived not a moment too soon. A glance towards Monterrey confirmed for Barlow that what he'd suspected was right—the dragoons were advancing, in column four abreast. Barlow caught himself wondering if Captain Rodriguez was among them. He had to assume that this was so. Looking around, he realized that he and the artillerymen were at least a half-mile from the nearest friendly troops.

The gun crews unlimbered their cannon along the ridge, spaced about thirty feet apart. The captain in charge of the battery, a man named Halloran, approached Barlow to inform him that they were ready. Barlow was using the spyglass to get a better look at the dragoons. He offered it to Halloran, but the captain shook his head.

"No thank you, Colonel. I'll see them plenty close enough, I'm guessing. Of course, they could swing right around us. There's nothing to stop them."

"Oh yes there is," replied Barlow.

Halloran looked about him. "Begging your pardon, sir, but we seem to be very much alone out here."

"Pride," said Barlow. "Those men will *not* go around your guns, Lieutenant, I can promise you that."

Halloran returned to his guns. Barlow put the spyglass in its hardened leather case, which was tied to his saddle, and climbed aboard his horse. Sitting there, he forced himself to look away from the oncoming dragoons, and checked the loads in the Colt Paterson.

"They're getting ready to charge, Colonel," called Halloran, an understandable edge to his voice.

Barlow looked up to see that the dragoons were changing formations, going from a column four-abreast to a line three-deep. They were, perhaps, a half-mile away, and Barlow figured the entire regiment had turned out. He could see the officers riding up and down their sections of their line, making sure that all was in order. An officer on a black stallion, whom Barlow presumed to be General Ampudia, whom he had briefly met prior to his incarceration in El Soldado, was about thirty yards in advance of the line, surrounded by aides and a color guard. The dragoons made an imposing sight. Barlow threw a quick look along the line of cannon atop the ridge. Most of the members of the gun crews were staring in awe—and fear—at the horsemen confronting them. A few of them, though, were watching Barlow, and Barlow knew from experience that his most important task at this moment was to act as though he had not the slightest doubt that they were going to prevail over the Mexicans arrayed against them. He suddenly remembered the cheroot that Churacho had given him at the officers' ball. It was in the inner pocket of his tunic, and until this moment he'd forgotten all about it. The cheroot was somewhat the worse for wear, but still intact. He clenched it between his teeth, and then realized he didn't have a way to light it. Steering his horse closer to the nearest cannon, he motioned to the Number 4 man, who stepped forward.

"You're the one with the responsibility of firing the gun, I believe," said Barlow.

"Yes, sir."

"You have any way of firing this up?" Barlow took the cheroot from between his teeth.

"Yes, sir, I reckon I do."

"Not with that, I hope." Barlow nodded at the friction primer in the man's hand.

Several of the other crew members laughed.

"No, sir. That would burn half your face off, sir." The No. 4 man smiled and fished a match out of a trouser pocket, flicked a thumbnail over the sulfur on the tip. The sulfur flared into life long enough for Barlow to get the cheroot lighted. Barlow nodded his thanks, looked up at the sky.

"I thought the desert was supposed to be dry," he said. "But at least when we get into Monterrey we'll have a roof over our heads."

"Yes, sir," said the No. 5 man, peering up at Barlow with rain steadily dripping from the visor of his cap. "That would suit me just fine."

"Well, it won't be much longer."

"Here they come," said Halloran.

Barlow looked across the plain, the sound of a bugle reaching his ears. The line of dragoons was surging forward, moving as one in perfect discipline, following their colors. The steady thunder of horses' hooves grew ever louder as the Mexican cavalry drew swiftly closer.

"Hold your fire, Captain," said Barlow.

Five hundred yards, four hundred. Watching them, Barlow couldn't help but feel a tremendous respect for the dragoons. They were the enemy, and his job was to kill them, but he still admired their courage. And in that moment before the blood began to spill, before the dying began, Barlow felt a fierce elation. The fear drained away, and he could think of no other place he would prefer to be than here, standing with brave men, about to engage in a life-or-death contest with other brave men—all of them willing to sacrifice everything for country and duty, in this moment of magnificent tragedy, with all of them hurled together by forces beyond their control.

Three hundred yards.

"Go ahead, Captain," said Barlow.

"Ready!" roared Halloran.

"Ready!" shouted the gunners.

Barlow watched the crew at the nearest gun. No. 3 removed his thumb from the vent and inserted a priming wire, making a hole in the cartridge bag that lay right below the vent. No. 4 stepped forward at Halloran's command; as he did so, No. 3 removed the priming wire so that his crewmate could insert a friction primer into the vent. He had already attached the lanyard to the primer, and now took one step to the rear and left of the cannon, taking up the slack in the lanyard. At the front of the cannon, No. 1 and No. 2 stepped away from the muzzle.

"Fire!" shouted Halloran.

"Fire!" roared the eight gunners, almost in unison.

No. 4 jerked the lanyard. Barlow knew that this pulled a serrated wire across friction composition within the primer, causing a spark, which ignited a fine powder; the flash went down the brass tube of the primer, through the breech, and into the cartridge bag. The main powder-charge exploded with a deafening roar. The twelve-pounder leaped backwards several feet, belching smoke and flame. All eight cannon fired nearly simultaneously. Barlow heard an odd, high-pitched whistling noise. It was the canister—projectiles, previously placed in the thin-walled cartridge bag—now hurtling through the air at the ranks of dragoons, like musket balls fired from hundreds of rifles. They struck the charging horsemen simultaneously all along the line—and wrought havoc. Men and horses screamed in agony. They fell, twisting, writhing, dying, in a bloody melee. Barlow couldn't believe that anyone, no matter how brave, could endure such horror and keep coming on. He expected to see the entire dragoon regiment—or what was left of it—reeling back towards Monterrey in complete disarray. But as the smoke cleared he realized that this was not the case. They were still coming. Many men had fallen in that first fusillade—many men and horses lay dead or dying, all in a ragged row. But the rest were not deterred. It seemed as though all of the dragoons were shouting—some sort of primal, incoherent yell of warrior rage. Some of them were firing their pistols. Most, though, brandished their sabers, eager to reach the line of American cannon, eager to wreak havoc of their own.

The gunners shouted the order to load. Barlow watched the crew at the nearest cannon. Number 3 tended the vent, placing his thumb, covered by a leather sheath, on the vent hole, to make sure that no air passed through the breech. This was done to prevent any lingering spark from being fanned by air passing through the vent hole and igniting the charge that Nos. 1 and 2 were about to insert into the barrel. First, though, No. 1 doused the sponge—a staff covered with sheepskin on one end—in a bucket of water, while No. 2 searched the piece with a wad-hook to remove any remnants of cartridge or cloth from the barrel. No. 1 shoved the dampened sponge down the barrel to extinguish any sparks left over from the previous shot. No. 5 carried a charge from the caisson to No. 2 who, when No. 1 had finished sponging the barrel, placed the charge in the muzzle. No. 1 rammed it home with the rammer head—the other end of the staff—so that the charge came to rest directly below the vent. At that point the gunner quickly aimed the

cannon, depressing the barrel slightly since the target—the line of charging dragoons—was substantially
closer than before. He did not waste time with a pen-
dulum hausse, but sighted the gun using years of experience. No. 3 inserted the priming wire into the vent,
making a hole in the cartridge bag—and the cannon
was ready to fire. All of this took about fifteen seconds. The gun crew worked like a well-oiled machine,
without a second wasted. Every man knew his job and
did it with swift expertise. Barlow had seen it done
many times before, but it never ceased to amaze him.
A good gun crew could fire three or four times in a
minute. And in this case, a minute was all that they
had. The dragoons were less than two hundred yards
away.

"Ready!" roared the gunners, all within a few seconds of one another. No. 3 removed the priming wire.
No. 4 stepped in with lanyard fixed to friction primer,
and inserted the latter into the vent hole.

"Fire!"

The cannon roared and spewed death into the ranks
of the dragoons. More horses and more men were cut
down as though by a giant invisible scythe. The
screams of agony and fear coming from man and animal alike sent a chill down Barlow's spine. The drift-
ing powder-smoke, virtually obscuring the battery
from his view, made his eyes sting. Immediately the
gun crews went to work, tending the vent, searching
the piece, sponging the barrel, ramming home the
charge. This time the powder-smoke seemed to linger,
so that Barlow could scarcely make out what was happening more than thirty feet ahead of him. But he
could feel the thunder of the dragoon horses still—it
came up from the ground, through his horse and into
his body, and he thought, *They're not going to quit.*

*They're going to run right through us and we'll all be
dead in less than a minute.*

Just as the dragoons came looming out of the mist
of battle, the battery fired again, and again the case-
shot whistled through the already decimated ranks,
this time at point-blank range, and all along the line,
men and horses perished. A few, on either end of the
charging line, escaped the brunt of the canister. Two
dragoons came thundering straight towards Barlow.
He wheeled his horse around and brought the Colt
Paterson to bear. He fired again and again, and both
the horses ran right past him, their saddles empty.
Another dragoon was coming at a slightly different
angle, saber raised high to strike him down. Other
dragoons had infiltrated the battery now, and the gun
crews were fighting for their lives, using anything at
hand to defend themselves against the enemy's sword
thrusts. Barlow fired at the dragoon coming for him—
and missed. The sword came down in a sweeping arc.
Reflex caused Barlow to kick his horse hard, making
the animal jump forward. The sword missed him by
inches, struck the cantle of his saddle—he felt the
breath of its passage on the back of his neck.

The dragoon's horse collided with his own, and both
lost their footing in the mud and fell. Barlow jumped
clear but landed poorly, jarring the wind out of his
lungs. The dragoon fell, too, but was quite agile, and
was up and advancing before Barlow could recover.
It was the horse that saved him—the sorrel got up
quickly, becoming a temporary obstacle for the dragoon, and giving Barlow a few precious seconds to
gather his wits about him. He had dropped the Colt
Paterson and couldn't find it in the muck, but he did
see a saber—a blade that had belonged to one of the
dragoons he had shot only a moment earlier. He

scooped it up and turned and parried a vicious downward stroke that would have cleaved his skull in two. Sparks flew as steel met steel.

The dragoon hurled his body into Barlow, knocking him backwards. Barlow lost his balance and sprawled. The dragoon advanced relentlessly, raising the saber again, bringing it down again—and once more Barlow managed to deflect it with a desperate lateral stroke of his own. He rolled, came up quickly. The dragoon thrust the saber, trying to run him through. Barlow parried the thrust and, spinning completely around, drove his blade deeply into his adversary's side before the dragoon could regain his balance. It wasn't a mortal wound, but the sudden shock of pain threw the dragoon off. He clutched at his side, hesitating a fateful few seconds before raising his sword again.

It was too late—Barlow turned his blade so that it would pass neatly between the ribs, and ran the Mexican through, piercing the man's heart and snuffing the life out of him instantly. He fell so abruptly that it wrenched the saber from Barlow's grasp. Barlow pried the dragoon's weapon from his dead hand and turned to face any new threat that might be coming his way.

But nothing was *coming*.

A gust of cold north wind swept some of the powder-smoke away, and he could see what was left of the dragoon regiment withdrawing across the bloody field. From virtually the mouth of the cannon out to three hundred yards, the ground was littered with dead and dying men and horses. Only a few dozen dragoons were retreating—the rest had been killed or wounded in the past few minutes.

Barlow stared in numbed horror at the carnage. He felt sick to his stomach, and he wasn't the only one. One of the artillerymen was retching violently, bent over double and clutching the wheel of a twelve-pounder.

There was no cheering from the gun crews, no celebration of any kind, and Barlow was glad of that. He didn't see anything to celebrate in what they had wrought. They had stayed alive, yes, and one might argue that they had slain all those brave men in self-defense. But Barlow wasn't thinking that way. He was wondering, instead, if Captain Rodriguez was among those men strewn like debris across the killing ground, and he decided not to conduct a search in order to satisfy his curiosity. No, he preferred to believe that Rodriguez was among those who had escaped.

Halloran hurried over to him, exuding barely contained excitement.

"Look there, Colonel! At the hill!"

Barlow looked. There seemed to be a great commotion atop Independence Hill, and the Mexican cannon fire, which had been a constant all day long, sounded much subdued. He looked around for his horse. The sorrel stood obediently nearby, seemingly none the worse for its recent experience. Barlow went to it, speaking softly to calm the skittish animal, and, reaching the saddle, removed the spyglass from its leather case. Halloran watched him put the glass to his eye, breathless in anticipation. Barlow smiled slowly, handed the glass to the captain. Halloran took it eagerly, and scanned the distant heights. He saw the Stars and Stripes flying above the Bishop's Palace— and let out a whoop of pure joy.

"They did it!" he exclaimed. "By God, they did it!"

Barlow nodded. Now General Worth would turn the guns captured atop Independence Hill on Federation Hill. The battle would go on awhile longer, but he knew the tide had turned. He could feel it in his bones. They had won. Ampudia's left flank would disintegrate, and then Monterrey would fall.

He was alive—and he was going home.

Chapter 33

The sun was a simmering red ball slipping down the darkening sky to the western horizon as Barlow walked through the still-smoldering ruins of El Soldado. There were bodies in the piles of debris, but most were battered or burned beyond recognition. By their uniforms, he could assume that all of those he checked were soldiers in Ampudia's army. And he was beginning to sense the futility of continuing his search for Zeke Fuller.

As per his instructions, General Worth had turned the captured Mexican guns atop Independence Hill on Federation Hill to the south, across the Santa Catarina River, and for several hours yesterday afternoon a fierce artillery exchange had occurred. Then, suddenly, the fortress known as El Soldado was wracked by an immense explosion. A store of powder and shot had gone up in flame and smoke, and no one was quite sure if the catalyst had been a lucky shot by an American gun crew or if it had been an accident. Whatever the case, the fortress became untenable, and the Mexicans fled the hill, streaming into Monterrey. By early morning, Worth could safely say that he was in complete command of the western approaches to the city.

Taylor had lost no time in launching an attack all

across the center of the Mexican line—and was surprised to discover the outer ring of fortifications abandoned. The rest of the day had seen fighting from house to house and street to street in the city proper. It turned out to be a rearguard action fought by some of Ampudia's best troops, who sacrificed themselves in order that the rest of the army could escape across the Santa Catarina and into the foothills of the Sierra Madre, on their way to Rinconada Pass beyond.

The fighting that day in Monterrey was a brutal business, with quarter seldom given, or asked for, on either side. Barlow was thankful that he'd taken no part in it. All day today he had been riding back and forth between headquarters—which was wherever General Taylor happened to be—and various units, as Old Rough 'n' Ready pressed relentlessly forward, giving Ampudia's soldiers no respite. By midafternoon, the Americans were in control of most of the city, with only pockets of resistance remaining—chief among them being a cathedral in the center of Monterrey, which had been turned into a stronghold. Taylor had all the cannon he could lay his hands on pulled up around the cathedral, and was prepared to reduce it to rubble, when the Mexican commander sent out an aide under a flag of truce. Taylor had insisted on unconditional surrender. Ampudia had balked. Eventually, it was agreed that the city would be surrendered to the Americans, while all Mexican forces were to be withdrawn beyond Rinconada Pass. An eight-week armistice was proclaimed. Barlow understood that Ampudia and about seven hundred Mexican troops were still in Monterrey; they would be allowed to leave on the morrow. Ampudia himself, fearful that the Texans among Taylor's men would want him dead, had a bodyguard of U.S. Army officers who would remain with him until he was out of the city.

Barlow's wanderings brought him to a man who was chipping away at the remnants of a wall with a pickax. The man then stepped back to survey the top of the wall. Barlow walked up to him.

"You're with the engineers?"

"Yes, sir," said the man. He identified himself and said he was with the Second Infantry.

"Are they intending to salvage this place?"

The man shook his head. "General Worth sent us out to see if there was anything worth saving. But there's no way. Best thing to do is bring the rest of it down with dynamite. That's what I'll recommend, anyway."

Barlow nodded, satisfied. Not that there was much he could have done about it had the generals decided to try saving the fortress, but he would have complained vociferously. He was glad to know that El Soldado would cease to exist. He could only hope that Zeke Fuller's remains were buried somewhere in the ruins. Not knowing for sure was troubling; Barlow suspected that he'd be looking over his shoulder for some time to come. But the day was waning, and he was tired of the fruitless searching. He had just decided to give up when Captain Armstrong appeared. The first thing Barlow noticed was that the captain's left arm was in a sling.

"I thought you'd be here," said Armstrong. "Find any trace of Fuller?"

"None. I don't think I will."

"Well, from what I hear, the war in the north is pretty much over now." Armstrong took a long look around at the smoking ruins. "There will be a strong force remaining here in Monterrey, but some of the volunteers will be going home soon, I think. And I thought you'd probably be doing the same."

Barlow nodded. "That's what I intend."

Armstrong took an envelope out of the sling and, hesitantly, held it out to Barlow.

"I was hoping you would do me a favor. If you know where Therese is, would you see that she gets this?"

Barlow's first impulse was a wholly natural one—to ask Armstrong what the envelope contained. But he caught himself; that was none of his business. And besides, he had a very good idea.

"Of course. I can see that she gets it."

"Thank you." Momentarily, Armstrong was at a loss for words. He watched Barlow stow the letter away under his tunic. "I know I'll likely never see her again. But I just wanted to . . . well, when we parted company there were some things I wanted to say to her, about the way I feel, but I didn't have the nerve. So I wrote it all down."

"Good idea." Barlow had mercy on the young captain, and changed the subject. "What happened to your arm?"

"Bit of shrapnel from a Mexican cannonball," said Armstrong ruefully. "Nothing too serious."

"But serious enough to warrant a furlough," said Barlow.

"What? A furlough? I wouldn't even bother asking. I'm afraid I'm going to be one of the men who'll be left to watch over this place."

"Fine. But you still deserve a furlough. I'll see what I can do. Put in a good word for you, and all that. And, if I'm successful, you can ride with me as far as Matamoros—and deliver the letter to her yourself."

Armstrong stared at him. If the thought of delivering his letter to Therese in person had ever occurred to him, he didn't show it.

"Are you serious?"

"Absolutely," said Barlow.

"I . . . I don't know if I could."

"I think you should."

"It's not as though I have any great expectations, you understand. I realize that she was in love with you. I suppose she always will be."

"No," said Barlow firmly. "She never was. So if I can arrange it, will you go?"

Armstrong hesitated. Barlow could see he was afraid—afraid of being rejected by the woman he loved. It was enough to make even the bravest warrior tremble.

"If you don't at least try you'll wonder for the rest of your days," warned Barlow.

"I'll go," said Armstrong.

By noon of the following day Barlow had it all arranged.

He managed to wrangle a few moments with General Taylor that morning, and informed Old Rough 'n' Ready of his plans. He wasn't sure what sort of reaction he would get, but Taylor seemed amenable.

"You've served me and your country in admirable fashion, Colonel. Do not think for a moment that I will forget what you did when I am writing the president a report of the battle we have just won. Had those dragoons gotten in behind General Worth, things might have turned out quite differently."

Barlow thanked him, and went next to Armstrong's commanding officer. He knew better than to ask Zachary Taylor for assistance in acquiring a furlough for his friend. He didn't know Armstrong's superior, but he'd been in the army long enough to understand that very few regimental commanders appreciated pressure being asserted from headquarters with respect to such matters. As it turned out, he had no problems. Armstrong was granted a two-week furlough. They were on their way north early that same afternoon.

Barlow was counting on Churacho and Therese being at the isolated adobe a day's ride out of Mata-moros. It was, as far as he knew, the closest thing to a home that the mustanger and his sister could claim. If they weren't there—if, instead, they were some-where on the plains of Texas hunting for the *mesteñ-aros,* then all would be lost, as far as Armstrong was concerned. Barlow could only hope that Churacho had the good sense to lay low for awhile—at least until the war fever in Texas had cooled down a little. Not that the mustanger had ever exhibited much in the way of good sense.

The bad weather cleared on the day they departed Monterrey, followed by several days that were uni-formly sunny and cool. They knew the way—they'd now been between from the Rio Grande and Monter-rey three times. Barlow enjoyed this particular journey far more than the others. He was on his way home, and it was as though a great weight had been lifted from his shoulders. His duty had been done, and he'd survived. Of course, it was still a dangerous trek— there was always the possibility that they would run afoul of Mexican troops—so they kept a vigilant eye on the countryside through which they passed.

They also kept an eye on the ground, for Barlow discovered, somewhat to his surprise, that he had de-veloped a habit of checking for signs. It was something he had picked up from all the days spent with Chura-cho and the mustangers—for it was, undoubtedly, a crucial element in frontier survival. It was because of this habit that Barlow came to the realization that two other riders were traveling in the same direction as he and Armstrong, preceding them by not much more than a day or two. Their trail was easy enough to see—the imprints of their horses' hooves were deep and clear, having been made in ground that was muddy from recent rains, only to have dried into hardpack during the sunny days that followed. Barlow and Armstrong crossed this trail not once but several times. On the third occasion, by sheer luck, they found a campsite where the horsemen had stopped only the night before—a determination made by Barlow after digging into the ashes of what had once been a campfire and finding that, down below, the embers were still warm. He took a few moments to study the ground. What he saw sent a cold shiver down his spine.

"My God," he muttered. "It can't be."

"What is it?" asked Armstrong, still mounted.

Barlow didn't answer right away. He circled the campsite, studying a larger section of the ground.

"What do you see?" asked Armstrong.

"A man with a cane," said Barlow. He looked bleakly at the captain. "Only one I know of is Zeke Fuller."

Armstrong looked skeptical. "How is that possible? Last we knew, Fuller had been captured by the dragoons. There's no way he could have gotten out of Monterrey alive."

"Why not? We did." Barlow stood up, scanned the desert's northern horizon. "He's headed north, just like we are. I expect he's got the same destination in mind. It's the only place he knows to find Churacho."

All the color bled from Armstrong's face. "Lord Almighty," he muttered. He didn't need to say more—Barlow knew perfectly well what he was thinking: Therese was in danger.

Chapter 34

They pressed on, pushing the horses to the limit of their endurance. But they couldn't push them too hard—Barlow was aware that if they lost one horse they would be slowed substantially, and if they lost both animals then they, too, were lost.

It took them another day to reach the adobe, and that with traveling during the portion of the night when a half-moon provided sufficient illumination to see by. Barlow didn't sleep the remainder of the night, and he didn't think Armstrong managed to get any shut-eye either. He was sure the captain was thinking along similar lines as he was—wondering what he would find tomorrow, when they reached the mustangers' adobe.

They got started before first light and by late morning were belly-down on a low rise two hundred yards from the adobe.

"Looks quiet enough," said Armstrong.

Barlow didn't say anything. There was no one in sight below—no one, alive or dead, outside the adobe. He noted that there were no horses in the corral, and he thought that odd.

"Maybe Fuller got here, found nobody was home, and moved on," suggested Armstrong.

"Maybe," said Barlow, but he was dubious. "We'll go in from different angles. Be careful. Keep your eyes open."

Armstrong nodded. He left Barlow, circling to the east. Barlow waited until he saw the captain come into view—on foot now, but leading his horse. Barlow nodded. That was smart, bringing the horse to use for cover, just in case—because there wasn't any cover to speak of. Barlow rose and walked toward the adobe, leading his own mount, the Colt Paterson in his hand.

They met in front of the adobe, and Armstrong was looking halfway relieved, as though he was willing to believe that nothing had befallen Churacho and Therese—that, indeed, Zeke Fuller had gotten here and gone away without having his revenge. But Barlow saw that the door to the adobe was ajar—and saw what he thought to be several fresh bullet-holes in the warped and weathered timber of the door.

"Watch my back," he told Armstrong, and ventured inside.

The room was a wreck, as though a tremendous fight had been waged within, and for a moment Barlow thought the adobe was empty—until he saw an arm, beneath the shattered, overturned big table. He shoved the pistol under his belt and tossed aside the wreckage and knelt beside Churacho, turning the mustanger over gently.

He thought at first that his friend was dead.

But then the mustanger's eyes fluttered open, and Barlow felt a brief surge of hope. He called for Armstrong. The captain came in, halted just across the threshold, and muttered a curse. Then he knelt on the other side of Churacho, and looked at Barlow.

"Is he going to make it?"

Barlow was trying to peel Churacho's blood-soaked

shirt away to check the wounds in his chest. "I don't know," he said.

"I am a dead man," said Churacho, wheezing with the effort to speak. "You must go, find Therese. Fuller has taken her."

Armstrong muttered another curse.

Churacho clutched Barlow's arm. "He said you would come for her. Is he right?"

"Yes, of course. Where are your men?"

"In Matamoros. They will not be back for . . ." He stopped and closed his eyes, his face a mask of pain, and Barlow thought he was going to slip into unconsciousness. But then the eyes opened again, and focused on him once more. ". . . For several days."

"Fuller isn't alone," said Barlow.

"No. He has a man with him. A big man. Very dangerous. Watch out for him."

Barlow nodded. He had removed enough of the shirt to see that Churacho had been shot three times in the chest. It was a miracle that the man was still alive. And Barlow knew, with sinking heart, that he wouldn't last much longer.

"I'm sorry," he said, "for what happened back at Fort Brown. I should have stood by you."

Churacho shook his head, and Barlow thought his eyes were beginning to lose their focus, were beginning to look right through him. "Who will take care of my sister?" he asked, his voice becoming frail. "She has no one now. . . ."

"That's not true, sir," said Armstrong. "I'll look after her. You can rely on me."

Churacho turned his head, looking for Armstrong, but it was as though he could no longer see anything— at least not anything of this world.

"Take me outside. I want to feel the sun on my face."

Barlow nodded to Armstrong. He got his hands under Churacho's arms while the captain took his feet and, as gently as they could, they carried him out of the adobe, out onto the hard-pack, where they carefully laid him down. Churacho smiled, and closed his eyes, like a man without a care in the world going to sleep. And then Barlow felt the life go out of him.

"Let's go," said Armstrong grimly, turning away.

"Wait. We have to bury him."

"There's no time. Therese . . ."

"Therese will stay alive. Fuller needs her alive as bait for me."

"But the longer she's in his hands . . ."

"Forget about that. We bury him. Then we go after Fuller." He glanced at Churacho. "And this time I'm going to make sure."

They found Zeke Fuller's trail and followed it—due north towards the Rio Grande. The old man intended to swing a wide loop around Matamoros, to avoid soldiers who might ask questions he didn't care to answer. Barlow figured Fuller only had a half-day's lead, and hoped to catch up with him before nightfall, but sundown caught them nearing the river with no sign of their prey. They crossed as the last light of day bled out of the sky, then pushed their weary horses to further exertion, aided by the light of an early moon.

Barlow assumed that Fuller was heading home—where else would the man go? That way, when their final reckoning occurred, he would be on familiar ground. But Barlow had every intention of catching him before he reached his destination. And early the following day, he accomplished that goal.

When they caught their first glimpse of the three riders it was from a distance of at least two-thirds of a mile—just three dark spots moving across the brown and tan expanse of a rolling prairie. Immediately, Armstrong kicked his tired horse into a gallop, ignoring Barlow's shouted warning. Barlow held his own horse to a canter, muttering an epithet that centered around young hotspurs blinded by love.

Ten minutes later, Armstrong's mount stumbled and fell. Barlow had been expecting it. They had pushed their horses to the limit and beyond. Armstrong was thrown clear, but the fall dazed him, and he was slow in getting up. The horse wasn't going to get up. He stood there, looking blankly at the animal, then up at Barlow as the latter approached. The captain removed his saber from the saddle and held out a hand, expecting Barlow to share his horse. But Barlow didn't slow the sorrel.

"You've as much as killed that horse," shouted Barlow as he rode by. "Finish the job!"

Armstrong shouted back at him, but Barlow wasn't listening. He focused all his attention on the three riders up ahead. Now no more than a half-mile separated them. As far as he could tell, his presence had not yet been detected.

That changed moments later. One of the riders split off from the other two. At first he thought that Zeke Fuller and the big man Churacho had warned him about were going separate ways. Then he realized that the lone rider was circling around to confront him. Barlow drew the Colt Paterson from his belt and kicked the sorrel into a gallop. The rider closed quickly. He, too, had drawn his pistol. It was Buell Fuller, but Barlow didn't know him or his name, and didn't care to. All he cared about was getting by him and reaching Zeke Fuller and killing the old man. Buell started firing first, when not more than two hundred yards separated them. Barlow held his fire, knowing that a man on horseback usually couldn't hit a target at twenty yards, much less two hundred. He waited until Buell was only fifty yards away, then started firing. He heard a bullet scream past his ear. Gripping the saddle-horn with his left hand, Barlow slid down the right side of the galloping sorrel and fired his last bullet from under the animal's neck just as Buell thundered by on his left. It was point-blank range, and the impact of the bullet lifted Buell out of the saddle and hurled him to the ground.

But Buell was a big man, as Churacho had said, and strong. One bullet wasn't going to put him down for good. Barlow checked his horse so sharply that its hindquarters nearly touched the ground. He turned the sorrel and, belting the empty Colt, drew his saber. Buell was getting to his feet. His horse was still running, so he turned to face Barlow with a snarl on his face, and lunged at him as he came near, but Barlow was expecting that, and he ran the man through with the saber. It didn't bother him at all that Buell Fuller was unarmed. A man that size could kill easily with his bare hands—and probably had. Besides, he'd played a part in Churacho's demise, and that had signed his death warrant. Heart pierced, Buell fell dead.

Barlow spun the sorrel around and was dismayed to see that Zeke Fuller had put more distance between them. He wasn't sure how long the sorrel could hold out, so he held it to a canter, guiding it with his knees and trying to load the Colt Paterson as he went along. Instinct made him look over a shoulder—and he saw that Armstrong had somehow caught up Buell Fuller's horse and was gaining on him. He looked ahead, and realized that Zeke Fuller was stopping. He couldn't believe it. The old man was dismounting, and forcing Therese to do the same. What was he doing?

Barlow got the answer a moment later. He didn't hear the report of Fuller's long gun until the sorrel was going down, killed in midstride. Barlow had time enough to curse—and then found himself hurtling through midair. He landed on a shoulder, lost his grip on the Colt. Stunned, he lay there a moment, listening to the thunder of hooves, catching a glimpse of Armstrong going by. By sheer force of will he got to his hands and knees. Fuller fired again, and this time Armstrong was hit. As he fell sideways he held onto the reins, and his mount fell, too, in a brief jumble of arms and legs and dust and blood.

Barlow got up, drew his saber, and began to run. He could see Zeke Fuller clearly, about eighty yards away, reloading his rifle. Armstrong lay still as death; his horse was trying to get up, but the reins were trapped under the captain's body, and prevented the animal from rising. Barlow reached the horse before Fuller could finish reloading. He slashed at the reins with the saber, freeing the horse, which leapt to its feet, blocking Fuller's aim—and giving Barlow the few precious seconds he needed to roll Armstrong over and mutter a thanks to God Almighty that the captain's pistol was still in his belt. He pulled the pistol free, whacked the dazed horse on the withers with the flat of the saber's blade to get it to move, and fired as soon as he had a shot at Fuller.

The old man fired back, but Barlow was moving sideways, and Fuller misjudged, and the bullet clipped Barlow's arm, ripping a gash in his tunic sleeve and grazing his flesh. He kept firing the pistol, and Fuller stood up, clutching at his chest. He stumbled backwards, then pitched forward. Therese was running now, toward Barlow; he grabbed her and pushed her down roughly when she reached him, and advanced on Fuller cautiously. The old man lay still, but Barlow wasn't taking any chances. He rolled Fuller over with a foot, holding the pistol on him. He'd been hit twice in the chest, but he wasn't dead. His eyes were open, and he focused on Barlow, smiling coldly.

"You're a hard man to kill, Colonel."

"So are you."

There was a pistol in Fuller's belt, but he was too far gone to reach for it; nonetheless, Barlow relieved him of it.

"What are you waitin' for?" asked the old man. "You gonna let me lay here and bleed to death? Put a bullet in my brainpan."

Barlow considered it, then shook his head. "I can't."

"Why the Hell not?"

"I can't kill a man in cold blood."

Zeke Fuller started to laugh, then coughed up frothy blood. "You've already killed me, damn it."

"Yes, I know." Barlow picked up the rifle and walked back to where Therese was kneeling beside Armstrong. He was surprised that the captain was still alive. "How bad are you hit?"

"Not too bad," said Armstrong. "But I think I broke my leg in the fall."

Barlow nodded. "So give her the letter, why don't you? That's what you came all this way to do, isn't it?"

"I don't think . . ."

"Oh, Christ," muttered Barlow. He bent down and plucked the letter from under Armstrong's tunic. It had some blood on it—the captain had been hit high in the shoulder—but he gave it to Therese anyway. "This is for you," he said. "I hope you'll take it to heart."

He caught up Buell Fuller's horse and rode out to collect the two mounts Zeke and Therese had been riding. In the process, he passed by Zeke Fuller, and in a glance knew the old bandit was gone. He brought the horses back to Armstrong and the girl, giving her the reins. By this time she had read the letter, and

Barlow could tell by the expression on her face that she had, indeed, taken the words it contained to heart.

"I'll send a message to General Taylor," Barlow told the captain. "Tell him you've been wounded in a scrape with bandits, and will be a little overdue."

"Good luck, Colonel."

"Luck to both of you." Barlow smiled at Therese. "Take good care of him. He's a good man. Just a bit reckless."

Armstrong scoffed. "Look who's talking."

Barlow gave them a final nod, then turned his horse toward Georgia.

SIGNET BOOKS

Jason Manning
The Long Hunters

In 1814, the fledgling U.S. Army is nothing more than a ragtag collection of veterans and boys, bound by blood, duty, and more than a little luck. The Army's commander in chief, Andrew Jackson, has turned his attention from the waning British threat to a conflict closer to home: "Old Hickory" hopes to capture and kill the Creek Indians responsible for murdering American "long hunters" on their home soil.

0-451-20723-8

Available wherever books are sold, or to order call: 1-800-788-6262

S696